# MY IMMORTAL LOVER

MAGGIE MUNDY

**My Immortal Lover**

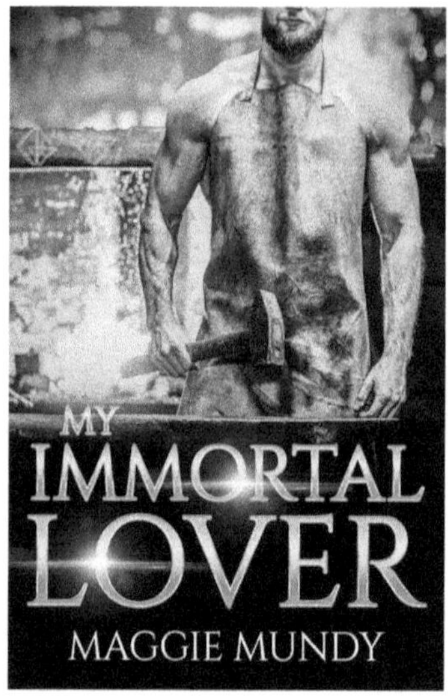


Maggie Mundy

Copyright 2021 Maggie Mundy
All Rights Reserved

This book is a work of fiction. Any references to real events, real people, and real places are used fictitiously. Other names, characters, places, and incidents are products of the author's imagination and any resemblance to persons, living or dead, actual events, organizations, or places is entirely coincidental.

This book was previously Published as Hidden Mortality.

Cover design by Designrans

# PROLOGUE

PrologueBath, 1849

Vincent's breath quickened. He needed to remain under control, but this experience felt more satisfying than opium. The heady sensation never failed to reassert itself whenever he killed. This time would be different. He had an audience. He wanted to smile but feared it might be seen as gloating.

His clients paid well, but lately they were getting bored consuming drugs and participating in orgies. Neither pastime had ever appealed to him much anyway. He liked control, which drugs took away and women or men sexually had never really interested him. Tonight he would show them the supreme thrill of how to take life. "Stand beside me, gentlemen."

The oil lamps flickered. Strange shadows formed on the brick walls of the cellar as his three clients staggered towards the table in the center of the room. These fops in their finery attracted too much attention in Bath. They thought him lackluster, but being boring had its benefits. Nobody noticed the commonplace.

The whore lying unconscious on the table before them looked pale, her chest hardly moving. Vincent cursed under his breath. He had given her too much laudanum. He hadn't wanted her to fight. She had been willing to have sex with them but he needed her more complacent for this next part of the evening. His clients didn't like to be bruised, but some form of awareness of her fate would have been more satisfying and more consistent with his exorbitant fee. He had no inheritance to rely upon so these men would provide the money for his home and travels.

He wanted this slaying to be as the book stated. This death would be a beautiful thing, just like the dagger in his hand. There were markings etched into the blade and the handle was the shape of two snakes, one black and one white coiled around each other. The way the black one devoured the head of the white one made him smile. It represented the way he saw the world. The weak would be devoured by the strong.

He had found the book and the dagger in a small book-shop in Bristol. When the owner had not wanted to part with it, he had persuaded him with a knock to the head.

Each cut, each stab, had to be precise.

The ritual was said to bestow immortality.

He didn't believe such things, or the reference to witches with odd colored eyes, one blue, one green. Who cared? It was just convenient the whore matched that description. It was all superstition from centuries past when the uneducated believed such things. The description of the sacrifice held within the plain little leather-bound book was suitably spectacular for what he required. He took a deep breath and savored the moment.

The whore's lips were slightly parted and blue tinged like irises. He hated the flowers. They had been all around his beloved mother's coffin. She had been the only woman who had meant anything to him and had died pointlessly in childbirth because of his father's needs.

He ground his teeth as he observed the fools before him. They were drinking too much and would not remember tonight. He peered back at their victim who said her name was Rosie. Who knew with these women? It was of no importance.

"Pick up your blades, gentlemen." Vincent indicated the four daggers placed beside the body. His heart beat fast with exhilaration and expectation. "Edgar, perhaps you would like to be the one to begin this sacrifice."

Edgar brushed the woman's hair back and placed the point of the dagger on one side of her forehead. At least he was not so drunk that he could not remember the instructions. His precise moves impressed Vincent. Edgar's cut was clean and without hesitation and caused Rosie to groan softly, but she still didn't move. Damn her.

Nigel and James made similar incisions just above Edgar's, from one side of her temple to the other. The blood oozed from the wounds. It pooled in her eye sockets and ran down into her ears. Little red puddles started to form. They flowed over her earlobes and down her neck to soak into the white tablecloth. Vincent wanted to lick the blood off of her body the way he did with previous victims. His clients were not quite ready for that just yet.

Untying Rosie's chemise, Vincent pulled it wide to reveal her breasts. James reacted with a sudden intake of breath. Edgar was always the first to be violent, whereas James was always the first to fornicate. Taking the dagger from Edgar, Vincent sliced Rosie from her chin to her navel, and then from her right breast to her left. Rosie whimpered and the men's faces lit up in anticipation of her enduring more pain but then she lay still yet again.

The next cut meandered down the body like a river around the previous wounds. The blood seeped to the surface, dark red in contrast to Rosie's pale skin. He wanted to rub his hands in it. Maybe he should have killed her on his own. The audience was not enhancing the experience but limiting it.

Vincent held the dagger above her heart. The knife was a magnificent weapon and the blade so sharp it sliced through the flesh with ease. It had needed fixing and he only had himself to blame. The bookseller he had stolen it from had fallen on the blade. Vincent was lucky the man's girth had not snapped the dagger in two. Nigel had had his local smithy do the job. An excellent repair.

"I want you all to place your right hands around mine as I hold the dagger. I'll say the words and you repeat them. We appeal to Kocshie, the Immortal Lord of death to accept this life so we can extend our own. In payment we give our own souls when our lives are complete, so he may once again return to the world."

On the second repetition, they were to plunge in the blade. Excitement showed in their gazes. Their eyes opened wide at the prospect. Vincent licked his lips as he struggled to control his breathing. He would not falter now when the means to the life of luxury he wanted was so close at hand. He needed their money and would not give up. As he pushed the tip of the blade beneath her skin, Rosie's eyes opened.

Vincent grinned. He relished the power over life and death. He needed her to know she was losing hers. Rosie's lips moved but no sound was emitted. He tried to tell himself fear stared back at him from her eyes, but it looked more like defiance. It was irrelevant; her life was about to cease.

James whimpered as the blood oozed around the blade. Someone helped Vincent push. That would be Edgar. The dagger slid beneath the skin with ease and Vincent moved his hand and angled the blade upwards so it would penetrate the heart. The lanterns flickered and weakened in strength. Rosie sighed and let out her final breath.

Vincent shivered. The cellar darkened. Shadows reached out from its very walls to grab them. Then a glow emanated from Rosie's chest, beginning to light the room. Blood around the dagger shone like molten metal flowing over their hands. His heart beat wildly with fear. This wasn't supposed to happen.

Vincent tensed with the onslaught of burning pain. It shot up his arm into his chest. The blood covering their joined hands disappeared. Somehow, he could still not loosen his grip on the dagger impaled in her chest.

Vincent gritted his teeth and tried to control his breathing as he watched. Even through the agony, he was fascinated. The skin on James' hand slowly peeled back leaving the bones white and bare as if maggots had stripped a corpse. James' screams filled the air. They continued while he ran from the table. He hid in the shadows in the far corner of the cellar.

Next was Edgar. He let go of the dagger and grabbed his left wrist yelling obscenities. His hand shriveled up like a rotten tree root. Vincent shook his head as he tried to think back to how much laudanum he had imbibed himself over the evening with these men.

They were all having hallucinations. They had to be. Edgar collapsed on the floor and curled up like a baby. Nigel stood silent as he watched his hand swell and the skin rip apart. As blood oozed, he laughed. The laughter continued as Nigel left the table.

Vincent gazed down to see his own hand. He held the dagger in his grasp, but what was in front of him appeared as a bloody stump cut off at the wrist.

The dead body of Rosie glowed. He had killed many times. He knew when life no longer lingered in a form and hers was gone. He tried yet again to let go of the dagger. He couldn't. His arms were on fire. A burning sensation flowed over his shoulder and towards his neck. The pain increased. A surge of power from Rosie's chest illuminated the cellar. It threw him against the opposite wall that he hit with a resounding thud. His chest ached where the wind had been forced out. Vincent shook his head to clear the dizziness that threatened to overwhelm him.

Rosie's ghost sat up but her body still lay translucent and flat on the table. The dagger protruded from her chest. Her ghostly gaze fixed on Vincent. Then her ethereal form glided across the room and stood in front of him. He pulled his knees up to his chin as he struggled to retain the contents of his stomach under her angry glare. Her blue and green eyes now looked red as if a flame burned in them. His body shook as the sight filled him with dread of what was to come.

Rosie's raspy voice echoed around the cellar. "You'd no right to take my power. I'll give what's left of my life to one who shall avenge my death."

Rosie's apparition disappeared as the lamps flared, lighting the cellar again. Vincent edged over to the table. He inspected the body. She was truly dead. Her chest didn't rise again. The dagger was still embedded in her heart. He had killed so many times, but he had never seen a ghost. He hadn't believed they existed until tonight. Fear surged through his veins at what this could mean. Would the spirits of all those he had killed over the years return to haunt him? He had his pride and would not let his concern show before these men. Edgar came and stood beside him, placing his tremulous hand on Vincent's shoulder.

"I'm impressed, Vincent. Whatever you mixed with the opium tonight was very effective. I thought she had come back to life and my hand rotted away." He laughed, but the sound appeared to catch in his throat. "I think I shall try and discover where Nigel's lurking. James is in the brandy again, I fear. I assume you don't need us to deal with the body." Edgar raised his left eyebrow as he looked at the dead woman with distaste.

Vincent shook his head.

"A most satisfying evening I think, don't you?" Edgar slapped him on the back. "My man will be here in the morning with the money we owe."

Vincent waited by the body until he was alone. Of course he would get rid of the evidence, but before he did there was something he needed to confirm. He went to the corner of the cellar where he kept his tools and knives.

Placing his hand palm down on the table he thrust the blade between the sinews and muscles. He clenched his teeth in pain. Removing the knife, he watched the cut heal. It left a faint scar. For the first time since seeing her apparition, he allowed himself to feel vindicated at this killing. He was long lived and so were his customers this evening. The story in the book had turned out to be true. He needed to know more. Knowledge was power and he craved it.

WESTBURY, *Wiltshire 1849*

S. SCANLON, BLACKSMITH. That's what the sign at the front of the cottage stated. Drunk, cheat and reprobate would have been a better way of summing him up. Seth wished death instead of drunken oblivion would take him. It was what he deserved.

Instead he sat alone at his kitchen table in the dark. He didn't have to accept what was missing in the dark. The forge was his refuge when the sun was high, but at night the guilt of what he had done to Rosie and Anne consumed him.

He wiped his wet cheeks with the back of his hand. He had no right to cry. This was his home, but a home was meant to be a place of love. The bed upstairs stayed empty and he would sleep with his head on the table again. With the stubble on his chin and the smell of the filth on his clothes, no one would have wanted him anyway. His large muscled body and stern face scared people. He had never frightened either of the women he missed. Which was more the pity, as they might have stayed away from him.

The light of the full moon shone in through the windows. Seth held up his hands. They were strong hands that should have protected others. Yet in the thirty years he had lived, all he had done was destroy the things he touched. Anne had never been happy wedded to him, but she deserved better than to die in childbirth.

Wild reckless Rosie. She needed his protection and he failed her. He should end it all before he caused anyone else more pain. Tonight, he would use one of the sharp blades he made on himself and end it all.

His fingers appeared a pasty gray color. Even in a stupor he could tell this was more than moonlight. With eyes half-open, he gazed towards the back door expecting to see someone enter with a lantern. No one was there. He rubbed his eyes as a shape formed, pale and insubstantial at first, but more recognizable as it became solid. It was Rosie. Seth jumped up. His chair tipped over, along with his beer. It spilled to the floor, the aroma filling the air.

As he held onto the dresser, his heart raced. Dizziness overwhelmed him. His legs weak, he squinted at the apparition before him. He shook his head but she was still there. She beckoned. He found himself drawn to the specter. He touched her face with his fingertips. Could she be real? Her skin was as cold as ice. Something beyond his drunken haze told him he should be afraid, but this was Rosie. She would never harm him.

With rough fingers he brushed blood soaked hair aside to reveal gashes cut deep across her forehead. He had run his fingers through her red curls in the past when love-making but never again. Who could have done this to her? Blood oozed from the wounds and dripped down her face in streaks.

Tears streamed down his face. His heart ached at what was before him. Seth glanced down to see her undergarments ripped and her flesh sliced open. The sign of a cross with a meandering wound like a red river on top cut deep into her skin. A curtain of blood soaked into her white chemise and petticoat. A dagger embedded to its hilt in her chest sliced into her heart. He wanted to turn away. He wanted to believe this wasn't happening but stood frozen in horror at the sight before him instead. Then she started to speak.

"I don't have much time." Her voice echoed around the room. Not the sweet lyrical voice he remembered, but one raspy and full of pain. "Give me your hands, my darling." She reached out and took his hands in hers.

"You're not real." His whole body shook at her touch.

He had wanted her to be with him more than anything, but not like this. For all his size he had never been so frightened in his life.

"I loved you. Find out who did this to me." She caressed his cheek. "Don't cry, my darling. You always doubted yourself too much. You are a good man. We just met at the wrong time for us both. Promise me you'll protect my descendants in case they come for them."

Seth nodded as Rosie placed their hands on the dagger in her chest and pushed deeper. His body became cold, as cold as the wind before snow comes.

"No" Seth screamed.

Not releasing him, Rosie lent forward and kissed him with icy blue lips.

Seth's strong arms bulged as he attempted to pull away. He didn't want his last memory of her to be this. Rosie pushed the blade deeper still.

"There were four of them, Seth. Promise me now you will do what I ask."

Seth nodded. "I promise I'll watch over your family. I'll find those who did this to you. They will pay with their lives."

Rosie became a dazzling brilliance of colors. Her hair glowed. Her eyes, one blue, one green twinkled mischievously. She laughed. All traces of blood and wounds disappeared, except for the dagger in her chest.

Seth smiled and laughed with her as warmth and power surged through his body. For one glorious moment, he was enveloped in a brilliant light and the happiness of what might have been.

"I'll give you life for as long as you need to avenge my death," Rosie said.

Then the kitchen resumed its darkened state. She was gone.

He stumbled toward the back door and pulled it open. The cold night air hit him. Dizziness overcame him again as he fell to his knees and emptied the contents of his stomach on the garden path. With the ale gone and the cold air sobering him, he leaned back against the wall of the cottage. He tried to remember Rosie's words through his muddled and intoxicated thoughts. What did she mean she had given him life?

He staggered across to the forge and lit an oil lamp to help illuminate the darkness. Its yellow glow caused the blades on his workbench nearby to gleam with sinister intent. Maybe he was still drunk. It felt as if the knives still called to him.

He picked one up and sliced across his wrist. He gritted his teeth at the searing pain. The skin glowed along the cut. Little veins grew out and pulled the edges back together. It was as if he watched someone else's hand heal. This couldn't be happening. He peered closer. All he could see was a faint scar barely visible in the light of the lamp.

"Rosie? What have you done to me?" He yelled the words, although there was no one to hear. On the night he was to end it all, she had saved him. In the past he had let her down, but not anymore. He had promised to look after her family and find her killers, and that was what he would do.

Now, he remembered something else about the apparition. The dagger plunged into her chest was one he finished repairing only two days before.

ONE

Cork, 2010

The bookshop buzzed with excitement as customers vied to get close to Nan. The early flight from Bristol to Cork had arrived late. So did Cara, but she was here now and planned to have some fun. She wanted to do a happy dance. It would probably attract a bit of attention and this was Nanna Kathleen's day.

The queue stretched to the exit as people stood clutching their copies of the Magic Touch Cookbook. Nanna looked wonderful in her elegant blue dress with her long auburn hair twirled up. No white-haired granny in an apron here. The hair color came out of a bottle these days. Cara had every intention of doing exactly the same when her dark auburn hair went gray.

The red hair and the odd green and blue eyes were what connected her to Nanna. It also made her feel a stranger with her own mother whose eyes were brown. Of course, there was also the fact they disagreed on about everything, especially her involvement with magic. Mum had never been able to access the power. It caused a grudge she wasn't prepared to discuss no matter how much Cara or Nanna tried.

Cara still couldn't get out of her mind that this wasn't your normal cookbook. Nanna made no pretense about accessing magic to enhance her food. She even went so far as to provide incantations with some of the recipes. Cara had always known that magic was real, with Nanna it was hard not to. She just didn't want to take the next step and practice herself. She suppressed a giggle at the thought of people buying the cookbook and going home thinking all their problems could be solved with a bit of sage and saying abracadabra.

Nanna glanced up and waved across the shop. The next customer was a man who put a single rose down on top of his copy of Nanna's book. Cara shook her head. The poor guy didn't know what he was getting into. The women in her family didn't do things by halves, eccentric Nanna, perfectionist Mum, and what about herself?

She reckoned she was slightly alternative with a love for vintage clothes, charity shops and Irish food. A quick glance around showed there weren't any men determined to walk her way with a rose in their teeth. It was just as well. If one showed up, she'd have told him that if he thought she was going to kiss him and get tetanus, it so wasn't happening. Someone touched her arm. Cara squeaked, then covered her mouth in embarrassment. She turned to find a smartly dressed woman beside her.

"I'm so sorry. I didn't mean to make you jump. You're Kathleen's granddaughter, Cara, aren't you? I'm Julie O'Donnell, from The Cork Examiner. Your grandmother said you're a chef and run your own business in the UK based on Irish food. We'd like to work on the connection. Say we found you first."

Julie kept talking but Cara couldn't concentrate. The place was crowded and warm, but a shiver passed through her body. Her back arched. For a second, the whole shop appeared to darken as if the shadow of someone's mind reached out to grab her. Cold seeped through her body making her lightheaded. Then the sensation was gone as fast as it had come. She leaned against a bookcase and took a deep breath as the room steadied.

That's what happens when you have an overactive imagination and no breakfast she considered. Julie was still talking but she hadn't heard a word.

"I'd love to do anything to help," Cara replied. What had she just agreed to do?

"Great, then we'll have you in the photo shoot too." Julie threaded her arm through Cara's and shepherded her across the room. "You know I'd never seen anyone with eyes of different colors, the blue and green are so different and so vivid, and now two of you in the same room. I can't miss that opportunity. Plus I love the green dress, so 1950's. You obviously have your Nanna's good taste."

Cara hugged Nanna who whispered, "This won't take long darling. Then we can have some time together."

"I'm fine, Nanna. Wallow in the glory, you deserve it." Cara took her place next to the book display as flashes went off from the cameras. The intimidating feeling from earlier completely disappeared. It was just as well because if someone good or bad was watching now, she would never see them for the lights in her eyes.

---

THE DAY SEEMED surreal once they were back at the family farm of Waterfall House. The whitewashed seventeenth century farmhouse oozed peace from its walls. Nanna had probably cast a protection spell that helped. The calmness always seeped into Cara's bones when she stayed here.

She had seriously thought of coming back after the breakup with Tony and losing the baby. Then the catering business had taken off and kept her going. Plus she wouldn't do that to her partner, Daniel.

Cara hoped the farmhouse wouldn't change now her grandmother was famous, especially since there were rumors of a television show. It was selfish, but Cara didn't like the idea of people rummaging through her memories.

"I saw you blush when the man gave you the rose, Nanna. You still have the golden touch. That twinkle in your eye gets men's hearts racing. Did you put a spell on him to make you look good in front of the reporters?"

Cara settled into one of the comfy armchairs in the sitting room, wine in hand. She'd changed from her dress to jeans and an overlarge jumper. The room seemed to shield them from the outside world with its coziness.

Her grandmother started a fire in the beautiful old inglenook fireplace. "He was charming, and had a lovely head of black hair just like Pop when I first met him. He was a bit too young for me though. Said he'd seen my website and traveled from England. And no, I didn't put a spell on him, you cheeky minx." Nanna wagged a finger as she sat opposite.

"He made you blush just like Pops used to." Cara's heart ached at the thought of her grandfather. The world still seemed less without him in it.

"I've never been interested in anyone else. Love's an elusive thing. I've no explanation why I found it with your grandfather, though the angel cards did tell me he was coming. I don't expect to love again now he's gone, but I'm open to offers. A little dalliance here and there might be fun. Your problem is you've never had a great love."

Cara sat back in the chair and pulled her feet underneath her. "We both know I've been extremely successful in finding exactly the opposite to love. My work is great. I'll stick with it instead. By the way, that reporter thought I was a witch, didn't she?"

Cara steered the conversation away from her love life, though magic was probably just as tricky as she couldn't deny her witch heritage much longer.

Nanna raised her gaze as she sipped her tea. "Didn't bother you, did she? She has this thing about the odd-colored eyes. It means nothing if you can't access the power."

"Daniel would've loved the photo shoot. I'm sure I was gormlessly grinning in the background." Cara pulled a face, trying to cross her eyes. She didn't succeed. That was a family talent that hadn't been passed on to her.

"How is Daniel?"

"Business is doing well and before you ask, Jeff hasn't proposed yet." Cara sipped her wine; glad the conversation was no longer on her love life.

"He will. I've seen it in my mirror. I'll give you an incantation to do the next time you cook for them," Nanna said, amusement sliding into her eyes as she grinned. "It'll speed things up a bit. I want to be alive when they tie the knot."

"No. I won't mess with spells again," Cara said. "I don't have the gift. I never did. It's more likely they'd probably never speak to each other. You've the knack of drawing in the power. I'm a disaster waiting to happen. Remember, when I gave the cat hiccups for two hours? Even you couldn't reverse it."

Nanna leaned forward, obviously she wasn't going to let up. "You know I didn't ask you back because of the book launch. A scrying might stop those dreams you told me about. Don't give me that look as if you're mumbling something under your breath."

"I'm not," Cara lied.

"I just want you to think about casting some spells," Nanna said. "While you do, I'll go and get dessert."

Cara had five bookings next weekend and needed to be focused. In addition, she was honestly scared of the power her grandmother embraced so easily. It seemed to be a double-edged sword as far as Cara was concerned. She didn't want to hurt the cat again, plus the dreams had started after her last go. The sexy ones with the dark well-built and mysterious man were okay. The ones with bodies being chopped up were another matter.

Nanna walked back in with the apple pie and cream. The flavors burst on Cara's tongue with the first mouthful. "You haven't put something in this, have you?"

"I'm shocked you'd suggest something. Are you insinuating my cooking's not good enough without magic?" Nanna wiped a fake tear from her eye.

"I'm eating it anyway. Life's too short." Cara shoveled in another mouthful. If Nan's pie was wicked, then she was more than happy to be sinful.

"While you do, I'll get ready."

Maybe, her grandmother was right and the scary dreams would go away if they did this. It would be good if she could keep the sexy ones though, Cara thought. They were as close as she got to romance these days.

Nanna went to the sideboard and brought out a box

made from a dark wood with a gold pentagram surrounded by a silver circle painted on the top. Cara glanced around and was relieved to see the farm cat was nowhere in sight. She didn't want to put it through agony again.

"You obviously weren't ready last time, Cara. I do believe you have the gift though. We'll see what we can do to help your business. To keep me happy, we'll do what we can about your love life. If you think you're up to it, we'll deal with the dreams as well."

Cara cringed at the thought, but kept eating. Nanna opened the box and took out two necklaces and placed them on the table. One was a delicate gold shamrock-shaped charm on a chain. The other looked to be made of silver or white gold, and had the shape of a stag's head. Cara had seen her grandparents wear them over the years and always thought them beautiful.

"I've been meaning to give you these since Pops died. He always said he was my protector. Sweet man couldn't even chop the head off of s turkey at Christmastime, but I let him believe it. I want you to have this so you can give it to your mate when you meet him."

Cara choked on a mouthful of food as she laughed.

"Come on, Nanna. I'm twenty-eight years old and look after myself. If not, I'll call the local security firm or the cops. I'll go along with this tonight but I'm not asking for some magical protector and 'mate' sounds so basic."

"Humor me and take them. I've imbued them with power. If you just want to wear yours as a pretty necklace, it will be fine." Nanna held out her hand.

"It's beautiful and I'll always wear it." Cara put on the necklace as Nanna took four candles from her box and placed them in the corners of the room.

"I want you to close your eyes and imagine a circle of

light surrounding us. I know it is how you like to imagine protection and I have called mine here already."

Cara's pulse started to quicken. Her hands grew clammy. The power had been good for Nan, so she had to think it would be the same for her granddaughter. If she was going to do this though, Cara thought, then she would barter. "Only if it gets me another piece of pie."

"That's my girl." Nanna smiled, reached out and squeezed Cara's fingers.

"Just don't be disappointed when nothing happens. I'm not paying the vet fees if the cat goes daft again." Cara closed her eyes and tried to envisage a circle around them. It was easier than she imagined.

When she opened her eyes, she could actually see a ring of light. It was probably just the effect of the candles and the fire. If Daniel could see her now doing this magic stuff he would crack up laughing. It was either that, or he'd be getting her to do spells to make them both rich and famous.

"I've called for the Goddess to protect us while we work. When you do this on your own, you must always ask a higher power to watch over you. Now, I want you to read this." Nanna took a piece of paper and a round mirror from the box and placed it on the table between them.

Cara picked up the piece of paper and cringed. "I thought we were going to do a spell for my business."

"We will, later." Nanna smirked as she raised an eyebrow.

Cara took a deep breath and read aloud. *"True love I have not found, true love I seem to fear. Banish the sadness of the past, and true love will soon appear."* She felt her heart pounding in her chest as she spoke. Did she really want to see her past and her failed loves thrown in her face again? Her hands shook as she peered at the mirror.

This was all hocus-pocus, so what was she scared of? Something other than a reflection of the ceiling above slowly appeared in the mirror. It looked like the main street in Bath. People milled around. One stopped and appeared to be staring as if he could actually see out of the mirror.

He was a tall well-built man with a somber brooding face, and hair cropped close to his head. Nanna might think those gray eyes appeared unapproachable, but Cara knew him to be incredibly passionate. She also knew he wasn't real. The mirror had conjured up her dream lover. So much for this spell finding her a real person to love. At least this dream guy wouldn't break her heart.

"He's not what I expected, but from the size of him, he looks as if he could protect you. You're blushing. You've seen him before." Nanna squinted at her.

"It's embarrassing. I've sort of seen him before, but it's not what you think. It's not possible for me to know him. He doesn't exist, except in some rather raunchy dreams I've been having."

Heat spread up Cara's neck. She felt hot in places she wasn't meant to when sitting with her grandmother. Thank goodness reading minds wasn't one of Nanna's abilities. She would be shocked at the man in the mirror and the things he had been doing with her granddaughter.

"Maybe you've seen him once and can't remember. The Goddess appears to believe he exists. She's never wrong."

The picture faded as Nanna handed her another piece of paper. Cara dreaded to think what might be written this time.

*"I request of you tonight, to let my business future be bright. Let the world my meals adore. Let them bring happiness, I ask no more."*

Another picture appeared in the mirror. She was in a

kitchen. It wasn't the one at her flat and there were TV cameras focused on her. Daniel stood beside her. They were laughing. Then the picture started to fade.

"That looked promising. You'll give all those other cooks a run for their money. Do you want to try and cast your own spell about the other dreams now?"

Goose bumps broke out on Cara's arms. Her gut clenched. She needed to do this before she panicked. Too late, she thought. She already struggled to take a deep breath. *"I have dreams of death and killing. I am the killer and seem pretty willing. Why do these dreams keep coming back to me? Tell me how to make them flee?"*

Nanna pursed her lips and shook her head. Cara ignored the silent criticism. The rhyme was the best she could come up with on such short notice.

A picture formed in the mirror of Nanna sitting at the book launch. In front of her was the man with the rose. Then the picture changed to the torso of a woman. The body had been sliced open with the mark of a cross and a meandering line cut through on top.

As in Cara's dreams, there was a dagger with an ornate handle plunged into the heart of the woman. Then the picture faded. All Cara could see was the ceiling and the tasseled lampshade above their heads reflected in it.

Nanna came across and hugged her. "Oh Cara, you poor thing. Is that what you've been dreaming? It's awful. Maybe, the man with the rose had something to do with it. I couldn't sense anything, but then again you did say you felt strange today."

It was only now, when she sat safely in her grandmother's embrace, that Cara realized how much her body was trembling. "Maybe, the dreams will stop. I have your necklace. Anyway, I can't go and accuse some poor innocent man of murder. It probably happened because I hadn't had any breakfast and felt a bit faint."

Nanna placed her hands palm down on the table and asked the Goddess to take the power back into the earth. She turned the light on again and blew out the candles. When she sat back down she looked like the cat that had gotten the cream.

"This confirms you've the power and you can control it. Then again I've always known that and so have you. There's one other thing I wanted to talk to you about. I've a box at my solicitors with some keepsakes in it. I think you should know more about our family's past. I was going to leave you the chest anyway if anything happened to me, but I think you should have it now. I'll phone my solicitor tomorrow and get him to send it to you." Nanna reached across the table. She took Cara's hand and gave it a squeeze.

"Nothing's going to happen to you," Cara said. "If you're going to insist on me being magical, then I've decided you'll live forever." A shudder went up Cara's spine at the concept of a world without her grandmother in it.

---

BACK IN BRISTOL DANIEL showed up at the flat with the menus for their upcoming meals. The weekend passed in a blur of jobs. Her feet would never feel the same again. The soles ached as if they were bruised. If she had any sense she should have wished for magic shoes to stop her feet from aching.

Tomorrow she would phone and confirm the bookings for next weekend. Plus the local paper, *The Bristol Evening Post* wanted to do a piece on the business because of the connection to her grandmother. Cara didn't have a clue what she would say. For now she just wanted hot chocolate and bed, but her daft cat Merlin, still hadn't come inside.

Cara stomped her feet on the pavement to get some circulation back into her frozen toes as she called out, "Merlin. Come on, you've had long enough." The sound of raucous meowing filled the air, followed by hissing and spitting. Then a bedraggled black and white cat limped across the road. "Sometimes you should learn to run away, Merlin."

Before she could say anymore he collapsed at her feet. Tears formed in her eyes and a lump rose in her throat as she wrapped him in her cardigan and carried him upstairs. His body, a heavy weight in her arms.

She gently placed him on the floor in the flat but he didn't make a sound. There was a long cut down his front leg and another one above his eye. Another deep gash on his abdomen covered the fur in blood. He was still breathing, soft shallow puffs of air.

Cara grabbed her mobile from the breakfast bar and started to search for the emergency vet's number. It rang when Merlin let out another howl of pain. Cara pressed 'end call' before the receptionist could answer. If there was a time to test her power, it was now. Closing her eyes, she made a circle in her mind, and asked the Goddess to protect her.

*"Merlin is laying hurt at my feet. Help me fix him up and make it tout suite." She didn't need Nanna here to tell her how awful that spell was.*

Her hands wouldn't stop shaking. She laid them gently on Merlin. Tears fell down her face. Did anything happen? Merlin stopped howling. He started to purr and lick his wounds. All she could see was a tiny scar when he cleaned away the blood on his leg.

She peered at his head as she wiped it with a damp tissue, but the cut had closed. His abdomen was healed too. Maybe it was the other cat's blood she had seen. That couldn't be possible though. She had seen the open wounds. Maybe someone was out to get Merlin. No, that was silly. Mr. Dewet's cat across the road was huge. Merlin had fought him before and it would probably happen again.

Cara knelt on the floor, placing her hands palm down. She offered thanks to the Goddess and Nanna. Then, Cara sent the energy back. Closing her eyes she dissolved the circle. She'd done it. She had performed magic all on her own.

It was probably her imagination, but her whole body tingled as if flooded with energy. Getting a wet, warm towel she finished cleaning Merlin. He meowed in protest at the attention. She picked him up and took him to the bedroom and laid him down on the bed next to her. The softness of his fur comforted her. She stroked him and drifted off to sleep.

THE BLOOD WAS WARM. It flowed away from the young woman's throat and over her fingers. Cara sat astride the woman. The annoying fool fought too much. Death needed to be savored with each cut or there would be ragged edges on the wounds.

Voices carried down the alleyway. Cara thumped the woman's face again with her fists. There wouldn't be enough time to finish the ritual. She wouldn't be caught over this trifle. As she stood up to run, she glanced back at the woman on the ground to see the face change to that of Nanna's.

HER OWN SCREAMS WOKE CARA. She sat bolt upright in bed. The sweat chilled on her skin as she reached out and turned on the bedside lamp. She expected her palms to be covered in blood when she held them up, but they were clean. Merlin moved onto her lap and pressed up against her chest. Her breathing calmed. She reached over and picked up her grandmother's book of spells and the stag necklace.

Whatever these dreams meant, Nanna wouldn't have protection anymore. She would send the necklace back. It had been silly to mess with magic. The dreams had come back so vividly it made her wonder if she could really imagine something like that. She'd never hurt anyone like that, so why did murder haunt her?

# TWO

Cara's stomach ached as if a rat had been gnawing at it all night. When she returned from the interview she would ring her grandmother and check on her. She looked at her watch. It was almost ten and the interview was at eleven.

She smoothed down her favorite blue pencil skirt and picked a cat hair off her cream jumper. The reporter would probably think she was going to turn up in green. Just because her cooking was from the Emerald Isle, it didn't mean she had to be clothed in green, even if it was her favorite color.

She also hoped they wouldn't make any comments about her differently colored eyes. This story needed to be professional. It wasn't about whether she was a witch, especially as she was sitting on the fence right now about the whole idea. Her mobile rang. It was Daniel.

"Where are you? You said you'd be here by ten and more importantly, what are you wearing?"

Cara laughed, hearing Daniel's voice. "I'm sorry. I'll be there in five."

Cara drove as fast as she could to Daniel's place and

hoped she hadn't gotten a speeding fine along the way. He stood waiting on the pavement outside of his apartment. He wore a black suit, white shirt, green tie, and tapped his immaculately polished patent-leather shoe. His short blond hair was perfect as always, but he was holding a cake box. She dreaded to think what was inside. Today was not the day for surprises.

"Love the outfit, Cara. Not exactly Irish though, is it? You have that lovely green vintage dress." He shook his head in mock disapproval of her.

"I decided it would look tacky if we dressed up in green with shamrocks everywhere. I just hope the publicity doesn't mean we have to lose our edge."

"With your cooking and my panache, we're not about to lose anything. I've always wanted to wear one though."

"Wear one what?" Cara stared at another set of traffic lights that had gone red as she approached. She was tempted to try and wriggle her nose like Samantha on Bewitched and make them change. Samantha would probably have been driving a fancy convertible rather than a Morris Minor van with a big emblem on the side saying Celtic Dinners.

"A kilt. The Irish wore them as well as the Scots, though ancient Celtic warriors used to go into battle naked. I was so born in the wrong time. Jeff said he would love to see me in a kilt." Daniel smiled wickedly.

"I'm sure he would and you'd take the whole "no underwear" thing literally. Anyway, before I go insane with worry, what's in the box?" Cara pulled into the car park of *The Bristol Evening Post* Building. She searched to find a space that might have been reserved for visitors.

"It's something I worked on while you were away."

Cara grabbed her briefcase from the back seat. Daniel

lifted the lid on the box to reveal a white iced cake decorated with a green Celtic Mandela. She loved the Celtic knot design. She was pretty sure this one showed a spiritual connection but knew some represented nastier things and she didn't need that today.

"It's the cake you did for the Morris couple. They said they didn't want it as the daughter ran off with the minister. I thought it would be a shame to let it go to waste. We could do weddings." Daniel grinned at her as they got in the lift.

Cara shook her head not so much surprised at what had happened with the Morris family, but at the idea of doing weddings. Daniel wanted his own wedding so much he had forgotten her attitude of avoiding them.

After leaving the lift and speaking to two more receptionists, they finally worked out where they were meant to be.

"I bet Gordon Ramsey would have been met downstairs," Daniel whispered.

Peter Connor, the editor of *The Evening Post's* "Good Food Guide", would be the one to work out if they were interesting enough to be in his pages. The thought made her stomach churn. Daniel's cake box was shaking so much, she was sure there would only be crumbs left. Maybe, that was a good idea.

"Why the hell are we here, Daniel?" Her stomach gurgled and her palms went sweaty.

"Because we want to be incredibly rich and famous." Daniel winked.

"No I don't. That's you." Cara's head started to thump. "I'll be known as the witch who can cook because of my Nanna and her spells. You know that's not where we want to go, not that I don't love my Nanna. Now I sound pathetic. I think I'm going to throw up." Cara's hand went to her mouth when an incredibly handsome man stopped in front of her.

"Hi, I'm Peter Conner. We meet at last. It sounds like a cliché but I've really heard a lot about both of you."

Peter offered his hand to both of them. Cara took it in her trembling grasp. She felt heat rising on her neck. He turned and motioned for them to follow him to his office. Daniel couldn't take his eyes off Peter's butt as they shuffled into his office. Peter turned and beamed at them with his perfect teeth, blond hair, and blue eyes.

He wasn't wrong when he talked about clichés, Cara thought. There was something about him that reminded her of Tony. Why was it her ex-lover kept popping into her mind even when she didn't want him there? It reminded her of everything she had lost. She had to hold it together. She couldn't deal with the past rearing its ugly head right now.

"I'm not going to ask you a load of questions about how you cook your culinary delights. My assistant Carol will be talking with you later regarding those details. I wanted to speak to you personally because I'm planning a dinner two weeks from Sunday. I'd like your company to cater it. I've some big names coming and we would do it as a feature."

"Yes, of course we can manage that." She dreaded the idea of cameras being shoved in her face. Worse still would be those startling blue eyes of Peter Connor staring at her all evening. It would be stupid to turn him down when they wanted to make their business a success.

"May I enquire what's in the box?"

Daniel beamed with pride as he lifted the lid. Thankfully the cake hadn't collapsed into a thousand pieces. "Cara's Irish whiskey fruitcakes are famous. I've been experimenting with some decorations with weddings in mind."

"Does the green design on top have any significance?"

"It's a Celtic Love Knot and conveys the intimate relationship of lovers." Daniel smiled, eagerly. "The lines cross over each other and wrap around each other so that everything is connected. The knots are beautiful and have no beginning or end. It can also show how there must be equality in a relationship or one will devour the other."

Cara shook her head. Why did he always have to be so dramatic? Peace doves would have been so much easier to live with.

"It'll be perfect for the photo shoot."

Peter pressed a button on his desk. His assistant, Carol, was immediately there ushering them out. Half an hour of questions followed. Cara drew the impression that Peter's assistant was looking down her nose at them as if they were gone off crème brûlée.

"I read your family comes from Ireland. Your grandmother recently published a cookbook. The talent runs in the family then," Carol said.

"I'd love to think someday I could reach the heights of my Nanna's cookery. She's gifted when it comes to food." Cara kept a straight face and guessed what was coming next.

"The article in The Cork Examiner mentioned that you and your grandmother have unusual eye coloring which in years gone by indicated witchcraft. You're not using incantations to mesmerize your clients are you?" Carol raised an eyebrow as she asked the question.

Cara sighed before answering. "I did try once to get one of our clients to sign a blank check after eating my Irish stew. I didn't do the incantation quite right and he refused to pay," Cara teased. "I've given up on magic and resorted to hard work again."

Daniel chuckled beside her. Cara was glad when the interview finally ended.

She pressed the button for the foyer as her mind wandered back to the photo shoot. The lift doors opened and she walked out before she realized they weren't in the foyer but in a narrow corridor. Before she could turn around, she bumped into a middle-aged man in a crumpled suit.

"What the hell," the man yelled, as his folder fell to the floor. Papers and photographs scattered across the corridor.

"I'm so sorry. I thought we were in the foyer," Cara said, as she helped him pick up the fallen items.

"Does this look like the bloody foyer? We are on the third floor, can't you even press a button right?" With that, he snatched the photographs from her hand and headed off down the corridor.

Daniel was still standing in the lift with his finger on the button. "What a grumpy old fart. Look he's probably not getting any. You're the closest he's been to a female in years. If he's gay, he'll never get laid in that suit."

Cara tried to smile at her partner and hoped she didn't look as dismal as she felt.

The lift opened at ground level.

"I need to go to the ladies. I won't be long." Once there, Cara sat in the cubicle and pulled the piece of paper from her pocket. It was from the reporter's pile on the floor. Her hands shook as she read.

*"Two women have died in the last six months in an identical fashion. Their bodies have been mutilated and dumped. The police are afraid of copycat killers, but surely their silence may cause something worse."*

The article went on to describe how the women had been mutilated. There was even a picture of a woman's body. Cara recognized the markings. They were identical to the ones in her dreams. She couldn't keep the bile down any longer. She turned and vomited into the toilet bowl.

Daniel stood in the foyer. He put his arm around her when she joined him. "You look awful. What's wrong?"

"I'm fine. I just let nerves get the better of me."

"You shouldn't worry. I don't think it went that badly, you know."

"Come on Daniel, I ogled Mr. Peter Perfect. Then I grinned my way through a photo shoot gormlessly."

"Come on, Cara." He hugged her quickly. "You're not gormless or you wouldn't be my partner."

She managed a weak smile. "Look, I need to give this piece of paper to the receptionist over there. That grumpy guy dropped it and I picked it up by mistake."

CARA SAT in her counselor Jessica's consulting room wishing she was somewhere else. The session wasn't going well. She had explained about the newspaper interview, but Cara knew her therapist's look of concern regardless of how well it was disguised. Jessica wasn't fooled that she was calm, cool and collected.

"Have you spoken to your parents since last month?"

"No." Cara said too quickly and wanted to take the word back and make up an excuse.

"What about the dreams?" Jessica asked, writing something in her file.

"They're less, maybe once a week." Cara pulled her hair on her neck. She knew Jessica was there to help her but she really didn't want to talk about it right now.

"Is the dream still the same recurring one?"

"Yes, but today I saw a photograph." Cara struggled to breathe as she remembered.

"So what was in the photograph?" Jessica probed deeper.

"She was."

"What do you mean?" Jessica stopped writing and leant forward.

"I saw a woman's picture today and she had the exact wounds."

"Are you sure about what you saw? You may have seen a newspaper article, or a news report, and it just resurfaced in your dreams."

"I'm a chef. When I use a knife, I'm particular about each cut or slice. The body in the photograph looked as if it had been dead a while but the slashes were the same." Cara's mouth dried up as she spoke. The walls of the room felt as if they closed in on her.

"Have you considered that the stress of the interview along with everything else may have led you to imagine the picture? You've been through so much this past year with your relationship ending, then losing the baby and the surgery."

Jessica was right. They could just be bad dreams. Someone didn't have to have died like that. It might be a shot from an old black and white movie. If that was the case then why was a reporter writing an article about two murders? Cara's head hurt as she rubbed her temples.

Jessica's phone beeped to let her know the next appointment had arrived. Cara was out of the seat and the room as quickly as she could walk. The next person waiting was Mr. Matcher.

Black hair hung over his face. Cara smiled politely at him. She received a glare for her effort. He would keep. He didn't look so cool today. In fact, he looked like he was about to throw up as he leaned against the wall.

"Are you all right?" Cara asked, expecting to be given the finger.

"Like you could help? You're not even normal."

The response was no different than what she expected, but it still annoyed her. She needed to get out of here and return home to cook. The preparation of food usually took her mind off any problems. She needed to forget interviews, counselors, dreams, photographs, magic and moody young men.

She took in a deep breath of air outside. It was good to be free of recycled air and emotions. Her mobile rang and Cara cringed as she saw it was her mother.

"Cara," Her mother hesitated.

"Hallo, Mum." She rarely phoned. Cara shivered with dread at what she was going to say next.

"I'm sorry, dear. Your grandmother's dead."

## THREE

Matcher sat opposite Jessica. Another tune came to mind and he flicked his fingers as if strumming his guitar. The music that always played in his head was something he liked about himself since the operation. He still wasn't sure about the new ability to read auras. He reckoned if he ever had a band he would call them Strange Glow just because of it.

"So you've moved into your flat?" Jessica asked.

"Yeah." Multiple colors swirled around his counselor aura. Maybe she had some bad shit going on. Then again, maybe he didn't want to know. In the waiting room he had felt like he was going to throw up but it was easing off now.

"How are you getting along with your flat-mates?"

"Great. The guys are cool." What was he doing here? He hadn't even told her he could read auras. It was just as well. She might get him locked up if she knew the truth. The hospital thought he was crazy after the operation. He yelled abuse and grabbed people asking where his Mum was. He only had one more session booked with Jessica, so he could cope.

"How's your father dealing with the move?"

"He said to call him if I needed anything."

Matcher let his mind wander to the woman he'd seen in the waiting room. Her aura was weird, like nothing he'd seen before. It was normal one minute and then went almost black. Maybe she was an alien. That was it. He'd been given this gift to make great music and save the world from aliens. Jessica waited.

"Went to an interview last week and I got a job stocking shelves." She smiled at him and he relaxed. At last, he had said something right. This was easy, he could blab on about his new workmates for a while till the buzzer went, then freedom.

Jumping in his old car an hour later, he headed for Filton and his dad's place. He needed his CD's. If he listened to any more of the guys' rap he'd go mad. He hoped Dad would let him have Mum's classical stuff. Julie answered the door. She was making Dad happy but Matcher's stomach still turned to knots, seeing another woman in this house.

"Your dad's at work, but he said you might call. Come on in. The box is out back."

"Can I use the loo?"

"Yeah, sure."

Matcher walked up the stairs. The bathroom was at the top and his old room was off to the right. His stepbrother Josh was a good kid and it was his place now. All the band posters had been replaced with footballers. Dad would be happy as Matcher reckoned he had always wanted a sporty kid and now he had one.

Back at the flat, he went straight to his room. This place wasn't much of a home but it was his. He looked around. He had one single bed, one desk, one bookshelf, one wardrobe, one comfy old threadbare chair and two bean-bags. Now, he had his collection of CD's and books, mostly fantasy. It was fun to escape from the real world. He put a CD on. Perhaps he would be able to convince his flat-mates to convert to some heavier stuff.

Most of the things in the box were odds and ends, except for a photo album. There was also a package wrapped in gift wrap and there was a note on it.

*"She loved them, and I think she hoped you would too someday. Love, Dad."*

Matcher eyes watered as he stared at the collection of his mother's classical CD's.

---

HIS FLAT-MATES MIKE and Pete were normal twenty-year- olds with two things on their minds, booze and sex. Matcher laughed to himself. At least, he'd managed to have sex before he lost his left ball to the big C at the tender age of eighteen. He would have something to compare his future capacity to, if he ever had sex again. God, he hoped he would have sex again.

It had been another good night down at the pub. Of course, he had no money left and couldn't eat for a week. He wasn't drunk, but he was close to it. Maybe, it wasn't such a good idea to move into a flat near a pub, especially with these two. Collapsing onto the bed, Matcher found something digging into his back. It was the photo album. He fell asleep listening to Mozart and looking at a photo of Mum building a sandcastle with him at Weston Super-Mare.

---

HIS BODY WAS SOAKED with sweat when he sat up. It was happening again. It was like someone tormented him by making him relive the experience over and over. He didn't need to close his eyes to remember everything clearly.

There were muffled voices in his dream as always. He couldn't move but still felt the excruciating pain. It was like a cannon ball hit him in the groin. They were chopping out the cancer. As the scalpel cut through the skin, the pain moved to his chest. He was dying and floating away above his body. Suddenly, the pain disappeared as his mother materialized beside him.

"Mum, what are you doing here?" Matcher said.

"Is that the only greeting I get, after all this time?"

She looked beautiful. Not like at the end when the breast cancer had taken everything, but like in the pictures of when he was a kid. This wasn't right. He could see through her to the tiled wall beyond. Matcher looked around. There was the big light and he was above it. Down there, on the bed was his body. The staff pulled in a machine and placed things on his chest.

"Stand clear," someone shouted.

The tortuous pain started up again as he turned back to his mother. She moved effortlessly forward and hugged him.

"I loved you so much. I never wanted to leave. It hurts to see you go through this pain, but you're not to come yet. I'll leave you with something to help."

"What are you on about? What's happening?" The agony in his chest swelled again.

He was back to reality and his room. Damn, he should have drunk more. Then he could slip back into oblivion instead of having the dream again.

The woman at the counselor's came to mind. He hadn't been too nice to her. Mum had given him the ability to read auras. So far, it wasn't helping him or anyone else. If anything, it just made him feel more separated from everyone.

He needed to pull his head out of his ass and do something. Maybe he had been given this gift to help the woman at Jessica's, but how the hell would he find her? Wait a minute. She had been talking to the receptionist about getting tickets to go to some Shakespeare play in Bath on the 18th. It was a long shot, but he had to try.

FOUR

The hammer smashed the metal again and again. Seth reckoned it would be a beautiful blade. After one hundred and fifty odd years he had perfected his skills. Making the swords and sculptures kept him sane some of the time. The swords were for decoration now, not killing. Killing from afar, not seeing your victim up close was preferable nowadays. Janet hovered by the door to the forge with freshly brewed coffee and homemade cake.

"Sorry to interrupt, Seth, but Robert Fetter called from London again. He says he'll be down next week to look at the swords. I suppose he has a buyer. Oh, and the stone company said they'll be delivering the soapstone block tomorrow. There's a letter from the solicitor as well. I'm off to the movies with Valerie."

Seth nodded and turned back to his work. He grinned and wondered why he kept attracting this kind of housekeeper. They always needed to organize every part of his life, whether he wanted them to or not. He loved each one of them. It always hurt when he outlived them and they died. Janet was as wonderful and eccentric as the rest. Maybe, they were all similar because it took a certain type of person to be willing to accept his longevity.

He sipped the coffee and then opened the letter from the solicitor. One of Rosie's descendants called Kathleen had died. He would go online later and book a flight to go to the funeral. It shamed him to admit it wasn't to honor Kathleen, but on the chance he might see Cara.

He had watched her for years but knew a relationship was not possible, or that was what he told himself. She wasn't Rosie and he had to remember his goal. He had to find Rosie's killer and die so he could be free of this torment. He always protected Rosie's descendants from a distance. He couldn't afford to let that change now.

———

THE COUNTRYSIDE BLURRED beside him as he increased the throttle on his bike. Grey bike, grey rider, he almost blended with the hedgerows as darkness approached. The lights of Bath ahead of him, beckoned as always. However, they never provided an answer of where the murderer lurked. Maybe he could ride into a tree, and fool himself again he could die.

He'd spend weeks in hospital. The doctors would state it was a miraculous recovery. It was all a lie. He parked the bike and walked the streets. When all else failed, it was reassuring to just plod all night. He could walk alongside others and make believe he was the same. He found himself near The Roman Baths again. It was the last place Rosie had been seen.

Seth shivered and pulled up the collar of his jacket. The

night air caused goose bumps to rise on his neck. He found a bar and sat down in the corner with his beer. People came and went, and as usual, avoided him. His muscular frame intimidated most onlookers. The shaved head and grey eyes caused many people to glance away. A group of woman giggled as two of them pointed towards him. Another couple sat quietly in a corner with eyes only for each other. Seth downed his beer and left.

Faces, he would observe everyone as they passed by. All these years. All the searching. For what? Once or twice he had come close to discovering the killers, but that was so long ago. After the night Rosie's apparition appeared, he visited James Rushton who had asked him to repair the dagger. Rushton twitched and wrung his hands but revealed nothing much. A week later James was dead. Rumors flew that the young buck had stabbed himself.

Seth's jaw clenched in frustration that he had missed his chance. He had been a fool back then. If he had known what the future held, he would have beaten Rushton until he got answers to his questions. Seth stopped outside one of the bookshops. A sign proclaimed, MAN'S YEARNING FOR IMMORTALITY. Is it MAGIC? SCIENCE? MYTH?

The window was full of books by assorted authors. They were surrounded by crystal balls, test tubes, a skeleton, and a large plastic looking red stone with a sign underneath stating it was the Philosopher's Stone. Every book, article, and Internet site he had studied did nothing to help him discover more about the dagger.

Perhaps one of these books might have another mention of the cult in Eastern Europe that seemed to be connected to the dagger. He had read one book that talked about taking lives to extend your own, but he hadn't taken Rosie's life. Yet he was still alive. What if he never found her killer? What if he went mad? He was close enough now. That was another reason to keep his distance from Cara, but he wouldn't, he couldn't. He was a fool who had lived too long. Now, he was in love with someone who didn't know he existed.

He walked on past Bath Abbey towards Pulteney Bridge. Leaning on the railing he glanced at the water below where he had tried to drown himself on more than one occasion. His last attempt was fifty years ago and he had lain beneath the water for an hour. It did no good.

A scream broke into his thoughts. It came from the other side of the river. He squinted at the grassy area that was illuminated by only one working lamp. It was a place where people would sit and relax in the daytime. It wasn't exactly the location to visit at night so he knew he was walking into trouble.

Seth had been there before. He remembered steps leading down to a raised walkway that skirted behind the trees. The canopy at the back of the grassy area provided darkness where perpetrators could hide. He should walk away. It was none of his business. Then again, what if someone had been there for Rosie? Another scream. A woman yelled but he couldn't make out the words.

He made his way down the steps two at a time. He hurried along the walkway until he was just above the disturbance. Two men stood over a woman sprawled on the ground. Anger bubbled up inside Seth as he clenched his fists.

The larger of the two men grabbed his friend's jacket. "What the bloody hell did you do that for? I just said keep your hand over her mouth, not hit her."

"She bit me, the cow."

"Well now, you've knocked her out. She won't be biting anyone. Shit, half the fun is when they fight."

"She'll wake up in a minute. It wasn't like I hit her hard."

The larger guy knelt down and ripped the girl's blouse open.

"Come to me, my lovely." He started to undo her jeans.

Seth jumped from the raised walkway onto the smaller man. He flattened him to the ground. Before the man had a chance to react and get up again Seth thumped him hard on the chin. He would be out for a while.

"Who the hell are you?" The lager guy shouted.

"No one you know. I've a problem with a man who doesn't treat a lady as he should though."

"She ain't no lady."

Standing up, the man lunged at Seth. The idiot forgot his pants rested around his ankles. Seth smirked as he watched him fall flat on his face. He pulled the man's head up and thumped him across the cheek. There was a satisfying crack as the bone broke beneath his knuckles.

"Bit clumsy, aren't we? Perhaps you should both lie there and rest."

The smell of cheap perfume mixed with cigarettes and alcohol wafted up from the young woman. As he pulled her blouse together and zipped up her pants, his action was rewarded by a slap across his face. He only just managed to move out of the way before her knee came up to connect with his groin. To be long-lived was one thing. He still didn't relish his nether regions being attacked.

"Piss off, you bastard." The young woman screeched so loud his ears hurt. She tried to slap him again.

"I suggest you look around. I thought you needed help." Seth stood back out of reach.

"Where's me purse?"

Seth found the small shoulder bag a few feet away. "Is there someone you can call?"

"None a yer business." She rifled through the contents of her purse, obviously checking to see if anything was missing. Then, she hustled away.

As she passed the two prostrate forms, she kicked each man in the groin. Seth cringed but stayed close behind her as she strode to the stairs. On the fourth step, she lost her footing falling forward and nearly hitting her head. He grabbed her arm and held her up so she didn't make contact with the concrete. She tensed at his touch but didn't push him away.

By the time they came out on the street above she was leaning heavily against him. She was probably concussed plus a little drunk or high. He recalled a taxi rank back near The Abby. All he needed to do now was get there without attracting the attention of any passing police car.

"The Royal United Hospital." Seth told the driver, as they settled in the back seat.

"What the hell? All right, I'm not asking questions. She up-chucks in the back, you're paying for it being cleaned."

When they got out of the cab she managed to stay upright until they entered the Accident and Emergency Department where her legs finally gave out. One of the nurses came over as Seth scooped the young woman up in his arms. Looking at the girl in the light, he thought she couldn't have been much more than sixteen.

"Bring her this way." The nurse pulled back a curtain to a cubicle where a trolley waited. Seth placed the girl on the mattress. She gave a little groan.

The Triage nurse eyed him suspiciously. "What happened?"

"She was beaten up. I stopped it. She passed out. I brought her here."

The nurse raised her eyebrows as she looked at him and then the young woman.

"A man of few words, aren't you? Just sit outside while I get a doctor to see her. Don't go though. We might need some information later."

As she pulled the cubicle curtain across, Seth turned to make his way out. He had no intention of staying. He had already done more than he had intended tonight. As he headed toward the exit, he heard an ambulance siren approaching.

Standing aside, he watched the paramedics bring in a woman on a trolley. They held padding across her forehead. There was blood on her chest but he could make out wounds he had seen before. Two seconds later they were gone behind doors of the Resuscitation Room. A while later, one of the paramedics came back to talk to the Triage Nurse.

"She's lucky to be alive. Some guy jumped her down by the Abbey. Police are still out looking for him." The paramedic peered across at Seth.

That would be his cue to leave. He didn't want to be noticed here tonight with attacks in Bath. With the nurse distracted by the gruesome discussion, Seth made his way out. All he needed to do now was face the long walk back to his bike. He could have ordered a taxi but needed the air to clear his thoughts about what he had just seen.

He rode home through the unlit country roads. The darkness clawed at him. There had been murders in the past with bodies cut up like Rosie's. They never yielded a killer.

Was it starting again? Was this just a random attack? Maybe, this time he would get lucky and find Rosie's killer. Maybe, this time death would get what it waited for, his demise. Then Cara would be safe from him, as well as the killer.

FIVE

Cara wanted to cry but her body seemed stuck in a stasis of disbelief. To feel any emotion would mean accepting Nanna's death. At any moment she expected the grief to hit like a bolt of lightning and tear her heart in two. *Breathe, you can do this. You can get through this.*

Nanna's instructions to her solicitor were for a quiet funeral service. It was typical of her not to want to leave the funeral arrangements to someone else, especially her daughter Anne. For years, Cara had been the go-between where the women were concerned. She hated the role for so long but would cherish it now. Mum had said she was going to come. At the last minute she said she was unwell. Cara wondered if the estranged relationship had finally taken its effect on her mother. Mum was disappointed it wasn't a church service. Her belief in the church was as strong as Nanna's belief in magic.

The local funeral parlor seated about seventy. Cara sat in the front row with Aunty Eileen who kept mumbling to herself.

"Are you all right?" Cara asked.

"Of course I am, dear. She's really glad you came, you know."

Cara clenched and unclenched her hands. They were cold and clammy as if her body was shutting down. Maybe talking to her crazy aunt might take her mind off what was happening. Eileen claimed she could talk to the dead. The fact that the dead person was Nanna was too much right now. Her aunt offered Cara a lace handkerchief. Nanna had never used paper tissues either. These two ladies always had embroidered lace hankies in their pockets.

Cara looked over her shoulder at the people who had known her grandmother. Most of them were family friends, but there were others who had recently made contact because of the cookbook. Looking down at the handkerchief, Cara saw it had her name on it.

"I found it at the farmhouse," Aunt Eileen said. "She says she had just finished it and to give it to you."

*To Cara, Love Nanna.* Cara ran her fingers over the fine stitching. The simple words caused the floodgates to open. Tears coursed down her cheeks. Her shoulders heaved as she gasped for air between sobs.

Outside the funeral parlor, people spoke to her. Their faces and what they were saying to her blurred together. The pain was unbearable. She felt as if her heart would physically snap in two. She always thought Aunty Eileen mad, but would give anything to be her right now, and be able to talk to Nanna.

Aunty Eileen took her arm. "You look pale, Cara. Maybe, you should sit down. All these people wanting to talk to you can be overwhelming. Even Kathleen's gone. I can't see her anywhere."

The tears kept flowing. Cara couldn't draw air into her lungs as her chest tightened. Her aunt was right. She needed to sit down or she would faint. Her legs turned to jelly as everything went out of focus. Someone was holding her. The steady heartbeat reassured her as she leant against their chest. Then, everything went black again.

Aunty Eileen was bending over her as Cara lay on a couch. She didn't recognize the room, but assumed it was a part of the funeral parlor.

"Thanks so much for helping. If you hadn't caught her, she might have hit her head. It's been such a rough day."

Cara craned her neck, but couldn't see who Aunty Eileen was talking to and then the door closed. Whoever it was, had left. It was strange. She felt so calm. The tears were gone. The terrible pain in her chest had eased. She wasn't sure why but she knew she would have the strength to make it through the rest of the day.

"Who was that?"

"I don't know, dear. I wasn't expecting so many people today. Kathleen was commenting earlier on the fact. I still can't see her, but I'm sure she'll talk to me later. In the meantime, we need to get back to Waterfall House so you can rest before more people arrive."

Cara didn't fight as she was helped up, but she didn't want to rest. She wanted to cook. It always helped.

THE FARMHOUSE SMELT WONDERFUL. The soda bread, the ham, the chicken and herbs, all the aromas fused together. People kept coming. The kitchen was a hive of activity. Cara could forget things for a while as she made salads, sliced up meat and served people. Someone tapped her shoulder. She dropped her knife. It fell to the floor with a loud noise and just missed her foot. Okay, maybe she wasn't quite as calm as she thought.

Aunty Eileen stood there next to her holding two large whiskeys. "Follow me, I need to talk to you."

They walked out of the farmyard and into the field opposite and sat down on the small rise. It overlooked the waterfall from which the farm took its name. Cara took her first mouthful of whiskey and spluttered.

"Drink up, Cara. It'll keep out the cold from sitting on the damp grass."

"What did you want to talk about?"

"She's back again. She said I had to tell you about what happened and give you something. By the way, I thought you were like me, but you're not, are you?"

"No, I can't see her. I wish I could," Cara answered.

"It's of no consequence. I was worried about you today. You grieve so and it hurts us both."

"When you say what happened, do you mean today, or when Nanna died?"

"Both. Today, I thought you were going to hit the step behind you. Then that man caught you. Huge he was, but had a lovely smile. He picked you up as if you were as light as a feather. He carried you into one of the waiting rooms and placed you down on the couch and was gone. I think he thought he was intruding."

"You said earlier you needed to give me something from Nanna."

"It's this letter. She gave it to me a week ago. She said to give it to you if anything happened to her."

"What really happened then? I was told there was an attempted break-in at the farmhouse. She had a heart attack, didn't she?"

"She says she knew his face when she opened the door.

He'd been at her book signing. She tried to fight him, but he overpowered her. He was going to cut her up and take her power. Her heart hadn't been well for a while. She just let it stop. She worries he'll come after you though."

Cara sipped on her whiskey unsure what to say. It seemed farfetched, but Aunty Eileen appeared convinced it was true. "I'm going back home to Bristol tomorrow, I'll be safe there."

"You're wearing her shamrock, I see." Eileen took her handkerchief from her sleeve and blew her nose. "Cara, do you know the story of your great, great-grandma Margaret?"

"Just what Nanna told me a long time ago, but not much. She said Margaret was working the streets in Bath when her sister was killed. Margaret believed someone was after her and came to Ireland. What's that to do with Nanna's death?"

Aunty Eileen twisted her cardigan between arthritic fingers. "Kathleen says the man who planned to murder her, killed Margaret's sister, Rosie. Somehow, he's immortal."

Cara shook he head. "I'm finding it hard enough to believe in witches. Now, you're saying people can live for forever."

"He wanted her witch power because he was getting weaker. That's why you need a protector. This man will be hard to fight on your own until your power is stronger."

*This is getting more ridiculous by the minute, Cara thought, or maybe it was the whiskey.*

"Your Nanna's gone again, but I wanted to say something to you. When I pass on, don't come back here. I've had enough of this gloom and doom. I want you and your friends to get together and have a whiskey on me. A good one mind, I'll be watching." The wicked glint was back in Aunty Eileen's eyes.

"That will be a long time off yet."

"Not as long as you think." Eileen's hand went up, stopping further discussion. "Now, listen here, Cara. I know you think this is all gibberish. You can humor an old woman now, can't you?"

"Yes." They hugged and Aunty Eileen held her tight. Had she seen her own death as well? Cara didn't want to know.

Cara gave her a kiss and then watched as Aunty Eileen waddled away to her car with her son Tim. Sneaking in through the front door, she peered into the sitting room and then the parlor. Both were full of people. She crept past hoping no one would call out her name. She grabbed the unopened cards from the hall table and made her way upstairs. At the top of the twisting staircase, she saw a set of large doors.

Opening them, she found the single bed inside that filled the whole cupboard. Nan used to call it the snug. Cara remembered sleeping there as a child, pretending she was in a cave, or on a ship at sea. She turned on the light and looked at the envelopes. Her name was written on one from Nanna. The sight of it made Cara bite her bottom lip to stop it from trembling. She opened the envelope and read the letter.

*My dearest Cara,*

*I'm so glad you're here. Don't worry about your mother. I honored your Grandpa's wish to bring the children up Catholics, but my heart was never in it. I'm sure Anne picked up on it the day she met your father. He was her way out of here. I love your Aunty Eileen. But I don't think she's going to be able to help you with what's to come. If my vision was right, my killer didn't attain my power.*

*Love, Nanna.*

Panic was coming back again. Cara's breath caught in her throat. Grasping to get a hold of something solid, her hand touched the greeting cards spread out on the bed and her breathing eased. She might be an inexperienced witch but there was power here amongst the cards. It was calming her.

A half an hour later and there was nothing. The cards were all the same. *We are sorry for your loss.* It showed Nanna was well loved, but it didn't help with what was going on here. There were just four cards left. One was from Nanna's solicitor, another from her publisher, another from an admirer of her food. The last one made Cara's fingers tingle as she picked it up. It wasn't signed and simply said.

*From someone who will always be there to protect your family as was promised long ago. That was all she needed, Cara thought, someone else being cryptic.*

AS THE PLANE took off back to Bristol, Cara tried to make some sense of the funeral, the note, the card and the talk with Aunty Eileen. No sense came, just confusion she could only explain if she believed in the unbelievable.

Her flat was cold after the crowded farmhouse. Daniel had left soup to be heated up. It was her favorite, potato, bacon and leek. She grabbed her nightgown and fluffy slippers. Then, she turned on the heater to take the chill off the place. Daniel would be fascinated by the family stories. He was into the supernatural. The trouble was some of this stuff felt a little too real right now.

Cara went to the bathroom and found her makeup mirror and took it back to her bedroom. She picked up the card from the mysterious protector and placed it next to the mirror. Sitting cross-legged on the bed she created a protective circle in her mind.

*"I don't want to see my own death. I don't want this to be my last breath. Show me what you mean to me. Help me find my history."*

The mirror remained clear, reflecting what was around it. That was the way things were meant to be and it was good. Then it went hazy. Cara held her breath but she couldn't turn away. She had to know. The picture in the mirror became clear as she stared. She was naked in the arms of her dream lover. She would love it if he was real, and she would love it if Nanna was still alive, but she wasn't.

Her imagination was working overtime because of the crazy stories and weird notes. She had been so long without a guy, it was no wonder she was making one up. He wasn't real and her grandmother had just died from a heart attack. Cara knew she would just have to accept it even if it still tore her up inside.

CARA WRIGGLED her feet on her wheat bag. It was only nine o'clock. Yet her eyes drooped like it was two in the morning. Eventually sleep came.

The night air-cooled the sweat on her skin as she sat up. For a moment she didn't know if she was still in the dream or this was her room. The dream had been so vivid. Her cousin Tim was driving around a corner. Aunty Eileen sat in the back of his old station wagon. Then a truck had come from nowhere, headlights blazing in the dark. It missed the car. A long plank of wood flew from its stack on the back of the truck and smashed through the windscreen.

Tim's neck was bent at a strange angle. The plank of wood hit him with such force that his head was bent round. He stared with dead eyes at his mother. The right side of Aunty Eileen's face was splattered on the plank and inside of the car. Bone, blood and shredded pieces of skin were all that was left of her smiling face.

Cara clutched her hand to her mouth. She ran to the bathroom and vomited into the toilet. Waves of nausea passed over her as she retched until there was nothing left. It just had to be a bad dream. She kept repeating those words to herself like a mantra. It worked until the phone rang.

## SIX

Cara surveyed her flat and her efforts at cleaning. Her place wasn't big. It was cozy, with two couches opposite each other and a large beanbag at the end against the wall. The couches were covered in big floppy cushions and there were throw rugs on the floor. Photos and large colorful picture covered the walls. It was colorful organized clutter as far as she was concerned.

Daniel didn't see it that way. The kitchen was big with lots of preparation surfaces. The small table made for intimate dinners. The spare bedroom made a great office and storage space. It would have been good to be on the ground floor, but the stairs were brilliant for exercise, or so she kept telling herself.

Daniel wanted to attack the place. He would have done a great job, but she had had enough change in her life right now. Her bedroom was clean, but disorganized with clothes everywhere. It didn't really matter as no one had been invited in there in a long time. Daniel arrived first. He held a basket of soda bread to go with the Irish stew she made. He lifted the lid to her large pot on the stove.

"Oh my God, that smells good, so much better than nibbles. Better for soaking up the whiskey, and it's just what I need to warm up my insides, apart from Jeff that is." Daniel winked at her.

"Did I hear someone say my name?" Jeff walked in carrying six cans of Guinness, and a bottle of Glayva scotch.

"I think it was a compliment, but with Daniel you can never be sure." Cara tried to smile knowing that wakes are occasions when you want to remember good times. The reality was that at one minute numbness chilled her to the core, the next emotions stripped her bare like a raw wound.

Jeff placed the booze on the breakfast bar. He gave her a cuddle. Her eyes watered. "Don't get me started again, I've only just stopped."

Once her cousin Shona arrived, Cara had a feeling she would be a blubbering mess. She needed to share some of the crazy things that were happening or she would burst.

Jeff touched her arm. "That's funny, because Daniel said that's what tonight was about. His precise words were and I quote, "we will get pissed and cry our eyes out." Then, again he's been known to be a bit of a drama queen." Jeff gave a sideways glance toward Daniel who raised one eyebrow, blew him a kiss and then whacked Jeff's backside as he walked by.

Cara reckoned it had caused more pain to Daniel than Jeff's rear.

"Truth always hurts." Jeff grinned back at him.

Daniel started to get out the plates while Jeff sorted through the glasses. Cara sat at the breakfast bar with her tumbler of whiskey. She stared at Jeff and Daniel. These two men were so different. Daniel was slight and fair. Jeff was this gentle black giant who ran his own IT Company.

Talk about opposites attracting. They were happy though and at least they proved love was possible.

"You know you're supposed to drink that, and then you might look slightly less like a coiled spring." Daniel smiled and touched her chin with his forefinger.

Cara nodded and took a drink, spluttering on the first mouthful.

"Don't blame me. You asked for it straight." Daniel shook his head.

Cara wiped her lips. "I had strict instructions from Aunty Eileen. She never drank it watered down."

Daniel poured himself a large drink. "Here's to Aunty Eileen and let's hope her hangover remedy works. More importantly, why wasn't I ever introduced to her?" Daniel gulped back and then started to cough. "Oh my God, my throat's on fire. Now I know why I stick to a nice glass of red."

"I've never known you stick to a glass of red. A bottle maybe," Jeff laughed. "I think I'll start with a Guinness. Someone's going to have to stay a little sober around here."

CARA DABBED the soggy tissue to her eyes again. Her tummy hurt from laughing. Her eyes were red from crying and the room spun from too much booze. Jeff kept coming over with intermittent glasses of water and coffee. He was her savior. They had eaten and sat down again. It wouldn't be long before they tried to squeeze things out of her.

"Okay, what happened in Ireland?" Shona leant forward and picked up the whiskey bottle and poured what was left into their cups of coffee.

Cara remembered drunken nights trying to drown the

sorrows of losing a baby, and Tony leaving her. She wouldn't have made it through without Shona. Cara wished she had the same devil-may-care attitude as her cousin. The eclectic mix of jewelry and clothes Shona wore made her look like a gypsy. She lived life to the full. She always had lots of men around, saying she was having too much fun playing the field because she wasn't ready to settle down with just one guy.

"I'll just get some cream." Daniel stood up, swayed and sat down again.

"I'll get the cream, and you can stick to my straight black." Jeff took Daniel's coffee away and replaced it with his own.

"Have I ever done anything else? I love it when he's bossy," Daniel giggled.

"I heard that," Jeff called from the kitchen.

"You were meant to," Daniel countered.

Jeff sat back down. Silence. They were waiting for her to talk but what would she say. Cara's stomach turned and it wasn't the whiskey.

"I don't know what happened, really. I mean, I know what happened. I just don't understand it." She knew she was waffling. Her mouth was dry despite the alcohol and coffee.

"So tell us, and we'll try to unravel the mystery." Shona pulled her legs up on the couch and spread out her tiered skirt.

"It wasn't a mystery. It's just a bit strange that's all." Cara bit on her lower lip.

Daniel shook his head. "A bit weird. The woman forecast her own death and said your Nanna stopped her own heart. Then there's the whole murder thing and immortals." Daniel did a fake shiver as he sipped his coffee.

"Nanna had a heart attack. It was just coincidence they had a crash. Trust me, Tim was a crazy driver." Cara could sense the blood drain from her face and didn't need to close her eyes to relive the dream of their death again.

"But you said your Nanna Kathleen's recipe book arrived the day after her death and it had a note inside." Daniel reminded Cara.

"Yes it did. The note said. *Dear Cara, Use my recipes wisely.*' It's just coincidence. That kind of stuff isn't real. It's only in books and on TV." Cara couldn't look at any of them for fear they could see the doubt in her eyes. Shona wasn't convinced. Cara knew it from the way her cousin peered at her.

Shona took her hand and squeezed. "Tell us what happened. We'll work it out with our alcohol-befuddled brains."

It all spilled out and no one interrupted. Cara described the dream and how she saw their deaths before it happened. They probably thought this was just like an episode of *Supernatural* and all very interesting. She didn't mention the picture of the dead woman at *The Evening Post* and the other dreams, horrific or erotic. Or the fact she had started to try and perform some spells. She did mention the necklaces though.

"Have you had any more dreams?" Shona asked.

"No," Cara said.

Shona raised an eyebrow as she glanced over. "Really?"

"It's a pity, because if you really were starting to foretell the future, I'd get you to find out what the Lotto numbers were for this weekend," Daniel piped in. "The businesses could do with some topping up."

"I keep telling you to let me invest," Jeff said.

"And I keep telling you I don't like to mix business with pleasure," Daniel replied, elbowing Jeff in the ribs.

"That wasn't pleasurable." Jeff winced.

Shona interrupted. "So where are these necklaces?"

Cara went to her bedroom and grabbed the necklaces off her bedside table. For some reason, she couldn't bring herself to wear hers in the last week since Aunty Eileen had died.

She sat back down on the couch as Shona held up the shamrock. "That's not unusual. It's to do with St. Patrick teaching about the Holy Trinity. My good Catholic mother would be so proud of me, even if she isn't so proud of the fact I haven't been to church for six years. It also symbolizes the three females of Wicca, the maid, the mother and the crone." Shona shrugged and handed it over to Daniel.

"The whole witch thing is a bit too close for comfort for me to discuss right now." Cara said.

"Your Nanna believed that stuff though, even if you didn't." Shona said. "Pity my side of the family is so boring."

"So what does this one mean then?" Daniel picked up the stag necklace.

Cara smiled, as she looked at it. "Nanna said I must find the one to wear it. He will protect me till I become stronger as a witch. How melodramatic is that? My life so far has taught me there are no white knights on chargers coming to protect me."

"I prefer black knights." Daniel winked at Jeff who shook his head in dismay.

"Protect you from what? A bad menu plan or a mass murderer," Shona asked.

"I don't know, but I don't like either of those scenarios," Cara answered.

"I'd offer, Cara, but I have my hands full with lover boy

here," Jeff answered as he put his arm around Daniel who snuggled in and looked as if he was falling asleep.

Shona held up both necklaces studying them. She was slightly cross-eyed tonight. Whiskey did that to her every time.

Shona finished her coffee and said. "Listen Cara, I know its crap. People don't talk to the dead and see their own deaths, but you might be psychic. These psychics in magazines make shit-loads of money. Most are just people on the dole doing it as a fill-in job. If you're the real deal you'd do well."

"I'm not psychic. I accept I may have some skills but without Nanna around, I'm not doing anything. I'm just emotional at the moment." It was true and as good an excuse as any. The real truth was she was petrified.

"If you come to Bath, the bookshop, W.H. Smiths has a display in their window all about witches, immortality, death and things that go bump in the night. You could have a look."

"Honestly, I'd rather let it all rest, Shona. Bad things happen in people's lives. I have to accept it and move on." The conversation turned to other things and Cara was glad. When they all left, she went to bed. She cried herself to sleep holding the necklaces in her hand.

<h1 style="text-align:center">SEVEN</h1>

It was four days since Aunty Eileen's wake. Cara's tears had finally stopped, since there were no tears left. The air was fresh. The sun was out and she needed a break. A visit to Bath to see her Shakespeare play would be perfect. She just wished there weren't quite so many tourists.

The first two acts of the play at the Theatre Royal were fantastic. She waited in the queue in the coffee shop in the interval and thought about the other reason she had come to Bath. She intended to visit the bookshop Shona had mentioned. It was silly but she couldn't get it off of her mind.

Someone kept sighing behind her in the queue. They were probably entitled to sigh, due to the fact the lady in front of her at the counter was going over every single item on the menu. Cara looked around and gasped.

"Matcher." The name slipped out before she remembered they didn't really know each other. He didn't look away. In fact, he peered at her even more closely. "Sorry, you're my follow-on appointment at the counselor's. Look, ignore me. It's okay, I didn't mean to intrude."

He stayed silent, staring. "I was rude that day, sorry." Matcher mumbled.

It wasn't the comment she had expected and she couldn't stop herself from smiling.

"Thanks. So you like Shakespeare?"

"Still not sure I understand what the fuck he's on about, but he's deep. Says things in five words the rest of us can never say."

Again a reply she didn't expect.

"Can I help you?" The woman behind the counter interrupted with a fake smile. Cara managed to return an equally fake one. They didn't get a chance to say much more as the bell rang to say the show would be starting again soon.

When the show was finished Cara waited outside the theatre for Matcher. There was something about him. Insanity most likely. It made them more compatible as friends. Her life was weird and she needed all the help she could get. Matcher fitted weird. He stopped in front of her, peering again. She needed to say something.

"I was going to a bookshop. Would you like to see what they have there? Then we could have something to eat."

He shuffled from one foot to the other, before he glanced up and down the street. She wasn't going to bite him. He could go if he wanted. Finally, he spoke. "Sure."

---

BROOMSTICKS HANGING from the ceiling showed the area of the bookshop they should head toward. Matcher just kept browsing. The book she wanted was called *Immortality and Witchcraft, Fact or Fiction*. The website said it contained information on cults believing in immortality. It also mentioned a connection with witches, plus the modern medical views on living longer. Sounded like perfect bedtime reading for the lonely and depressed. *That was her all right.*

There was a bunch of schoolgirls giggling and flicking through the pages of a book, called *Love Spells*. Casting a spell and making sure your romance was going to work could save a lot of time and effort. Maybe she would be able to make her dream lover real. That might not be such a good idea. She would be tired all the time and never get any work done. She smiled. What a way to get exhausted.

Matcher dislodged one of the books on the table. He sent the pile spilling to the floor. The schoolgirls continued to giggle, as he scrambled around trying to pick the books up. The half of his face not covered with a long black fringe glowed red with embarrassment.

"Here let me help." Cara offered.

"Thanks," he answered, avoiding the stares of the schoolgirls. "I'm going to get this one. I'll meet you outside."

Cara kept searching but couldn't find the book she wanted. The assistant at the empty counter smiled politely as she approached.

"I'm looking for a book called *Immortality and Witchcraft, Fact or Fiction,*" Cara said.

The woman typed the title into her computer. As Cara waited, someone walked up to the other counter beside her. She turned to look. Her world stopped as she met the slate gray gaze of the man staring straight at her. This wasn't possible. He couldn't exist. He was just a dream lover. Yet there he was, standing next to her as big as life.

She tried to smile, but it probably came out as more of a grin. He didn't smile back. Her legs turned to jelly. If she didn't breathe, she would pass out. She reached out and gripped the counter. One of them had to look away but she couldn't bring herself to do it. Someone was talking to her and the moment was broken.

"Excuse me."

"Sorry," Cara replied, as she forced herself to look at the salesperson. She was afraid if she glanced back, he would be gone. Her imagination must be playing tricks on her.

"It looks like we should have one copy left." The woman said.

"I think I'm just about to sell it." The other shop assistant said coming up to the register. "We could order it in for you. It might take a couple of weeks."

"Please, take my copy." The man at the other counter held out the book. His voice was deep, exactly as it was in her dreams. She was caught again in his gaze. The world disappeared and for a moment they were the only two people alive locked in the look they shared. Her hand went to her chest. She could feel her heart racing at the thought of him being near.

"Thank you, but no I couldn't. You had the book first."

"Please, take it. I have plenty of time to wait for another copy to come in."

She found it hard to say no. Perhaps, it was the fact he was about six three and wore grey bike leathers. They added to the effect of making him look powerful. The shaved head and the stubble on his face gave a menacing look, but she wasn't afraid of him. This wasn't right. Her life was wild enough without dream lovers becoming real.

Plus, she wouldn't want her other dreams to become real as well. She needed to say something, or he would think she was an idiot standing there with her mouth gaping. He held the book out to her. As she took it, her hand touched his. It was such a tiny touch and yet it meant he was real.

She felt the heat rising up her neck as she blushed. She also sensed another heat inside her. It was the same way he had made her feel in her dreams.

"Thanks." Cara paid for her book and listened as he confirmed his contact details. Seth Scanlon. She had a name. She wasn't really stalking. Taking another book off a shelf, she flipped through the pages. He glanced her way before he left and caught her gaze once more.

She couldn't fool herself. The look he gave her was so intense she felt he was seeing inside her soul. Her breath caught. She shivered although the shop was warm. For a split second, she considered following him and saying he must remember all the times they had made love.

She could just imagine the expression he would give her. He didn't know her. She was a stranger. The shop became suffocating as she pulled at the collar of her jumper. She needed to be outside. There was no sign of him on the street. For a moment, she wanted to cry. At this rate, she would give the silly schoolgirls in the shop a run for their money.

"Take my word on it. He's dark," Matcher said, behind her.

"What?"

"Look, it's nothing to me. I just wondered, that's all." Matcher shuffled from one foot to the other.

"Wondered what?"

"You need to ask. I don't need to wonder." He turned away.

This made no sense at all. "Do you still want that coffee?" She asked.

"If you're paying, why not?"

They made their way down to Sally Lunn's Coffee Shop, which as always was warm and full of noisy customers. The Sally Lunn buns in the cabinet looked tempting. Her newfound company could do with some fattening up. Their cups of coffee arrived.

"I thought Matcher was your surname. Jessica's receptionist called you Mr. Matcher."

"Matcher's fine. I don't like my first name."

"What is it?" Silence, surprise, surprise. Cara watched as he took off his fingerless gloves and put three sugars in his coffee. He cradled the coffee cup in his pale hands.

"Do you mind if we don't talk about the stuff with Jessica."

That was fair enough. She didn't want his past medical history anyway and was sure he wouldn't want hers.

"Can I have a look at the book you've bought?"

He pushed the bag across the table. Cara offered her purchase for him to look at. His book was entitled, *Near Death Experiences, When the Light Calls You.* She wondered if there was a section on mutilated bodies. She doubted it. Matcher glanced through her book. Cara had an irresistible urge to push his fringe back so she could see his eyes.

"You said the man in the bookshop was dark, the one who had bought this book. What did you mean?"

Matcher stiffened at her question. "He's different, like you. I thought you could see it, but you can't." Matcher put his cup down and stared at her.

"In what way am I different?"

Matcher shrugged. "You're open. People who see stuff would think you were the same."

"You mean people who see ghosts and things would think I was their friend."

"I see people differently. I don't know, probably like those aura things. I see colors around bodies. I thought you saw his. It was grey like his bike leathers." Matcher picked up his bun and started to pull it apart. He groaned in pleasure as the flavors hit his tongue.

"And what color's mine?"

"I'm just starting to learn this stuff. You're all the usual colors, except your higher plane is so bright a blue; it hurts to look at it. You've got a couple of dark spots on your physical plane. Your inner plane's grey like his. Do you know him?" Matcher shoved a large piece of bun in his mouth and when he had finished it said. "Oh my god, this is so good. How did I not know this place existed?"

"Look, I'm going to get another coffee, you want one?"

"Yeh."

Cara glanced over at Matcher as she stood at the counter. What would she tell him? It didn't really matter in the long run. She was probably never going to see him again anyway. There was something slightly comforting that someone else had peculiar things happening to them. Sometimes, it was easier to talk to a stranger who had no preconceived ideas. Maybe she was reassured by the fact he could see auras like she could do magic. She should be scared but instead felt as if she had met a kindred spirit.

It didn't seem quite so ridiculous repeating all the things that had happened. Matcher sat listening to every word as if he were soaking it up. She even found herself telling him about the photograph and some of the dreams and that she had seen Seth in them, but not what they had done. She kept the magic to herself though for now.

"Jessica must think you're really fucked up if you come out with this stuff. She'll be asking for a holiday with the two of us on her books."

Cara breathed a sigh of relief that he hadn't gotten up and run away, then again he was odd too.

"She only knows about the dreams and the picture. The day I saw you at her office and you looked unwell was the day I learned my grandmother died. I doubt I'll repeat any of this to her. I went to the bookshop today to get this book so I could make some sense of this stuff that's happening. Then, I'll forget it and get on with my life."

"You can try forgetting, but it won't work. I thought at first there was some reason for me to see auras. Mum believed it would help me, but so far it hasn't. It's just happening. If you're like me, it won't go away. Let it take you somewhere."

The loony bin was where it would take her. "And where has that attitude taken you so far?"

"It got me here sitting with you, and you're the first person who believes me."

He was biting his nails. Maybe he needed her more than she needed him, but she wanted to keep in contact. "How old are you?"

"Eighteen. Why do you want to know?"

"You working, or still studying?"

"Gave up school when I got too far behind. I've a job stocking at a supermarket." He wouldn't look up and stared into his coffee.

"I run a catering business. I need a waiter to help out with the dinner parties. Would you be interested?" Daniel would probably kill her for this.

"I suppose so. Why are you doing this? You don't know me." He looked up at her and pushed his fringe back so she could see both of his eyes.

"I think we've both had it rough, and I'd like to help."

"Been a long time since a stranger wanted to help me. Trust it to be an odd one." He laughed.

She wasn't sure if that was a compliment or not. "This is our card. If you're still interested in a few days, then call."

"Ours." Matcher started to bite what was left of his thumbnail.

"Daniel is my partner in the business. He's vicious if you don't come up with the goods. Be forewarned." Cara said. "He is also meticulous about presentation. The piercings and the fringe would have to go."

"I reckon if you're going to take a chance on me, I'll take one on you. I'll phone." Matcher leaned forward and hugged her, and then quickly jumped back. "Shit, that was awesome. Your aura's so powerful."

"I never felt a thing. I'll just have to take your word on that." Cara watched him walk off, then finished her coffee and started to make her way back to her car. There was a newsagent on the next corner. Their new advertisement for the business should be in *The Bristol Evening Post*. Her stomach clenched. Bile rose in her throat as she looked at the news board out the front of the shop.

*"The Slice and Dice Killer Strikes in Bath."*

Beneath the words, was a drawing of the symbol she had seen too many times in her dreams, and on a photograph belonging to a disgruntled journalist.

# EIGHT

Another meal had gone well. The clients were pleased, and for the first time since she started the business, it meant nothing. It was midnight as she unpacked the dishes with Shona.

"There's a message on your answer machine. You want to hear it?" Shona asked, as her finger hovered over the button.

Cara nodded.

"Cara dearest, I was phoning because a friend of your father's suggested your business to one of his clients. This is the date he would like for a Sunday evening for an intimate meal for two. I gave him your number. I also want to talk to you about a dinner party for us. Take care my dear, and do call if you need me." Click. "You have no more new messages."

Cara had tried to talk with mum after Nanna's death but she had clammed up. She thought they could have shared their grief together but it wasn't to be.

Shona gave the phone the finger. "My dearest Auntie Anne has a way with words. Her message is sparse and littered with, "don't you dare call me." Shona opened the fridge and found a bottle of white wine. "Looks good. Think we'll try this one."

Cara bit her lower lip and contemplated a life far away in Australia where the wine originated.

"Will you come talk to me? Must I drag you over?" Shona sat down, a glass of wine in her hand. She relaxed back on the sofa, pulling her long hair from its tight bun. "That feels so good."

Cara went to sit next to her cousin and picked up the second glass. There had been times in the past when getting drunk and forgetting what was happening was a solution. It didn't seem so now.

"The other night when we talked, I didn't exactly tell you everything." Cara gulped her wine.

"I guessed that much."

"I told you I was having dreams about dead bodies. I've also been having dreams where I kill someone with a knife, or I watch someone else kill them. I carve a symbol into their abdomens and stab them through the heart. So if you want to leave and go home now and not be around a mad woman, I understand." Cara gave a feeble smile, hoping against all odds Shona would understand.

"That's some intense dreaming, girl."

"I told Jessica about the dreams. She believes it's related to the stress of the surgery and the loss of the baby. She says I'm torturing my own body. The day I went to *The Evening Post,* I saw a reporter drop a picture with a body that had the same marks I dream about. I read his article. He described a copycat killer, a murderer who killed like that in the past. The reporter wrote the police are holding back. I'm starting to think he was right. The other day, the paper said they have another body with the same symbol on it." Cara emptied her glass and refilled it.

"I saw that in the paper too. It's just some sicko doing creepy stuff. Anyway, what are you saying? Do you think you're slipping out at night in some strange dream state and killing people?" Shona raised her eyes to the ceiling.

Cara told Shona about Matcher and her strange afternoon with him. It all seemed a bit bizarre now. She wasn't sure she really believed he could see auras. Shona was right, Cara thought. She had probably seen the symbol in some old book. With the operation and her own abdomen being opened up, it had probably caused the dreams. Now some random person was killing people and leaving the mark on them because they had seen it in a book too. Shona had made sense of it all. It was what she needed, Cara decided.

"I drew a picture of the knife from my dreams." Cara got the picture and placed it down on the coffee table.

Shona leant forward to get a better look, picking up the drawing. As Shona worked in an antique shop she had probably seen something like it before. Boscombe, her boss, loved old weapons so it was likely.

"I'm surprised you could find anything in that bedroom of yours."

"It was in the study. Even I need some order amongst the chaos." Cara peered at Shona to try and gauge what she thought of the picture.

"It looks old. I'm sure I've seen something like it. I'll ask Boscombe to have a look. He specializes in daggers and swords. Can I keep it?"

Cara hesitated. "Sure, I've got a copy."

"I'm so glad you've found this Matcher guy. I won't feel so bad about not helping out anymore." Shona folded the picture and stuffed it in her purse.

"I know you've never been that keen on waitressing."

"You're right. I wanted to help out with your business when you were getting started, and the extra cash is good. It's been so hectic recently at the shop. Every other week we're off to some antique fair. I love the job, but it's exhausting. So what do you think of your mother's message?"

"It's just a dinner party. There will be some eligible man there with a decent background. They don't get it. It's my choice who I want to be with, or without, as the case may be." Cara took a large gulp of wine.

"You could always introduce your young emo as your new boyfriend." Shona laughed.

"You know it might be worth it just to see the look on her face." They both cracked up. "Thanks for being here tonight. It's been good having someone to talk to." Cara reached out and grabbed Shona's hand.

"Well we've sorted out all the other stuff so what about the witch stuff? Do you mean to tell me you did spells with Nanna since you were a kid and didn't tell me?"

"Yes and I've done a few recently, just to help me understand what was going on. They could just be my imagination playing tricks on me though."

"Do one for me now." Shona sat forward with a wicked grin on her face.

"Nanna used to say magic should never be taken lightly. Anyway I thought we were trying to prove this was all make-believe." Maybe doing magic drunk was against the rules.

"Just a little spell. We'll know for sure it's all rubbish if nothing happens and you really are imagining it all."

"I have to create a protective circle around us and call on the power of the Earth." Cara didn't know why she was explaining but Shona looked keen to see something. Cara pulled up her sleeve to show the big purple bruise on her forearm where she had dropped a heavy casserole dish. "On my arm is a bruise from yesterday. Use the power of the earth and make it go away."

Shona screwed up her face, totally unimpressed. "Is that it? All you have to do is make up a rhyme and things happen?" "I know you wanted a Lotto ticket but I'll start small." They watched as the purple bruise changed color to blue, then pink and was gone. She couldn't believe she had shown someone this, even Shona. This really was her and she had to accept it.

"Oh my god you really did that. Why aren't you doing more? I need to pee. Tell me more when I get back."

"I'll take Merlin out for a wee too. Then I'll make the bed settee up," Cara called after the wobbling Shona. She would wait for Merlin outside. Since the attack, she wanted him in as much as possible but he would drive her insane sometimes scratching to get out. He never went beyond the garden at the front of the house now, which was good.

Later, Cara lay in bed unable to sleep. Shona had badgered but she wouldn't do any more spells. It seemed wrong to use the magic just for entertainment. Maybe she would wake up in the morning and be in a straitjacket somewhere, because her mind certainly couldn't calm down.

She turned on her bedside light and fumbled around on her bedside table until she found the shamrock necklace. She put it on and lay down. The pendant felt cool between her thumb and forefinger. Touching the pendant made her think about Seth and her dreams. He was one thing she hadn't shared with her cousin, no matter how much wine they drank.

TWO WEEKS and no nightmares or strange things happening. It was good. Maybe life really was returning to normal, whatever that was. It had obviously just been one of those times when things were out of kilter. She wanted to believe strange things instead of the sensible ones, just because the sensible ones were unpleasant. Okay she had accepted her witch side, but that didn't mean she had to do spells all the time. She also didn't want to accept chopped up bodies and her involvement with them.

What was more amazing was Daniel even liked Matcher. They had a rather heated discussion on snakebite piercings, and the eyebrow ring had to come out. Matcher agreed. He didn't even complain. Cara still wondered how he was going to see what he was serving with hair covering half of his face.

There were going to be eight guests for the dinner party at her mother's apartment. For once, Cara was going to be allowed to choose what she wanted to serve. When Matcher walked out of the bathroom at her place that night, she almost didn't recognize him. His long fringe was gelled back and she could see both of his lovely brown eyes.

"My goodness, you scrub up good." She hugged him. "It won't be too bad today, I promise. This isn't a meal with too much detail. We rely more on the taste to bowl them over. Oh, and by the way, don't, believe Daniel. My parents only turn into dragons at midnight." Cara laughed and hoped Matcher didn't pick up on the fact she thought they were dragons already.

"You know Cara, Daniel and Jeff have the most combined aura's I've ever seen. I like him. I like them both. They're a bizarre match though, a bit like you choosing me as a waiter." He shook his head at her.

She wanted to ask him something she had wondered

since she met him. "If you look in the mirror, can you see your own aura? I'd be interested to know what it shows."

"Can't see a thing." He shrugged.

---

HER MOTHER WAS the elegant and knowledgeable hostess to her friends and somewhat dubious acquaintances as she always was. The meal was perfect and suitably extravagant for her parents who were all about impressions. Sometimes Cara wondered if she had been adopted.

The starter was smoked Irish salmon mixed with swirls of cream cheese flavored with chives and dill served on thin slices of toasted soda bread. The main was one Daniel excelled at, Guinness and honey glazed duck accompanied by parsnip, potato and mint fritters covered with goat cheese, plus spiced kale and honeyed carrots. Now, the guests would be tucking into the best apple and rhubarb pie and rich Irish cream they had ever tasted.

Peeking through the dining room door, Cara viewed them at the table. Mother, Father, and next to them were their long-time friends, Carol and John Churchill.

Seated by them was the other partner in her dad's law firm, Doug. He wasn't there with his wife tonight as expected. The older woman he had brought with him was called Tarin. She didn't speak much English, but held herself with such dignity.

Doug was obviously mesmerized by Tarin. Cara reckoned the woman was going to eat him up for breakfast. Talk about going from the frying pan into the fire. Mum apparently didn't like his new choice as she had been friends with his previous wife. Anne said she thought Tarin opinionated which in mum speak meant, she was not the polite little wife.

Lastly, were two men intended to be prospective suitors. They were probably annoyed at this moment for the lack of available females present. One looked like the typical candidate her parents always chose. His name was Thomas and he was an accountant. Surprise, surprise!

The other one wasn't talking. He just watched everyone. His clothes were expensive and fit his firm physique well. His black hair was well cut, with a slight touch of gray at the temples. Mother had said his name was Vincent. He had bought the house next door. In Sneyd Park, an elite area of Bristol, owning property meant money, lots of it.

Daniel didn't think Vincent was gay, and her partner's radar was usually good. Someone tapped her shoulder. Cara jumped and let out a little squeak.

"Becoming a peeping Tom, Cara?" Daniel grinned, as he stood next to her, peering through the gap. "Just because we're on dessert doesn't mean you can slack off, Anne's going to expect you to make yourself glamorous to show off to the prospective mates."

Daniel groaned, as she dug him in the ribs with her elbow. "Matcher's been good for his first evening, but tell him he's on trial for a month. By the way, are you going to tell me now where you met him?"

"No." Cara poked out her tongue.

"Don't worry, I love a challenge. There's something about him that's different. Saw his name on his tax file. It's beautiful. Why he doesn't use it is beyond me."

"Trust me, Daniel, for once in your life, leave it alone." Cara hoped her steely look would dissuade him but doubted it.

At that moment Vincent turned and peered at the door.

Cara moved away, her heart beating fast. She needed to work, not dawdle anymore. She started to prepare the coffees. Then, her mother walked into the kitchen. She gave her regular ingratiating smile to Daniel, before coming across to bestow the obligatory hug and fake kiss on each of Cara's cheeks.

"Cara, the meal was wonderful."

"Thank you." Cara winked at Daniel over her mother's shoulder. He blew her an over-the-top kiss back. The only partner her mother considered appropriate was one Cara could marry. She would have liked to take credit for choosing a gay business partner on purpose to annoy her mum, but it had just been pure luck. "Daniel and I do our best."

Mother nodded to Daniel. He had accepted long ago it was the only acknowledgment he would ever get. "I want to introduce you to some new friends of ours. I think they might help your little business venture."

"If anyone out there is offering free financial advice, we're always willing to listen for the cost of a meal." Cara smiled sweetly.

Her mother pursed her lips and looked her up and down, frowning. Cara didn't want to look like the classic chef with white top and check pants. Anyway her hips were too big to make those pants look acceptable. She opted for brown pants. They hid most stains. On top, she wore a cream v-necked T-shirt under her dark blue apron that had their logo printed in gold on it.

Following her mother into the dining room, she glanced back at Daniel. He was the only one to see her crossed fingers. Introductions to the known guests came first. Cara couldn't complain as they kept having plenty of bookings from her parents' close friends.

Then came the moment for her introduction to the prospective marriage partners her mother chose. First, was Thomas. He didn't stand up when they were introduced. The other guy Vincent wasn't there. Thomas toyed with his pie and cream until it resembled a milky congealed glue. Cara hoped he could see her eyes glaring at what he was doing to her food. Did he not realize that it wasn't just any apple and rhubarb pie? The pastry melted in the mouth as the flavors of the butter, cinnamon, and fruits rippled across the tongue.

Thomas put his spoon down and looked up from the plate. "The food was fantastic. I didn't know Ireland had such tasty offerings. I mean to say you tend to think their food is boring. It's the potato thing, I suppose."

The poor man looked so bored she thought he couldn't wait to leave. "Potatoes are wonderful," Cara replied. "Since I started this business, I realize that more and more. I've been thinking about looking for backing for a cookbook called '1000 Things You can do With a Spud.' What do you think?"

Thomas turned up the corner of his mouth in a fake smile. He wasn't going to be parted with his money for her wonderful venture. Somehow she wasn't surprised.

Her mother shuffled behind her. Thomas went back to his plate. If Matcher didn't come and snatch it off him soon, she would never give him another night's work.

Vincent was back. Mother was smiling. This guy must have a big bank balance. *I'm not doing this again.* Cara thought. She glanced to her father for support. It was nonexistent in coming as always. He was in deep conversation with his friends. There was only one person who existed in his world, and it was him. He was the fancy lawyer with the sociable wife who let him do what he wanted.

Mother might be annoying in her interference. He was more hurtful in his lack of acknowledgment. There was a pain, or rather an ache in Cara's chest at their lack of friendship. It would do her no good. They would never be any closer. Vincent sat down and smiled at her.

"Thank you for letting me join in this celebration of the senses. Your food was divine. I don't think I will eat again for a week. Please won't you sit down a moment?'

Vincent ignored everyone except her. He wasn't classically good looking. She would call him too smooth. Still, there was definitely something about him that required her attention. She perched on the chair next to him wishing to be back in the kitchen. Small talk had never been one of her talents.

"Thank you. Our aim is to please." Heat was rising up her neck. She would be coming out in blotches. He would think she had measles.

"I'll be having a get-together myself in a few weeks' time for some of my clients. If I could have your card, I could call and give you more details."

"Of course. If you don't mind me asking, what business are you in?"

"Antiques. I've collected many pieces over my lifetime. I've been fortunate enough to be somewhat successful."

Her mother interrupted. "Now, you're just being modest, Vincent. I hear you're one of the best experts around. No one knows quality and can age pieces like you."

Vincent shot a stern look at her mother. She smiled weakly and turned back to her other guests.

*That will teach her to interrupt after she had made him*

*sit through a boring dinner party except for the food of course, Cara thought.*

Vincent looked about thirty-five but wasn't going to bow to his elders. He oozed self-confidence.

"Did my parents mention my cousin Shona works with an antique dealer in Bath, Boscombe. Perhaps, you know him." If she could pass any business Shona's way she would.

"Yes, I know of him." Vincent answered abruptly.

"I'll go and get our card." Cara stood up, as did Vincent. As she turned away he took her hand in his, bringing it to his lips and gently kissing it. The blotches were coming back to her neck. *What kind of guy kisses your hand these days?* She wasn't sure if it was cute or creepy.

She opened the kitchen door. She chose to ignore the fact Matcher and Daniel jumped back and were cleaning glasses. These two were being more than a little disconcerting. She had expected they would have knives at each other's throats by now.

Instead they seemed to have just joined forces in the collection of people who knew what was best for her. She hadn't known Matcher long, but she was aware he watched all the people who surrounded her. Part of her wanted to know what their auras revealed. Another part didn't want to know a thing.

Daniel put down the glass, folded his arms and looked straight at her. "Is your mother up to her old tricks again? I can't say either of those two are your type."

"I don't have a type, Daniel."

"I saw him kiss your hand. I'll have to see if I can get Jeff to do that." Daniel said, and blew a kiss.

"I don't think you've a chance in hell. They weren't that bad. Mother's invited worse in the past. She pays well, and this Vincent guy wants to book us." Cara started to go through her briefcase to find her card and a sample menu. Matcher hadn't reacted to their conversation. He was giving too much attention to cleaning glasses. She would wheedle what was wrong out of him later.

---

ALL THE WAY back in the van Matcher was silent. He wouldn't look at her and even Daniel noticed.

"What's with you, Matcher? Cat got your tongue? Or is that big stud you have in there causing problems?" Daniel asked.

Matcher didn't take the bait. They pulled up in front of her flat and started unloading. Daniel said he would drop Matcher off on his way home. Maybe it had been a mistake employing him and he was still sick. After all she didn't know why he was seeing Jessica, maybe something else was troubling him. He looked strong enough though, as he brought the boxes of crockery upstairs and stored them in the office.

"There's just one box of glasses left. I'll get it if you'll sort out Matcher's pay for the night." Daniel headed back out the door.

Matcher stood by the office door, head down. That was it. She needed to know what was wrong.

"I'm sorry about my family. They can be a bit much. You seemed..."

"It wasn't them," he snapped.

Cara held her arms up, "Then what?"

"I've no right to say anything. You can believe what you like about the things I said before. It's the man who kissed your hand. Well, his aura is just dark. There's nothing good there at all. You're a nice person, Cara. This job is great. I just don't know if I can hack it. I thought this was cool, but I see stuff in so many auras, everywhere." Matcher started to bite his nails, or what was left of them.

"You can't lock yourself away," Cara said gently. "Life goes on. Look, if we get the job, I'll ask Shona to do it. She told me she'd help out when she could. You're not going to leave this job. I won't let you."

Daniel raised one eyebrow as he walked into the office with the last box. She hoped he got her look that said, not now.

Cara watched the two of them walk out the door. Maybe she should have asked Matcher to stay longer so they could finish talking. She wasn't one to offer advice much at the moment. Whenever she did a dinner at her parents, it always left her feeling unsettled. This was the final one. It was one thing when it got to her. She didn't want her friends to get upset.

She grabbed Aunty Eileen's book and settled into bed with Merlin purring at her feet. She had used some of the herb combinations in the food tonight. She wondered if her mother had picked up on it. Then again, Mum's eyes were the same color so probably not.

Cara switched to the book on immortality. She opened it to the chapter she was reading. It was about the Hellfire Club in the 1700's. The members had believed that some of the ritual killings they performed would endow immortality on the killer. She flicked through the next chapter on DNA modeling, and how doctors would be able to extend life.

The chapter after that was a bit unsettling. It had a section about witches and people who tried to kill them to attain immortality. It particularly mentioned witches with one blue eye and one green eye being more powerful. That was it. She needed to get rid of this book.

Tomorrow, she would send it on to Seth. His address was still on the order sheet the store employees had left in the book. Its contents hadn't really helped anyway. That last bit was just plain sick. As she remembered Seth, she thought of her dreams, the good ones. It was still a scary concept to believe he was real.

She had to accept that he was a stranger she must have seen around sometime. She'd started dreaming about him in her desperation for comfort. She didn't know anything about him. He knew nothing about her. It was the way it should stay.

# NINE

The back road into Bath via Ham Green was beautiful, even if the roads were narrower. There were a few country pubs along the way. She had frequented them with Shona on more than one occasion. She hadn't seen Shona since their boozy night weeks ago. Matcher was helping out and Cara needed to talk to her cousin about the dinner party at her mother's.

On the seat beside her was the book on immortality and witchcraft. She was coming as far as Bath so she might as well go on to Trowbridge, she told herself. Seth's house was just outside of town. She had wrapped the book up and put a note with it intending to leave it on the doorstep. That was a lie. She secretly hoped she might see him again.

As expected, the narrow side streets of Bath with their myriad of small specialty shops were crowded with tourists. Cara loved the smells, the colors. There was always some-thing different, from shops selling Chilean goods, to the best pasties around.

Shona smiled when she walked in, but turned back to a customer. Cara loved to browse in antique shops even if she could never afford anything. The shop dealt in paintings, pottery statues, plus weapons and jewelry. Cara reckoned there was something sneaky about antique shops. They never appeared well lit, as though they were trying to hide something. Shona swore it was true and her eyesight had gotten worse since she had worked at Boscombes.

Cara found herself drawn to an oval broach in the jewelry cabinet. The center was black with gold edging and had a gold daisy on it. Each petal of the daisy was a little pearl. It was so delicate, but Cara felt an overwhelming sense of sadness as she stared at it.

"You look lost in thought. What's caught your eye?" Shona stood behind the cabinet ready with a key to open it.

Forever the saleswoman, even when she knew she didn't have a chance. "It's the broach, Shona. It's beautiful, but sad."

"You're right. It is sad. Using your witchy skills to see things, are you?" Shona handed her the broach. "Turn it over."

On the back of the broach was the usual clasp but beneath it was a small compartment covered in glass. Inside the glass bubble was hair. Engraved on the gold back was Gloria Flores, wife of Francis Flores died 1867.

"Okay, Shona. That's amazing, but also kind of uncanny. That's a hundred and fifty odd year old hair. I like my knickknacks and memories about me, but I'd find being around personal stuff from so long ago would eventually freak me out. Just the fact they would make things like this, makes me think how different from us they were. Mind you now I come to think of it I was offered a lock of Nan's hair at her funeral service."

"It was a slower time where people could show how they felt, nowadays you just a get a text message to say they can't make a date or it's over." Shona shrugged her shoulders.

"You're getting cynical. Go on; tell me, how much?"

"About three hundred pounds, but we could do you a good deal. Say two fifty for cash." Shona was already putting it back in the cabinet.

"I'll stick to my simple necklace from Nana. I couldn't walk around wearing that kind of money." Cara fingered her shamrock pendant.

"Trust me, you could get used to it. All I need to do is to find someone who'll buy this kind of thing for me or get a better job. By the way those necklaces are old and would be worth something. So how did the dinner go?"

"Interesting." Cara bit her bottom lip not knowing where to start without sounding like the world's worst daughter.

"Interesting, that's it. I'm due a coffee break and with what I've managed to sell today the boss shouldn't complain. See you outside in five."

Shona slipped her arm in Cara's as they walked down the narrow side street and entered a little cafe.

"The coffee's really good, but the queues are long. It's worth it though if you can't live without your caffeine like me."

"I don't think I'm quite as bad as you, but I'm working on it." Cara followed Shona to a table in the corner. It wasn't quiet, but at least they were sitting down.

"So what happened?"

"The food was wonderful, of course. As usual, Mother had her normal collection of cronies plus a couple of marital candidates for me."

"So, tell me more." Shona sipped on her long black.

"One was an accountant, who I'm sure thought the

whole concept of the Irish having an official cuisine was a contradiction to the laws of physics. The other one was, well, I'm not sure what he was? His name was Vincent and he's moved next door to them, and he kissed my hand." The comment caused Shona to choke on her coffee.

"He kissed your hand. Now come on, that has to be a first."

"Yes it was, and he complimented us on our cooking. His eyes were strange though, like he was looking right at you. I don't know. It was like he could see more than you wanted him too, you know?" It sounded ridiculous but these days she usually did anyway so what was new.

"No, I don't know, but he sounds the most unusual candidate your mother has found so far. If he is rich and you are not interested, send him my way. Not that I'm saying you should take up with any of her choices. Did you do the herb thing?" Shona leaned forward eagerly.

"Yes I did."

"Did you use the aphrodisiac ones?" Shona giggled.

"Hell no. I used the combination that draws out honesty. It was more appropriate in their case. I don't think I should've done it. I'm messing with what Aunty Eileen and Nanna gave me."

"From what you have told me Nanna Kathleen had a great sense of humor and would have loved it."

"I finished the book on immortality and witchcraft."

"And?"

"It didn't answer any of my questions. It just rambled on about ancient sects and bloodthirsty young bloods in the seventeenth century. There was a load of medical stuff I didn't get, plus a section on witches with different colored eyes being sacrificed. I can't say I enjoyed reading that bit."

"That kind of stuff was done hundreds of years ago.

People don't do that now. What with forensics and every-thing, they'd never get away with it. You've got it out of your system and you're to become a boring person like the rest of us again, or are you still going to try the odd spell?"

"I'm going to drop the book off at the address of the guy from the shop. Then I'll return to my incredibly exciting life of cooking and slowly going insane."

"Do you think that's wise just going up to some strangers home?" Shona said as she raised an eyebrow and pursed her lips.

"It's a nice country drive and I thought I'd just place it on his doorstep."

Shona glanced at her watch. "Shit, I'd better get back. I'll call you tonight."

As they walked out Cara remembered about Vincent's business card. "I forgot to tell you, this Vincent guy is into antiques and I told him about your shop. I hope you get something out of it, he looks like money."

Leaving Bath, her heart raced with excitement. She loved these autumn days. They were cold, but the sky was clear and sunny. No grey clouds to dampen her feelings. It hadn't been a hot summer. Leaves were returning to their luscious varieties of gold, amber and dark green.

Trowbridge hadn't been too busy. Smithy Lane was just outside of town. Cara's heart swelled at the beauty of the place. Ivy cascaded down the stone wall at the front and onto the footpath. It was probably all that was holding the stones together.

The gate she would have to pass was in such contrast to the old walls. The intricacies of the scrolls and angles of the black metalwork took her breath away. The garden would look lovely in spring with daffodils and crocuses blooming.

The latticed windows made her feel like Gretel wanting

to take a peek inside the Gingerbread House. The thatched roof had eaves that hung down above the front door. Thatch always made her think of spiders. She'd hated spiders since she was small. One had fallen on her face and she remembered her screams as she tried to get rid of it.

The knocker on the solid wooden door was a collection of bent metal that might have resembled something once. With one hand holding the book to her chest, she reached out and almost touched the metal. An odd feeling stopped her, as if opening this door was going to reveal much more than the interior of the house. Common sense needed to kick in soon, or the cops would be called for a suspected burglar.

Taking a deep breath, she placed the book on the step and turned away. This was silly. She was acting like a love-struck schoolgirl. Her hand went to her bag. She fingered the stag necklace. Turning away, she heard the front door opening.

"Hello. Can I help you? Oh, I think you've dropped something."

A petite gray-haired lady stood smiling in the doorway. Cara bit her bottom lip. She cringed as if she had been caught with her fingers in the cookie jar.

"I'm Cara. I brought it for Mr. Scanlon." The woman raised her eyebrows. "He wanted it from the bookshop. He had a special order in and I got it. I wanted him to have it so he could cancel his order."

*Get it, got it, good, no, never mind. Message to self, Never get interrogated by the police, they'll need a translator. Cara thought.*

"Do come in then. Seth will be glad he didn't miss you."

The woman turned towards the interior of the house. She clutched the package in her arms. Cara glanced at her van. She could pretend she hadn't heard anything. Then the smell of baking assailed her. What was cooking inside? Something created a wonderful aroma. She had to find out what the woman was making. It was sweet, yet there was something spicy about it.

The woman from the front door was asking her to sit down in a beautiful cottage kitchen. There was an Aga cooker, and knick-knacks everywhere. The windowsill had potted plants on it. The dresser shelves were covered with everything from plates, thimbles, and candleholders to little statues. A beautiful embroidered cloth covered the table. Cara ran her fingers over the delicate stitching that depicted alternating red and pink roses. It reminded her of what Nanna used to make.

"Did that one years ago. We need a new one really. Hate to throw things out though. Where are my manners? I didn't introduce myself, Janet Markham, Seth's house-keeper; then again I suppose he told you that." Janet placed the cups and saucers plus a large mug down on the table. A tin was taken off a shelf and cookies arranged on a plate. "Freshly made this morning. Seth doesn't like shop bought as you would know."

"I only met Mr. Scanlon briefly." That was an under-statement. Janet was talking as if they were old friends.

"It's nice to have visitors. I keep telling him he spends too much time out in his forge, or on those statues. Men like to have their hobbies though, don't they?"

Cara suspected this wasn't a question Janet expected to have answered and just smiled in reply. She reckoned Janet to be in her sixties. She wore dark blue dungarees with brown marks on the knees from gardening. The brown jumper underneath looked as if it had been badly hand-knitted. Her long graying hair was done up in a French bun and she had gold jewelry draped around her neck. She gave the appearance of a stylish country gossip. She passed the plate of cookies towards Cara.

The cookie melted in her mouth as the flavors rolled across her tongue. Butter, cinnamon, nutmeg, ground almonds and something else she couldn't decipher. "These are delicious. I'd love the recipe."

"You like cooking then?" Janet sipped her tea.

"I'm a caterer."

"It's a family recipe my mother gave me. We used to call them yummy bites. Silly name really." Janet picked one up and bit into it. Her eyes closed, as she savored the first mouthful before she took the next. She opened her eyes and smiled. "There's something wicked about food, don't you think? It's like you're being naughty, and it's allowed." Janet laughed.

Cara liked this woman, even if she was in the kitchen of a stranger. She would have to explain later she really didn't know Seth at all but for now she would enjoy the cookie. The door behind Cara opened and Janet started to fill the mug with tea.

"About time you came in. You've been out there for hours. Why didn't you tell me Cara was coming? I like to know if you're expecting visitors." Janet picked up the cake tin and refilled the plate.

The fun of talking with Janet disappeared with the presence of Seth Scanlon. Cara's heart pounded and her breath quickened. *Stay calm, yeah like that was going to happen.* The sun shone through the window behind him. It threw his imposing shadow across the table in front of her. Cara studied her empty cup and tried to remember to breathe.

His footsteps indicated he had moved around to the

other side of the table directly in front of her. She tried to remember what he looked like. All she could come up with was the man having sex with her in her dreams, not this stranger who had frowned at her in a bookshop.

"I'm sorry. I didn't know you were coming today. I would've told Janet to expect you."

Seth's deep voice betrayed nothing but made the hair on her neck stand up. Cara looked up, and smiled her brightest smile. Seth's expression was deadpan as he stood leaning back against the dresser with his mug in his hand. His gray T-shirt and jeans looked grubby. She had visions in her head involving no clothing at all. His piercing gray eyes studied her as she crossed her legs. She tried to control the ache building up in her core. He didn't need to do a thing. He was turning her on just standing there.

"I brought the book. I thought it only polite that I pass it on to you now." Her voice came out like a squeak. What was wrong with her?

"I'll shower and change. Then we can talk." Seth put his mug down and left.

Her breath was coming too fast. She wanted out of here. It was like stumbling into one of those T.V. murder mysteries with strange characters. She didn't want to be the red herring in the plot. Seth was exactly like the man in her dreams, except he didn't look at her with love, but suspicion.

"I noticed the roses in the front garden. I've never been able to grow them. I was wondering if you could give me some tips." Cara smiled at Janet. She needed to go and grabbed her purse and headed for the front door. All she could do was hope Janet would take the hint. Once outside she could make an excuse to get away.

"I know what you saw. It's my climbing rose. I stole some cuttings from a country house around here that won't be named. Trust me. They're not difficult to grow." Janet was right behind her. "Since autumn is coming, they are over the best.

Seth's friendly housekeeper kept talking and Cara guessed she was giving Seth time to get respectable. Cara clutched the gate latch. She sensed Janet walking away and heard Seth's heavy footfalls on the gravel behind her. She wanted to turn and throw herself into his arms and feel those lips come crushing down on hers. All she could do was take a deep breath and close her eyes for a second.

"I'll leave you two to catch up then. I want to go check my emails. It seems a gentleman in Paris thinks I understand art. I just tell him when I think it looks silly. Personally, that's most of the time, to be honest." Janet chuckled as she walked away.

Taking her hand off of the latch, Cara leant forward and smelt the cream colored rose in front of her. She wanted to do anything other than look at Seth for fear he would be able to see the need in her.

"It's beautiful, isn't it?"

"Yes." She wanted him to say she was beautiful. She wanted him to pick her up and take to his bedroom and seduce her. Seth leaned forward and sniffed the flower. He was so close and smelled so good. Then, he sighed and moved away. She had to look up. She wanted to look up.

"I'm sorry Seth, I mean Mr. Scanlon. I didn't mean to intrude. I finished the book. I was driving nearby so I thought it would be a good idea if I dropped it off. I got the impression the bookshop wasn't going to be able to get you another copy for a while. It wasn't any help anyway. I'm sorry. I should introduce myself. I'm Cara O'Donovan." Cara put out her hand aware that she was babbling on.

"Seth Scanlon. I'm pleased to meet you."

He shook her hand briefly and gave a slight nod with his head. He was real and she had touched him. Her dream man was really here before her.

"I've read many books on those particular subjects. I've found the people around me teach me more than books. I'm more interested in how you obtained my address." Seth opened the gate.

He turned away from the van. Cara felt obliged to follow. Walking down some dark country lane with a person she didn't know was not her best move to date. Then again, she didn't have many good moves.

"The people in the book store didn't say anything. Don't blame them. They left your order form inside the book. I'm sure it was just a genuine accident." Cara glanced back at her van but in truth wanted to stay near him.

Seth kept walking. They were only about fifty feet from the cottage when he walked towards a field and leaned on the gate.

Cara stood back a moment. Then, she joined him silently, taking in the country scene. They didn't talk. They just listened to the birds and watched the shadows of the clouds move across the field. The horse from the other side of the field came across and let Seth stroke its neck. The horse was huge and just the sort she would have imagined him owning. She reckoned they were called warm bloods and were incredibly regal.

Cara watched the scene. She put her head back and closed her eyes so she could take in the sounds around her. When she opened them, Seth was staring at her. She could feel the blotches coming back on her neck, but he was smiling. How long had he been standing there watching?

"It's a problem with people these days. They don't

stop." He smiled. "You said you didn't find what you wanted in the book?"

What would she answer? Janet was endearing. The cottage and the field were calming. She didn't want to tell this stranger about the things happening to her. Or the dreams she'd been having. "It explained a few things, just not what I wanted."

"So tell me, do you believe in magic and immortality?" He grinned.

He probably thought she was some idiotic new-age devotee. Perhaps she should lead him on and say she was going to perform some strange rite to bring some dead person alive again and freak him out. "I'd like to think it was true. The problem is if we all lived forever, then you would be stuck with some of the people you'd never like to see again."

He raised an eyebrow at her comment, then turned back toward the cottage. "I'd like to thank you again for giving me the book."

Cara followed him back in silence. It was ridiculous, but she wanted him to reach out and take her hand. She looked away from him. Suddenly, she noticed a building behind the cottage that was built from the same old stone. "What's that?" she blurted.

"It's my forge."

"You're a blacksmith?" The place was called the Old Smithy. Talk about appearing ignorant. That would explain the muscles, the big muscles. *Don't go there.*

"Among other things."

More silence again as they walked back to her van.

"Could I see it? I've never been in one before." Would he pick up she just wanted to be with him a bit longer? *Just because he wants you in dreams, doesn't mean he wants you awake, you fool.*

"If you wish."

Who the hell says, if you wish outside of the movies? This guy was too gorgeous and too strange. She needed boring and normal. Seth was neither.

She gasped at the sight of the statues in the garden at the back of the cottage. Each one was about three foot tall and made from a black colored stone. There were four of them, all naked women either standing, kneeling or lying down.

The one thing that connected them was their outstretched arms as if they pleaded to the world for an answer. The only male form was a statue of a man with a sword impaled in his chest. It looked like Seth. Maybe walking into the workshop of a deranged blacksmith wasn't such a good idea after all.

Cara struggled to keep the alarm out of her voice. "You made these statues?"

"Yes," he answered as he touched each one with his fingertips as he passed. It seemed such a sad gesture. Seth pushed open the door to the forge.

Cara loved it, the smell of the coals, the heat of the room, the humidity. There were no statues in here, but swords and daggers on the tables. It was almost as if there was a tang of metal in the air you could taste on your tongue.

"People buy them and hang them on their walls," Seth said, "or they play games at tournaments dressing up as people from a bygone era."

"They're exquisite." She reached out but didn't touch anything.

There were rapiers with ornate handholds. The knights of old would have developed muscles chopping their opponents in half with the heavier swords. Cara's guts clenched as she saw one of the daggers on the table. There was no mistake. It looked exactly like the one from her dream that she used to slice open people. She had to pick it up and prove to herself it existed. She was a fool. If Seth existed then why wouldn't the knife exist? Why wouldn't the murders have happened?

"This is an unusual design." Turning the knife over in her hand, Cara forced out the words. Her mouth felt dry. She looked to Seth for a reaction, some reassurance, but there was none.

When he touched her hand to take the dagger, heat flowed over her as if the furnace had exploded. The room became hazy. Seth's face drifted out of focus. It was no good. She was going to faint.

THEY WERE IN THE KITCHEN, but it looked different. It was dark. Only a lantern on the table illuminated the room. Cara wanted to move from the chair, but her legs felt like lead. The cupboards were bare. All the trinkets covering the shelves were gone. Where were Janet and Seth? It was dark. She must have been out for hours.

She heard footsteps. Someone was coming. Seth entered with another man. At least she thought it was Seth. He had long hair pulled back with a cord. Their clothes were so old-fashioned. Seth wore an old leather apron, shirt and loose pants. The other man was in a fancy jacket that was almost like a tailcoat you would wear at a wedding. Underneath he had a high collared shirt with a bright red cravat. It was as if she watched a television version of an old novel. She tried to speak. No words came out.

"Have you repaired it?" The stranger asked.

"Said I would." The old-time Seth took down a cloth from the dresser. He unwrapped the material. He placed the dagger from the forge and her dreams on the table. The man went to pick it up, but Seth grabbed his wrist. "Not before I get paid."

"Of course. You've done an excellent job." A purse was thrown on the table.

"It was a strange design. Who is it for?"

"Why should it bother you who owns it as long as you get paid?"

"Took a while to fix, that's all."

"I'm just the person collecting it. I've been paid like you. It's a dagger though. I would imagine it will be used to kill something," the man snickered.

"Take it and get out."

With the man gone, Seth went to the cupboard and got a jug and tankard. He took a knife from one of the dresser draws. Sitting down, he drank a tankard of ale straight down, followed by a second one. Picking up the knife, he held it over his left wrist. He was about to cut through the skin when Cara tried to scream.

---

"IT'S ALL RIGHT. You just fainted." Janet stood in front of Cara in the kitchen. It was still daylight. The sun streamed in through the window making her screw up her eyes.

Looking up, Cara realized Seth was holding her in his arms, concern etched on his face. She struggled to breathe and glanced down at his wrists. She didn't see any evidence of scars. *This wasn't good.* She was starting to have these crazy dreams in the daytime.

He was so close. She smelled his aftershave and heard his heartbeat as her head pressed against his chest. It was strange but for a moment she felt as if she had been in this position before, but that wasn't possible. She wanted to be in this man's arms too much for this to be happening. Their gazes connected. The coldness she had seen in his eyes before had vanished. She should look away but she didn't. Instead, she looked at his lips. She wanted him to kiss her right there in front of Janet.

"I don't know why he took you out to that forge. The heat was bound to get you lightheaded." Janet followed them into the lounge, carrying a glass of water.

Cara took her arms from around his neck as he placed her on the sofa. He stayed close, too close if that was possible. She accepted the glass Janet offered. "I'm fine now, honestly. I've been more than enough trouble."

Cara sipped the water. "I really should be going." She looked around. Her purse was missing. "Where's my bag?"

"It'll be in the forge. I'll get it for you." Seth left.

"It scared me half to death when I saw him carrying you into the kitchen," Janet said.

"I'm fine, honestly. I need to be going soon anyway."

"I think you should stay longer. You still look pale." Janet's brow furrowed as she peered closely.

"I have someone coming over tonight about a dinner I need to cater and I really do feel better. I need to start home."

Seth walked back in with her purse. "It had emptied onto the floor." He said.

Cara glanced in. He had put everything back neatly. She tried to stand, but fell back. Seth's hands were around her once again, lowering her onto the couch. Every time they touched her heart sped up.

"I'll get her some more water." Janet ran from the room.

"You were leaving?" Seth asked.

For a second, she thought she heard sadness in his voice. She couldn't think straight with him standing so close. He watched her as if he knew something about her that she didn't. His lips were so near as he leaned in towards her. Cara swallowed as she struggled to control the urge to kiss him.

"Here, I've got some more water. I think she should stay for tea, Seth, but she won't listen to me." Janet handed the glass over.

Seth moved to the far side of the room and stood by the fireplace. Cara drank the water as Janet talked until the phone rang. The elderly housekeeper left them alone. Silence.

"I really must get back to Bristol." Cara needed to be away from here. She couldn't think straight and would say something she would regret soon like *'Are you sure you don't remember the sexy dreams? Did you used to have long hair? Or did you ever try to cut your wrists?'*

"Let me walk you to your van." Seth offered his arm to support her.

Cara couldn't refuse. She didn't want to anyway. She wanted any excuse for her body to be near him for a moment longer. Her mind was a different matter.

Seth was still standing by his front gate when she drove away. The thought of seeing him again scared her. The idea of never seeing him again was worse. How could she be so foolish as to go to his house? What made her faint on him? What must he think of her?

Once she was at home and made coffee, it all seemed a

world away from what was real. The phone rang. The sudden sound caused her to spill some of the steaming beverage on her pants.

"Ouch! Damn that was hot." She grabbed the phone. "Hallo."

"Cara, are you all right?"

It was him. She would know that deep voice anywhere. He wasn't even with her and her body was reacting by heating up. It was like phone sex, except he didn't know he was having that effect.

"Yes. I'm sorry. I didn't mean to snap. I was just being a klutz and spilt some coffee on myself. It's Seth, isn't it?"

"Janet had your business card. I was ringing to make sure you'd gotten home safe."

"I'm fine. Janet was probably right. The heat must have gotten to me."

"I'd like to thank you again for bringing the book to me."

"It was no trouble." Silence and she tried to think of something brilliant to say. "Well don't forget us when you want your next dinner party organized."

"I won't forget you. Thank you again."

Then he was gone. Cara sat down staring at the phone. He had called her. Maybe, there was some way they could stay in contact without her looking like a total stalker, but she doubted it.

# TEN

Seth put down the phone and popped the business card back in his pocket. Janet would know he had used the extension in the forge. She would also work out who he had phoned. He couldn't go back inside yet. Talking wasn't what he needed right now.

He had watched Cara since she had arrived in Bristol with her parents as an eighteen-year-old. He had watched her fall in and out of love. Then, he had fallen in love himself from a distance. Now, that they had finally met, he knew things were going to change no matter how he tried to stop it. Why was she reading books on immortality? There were too many unanswered questions here. What did she know?

The forge was cool. Anyway, he wanted to work on his latest statue. He ran his fingers over the cool surface of the new slab of soapstone. As before, his mind could almost make out the shape waiting to be released. The slab was about eighteen inches high and four foot long. He had intended to turn it upright. Now, he knew that wasn't necessary.

Easing the slab onto a trolley, he moved the cart by the window so he could get the benefit of the natural light. His chisel and hammer became extensions of his fingers as he set to work.

The next hour passed in a blur. He didn't even notice the sunlight fading until Janet turned on the light. He smelled coffee. She placed the tray down on the chair near him. It held a bowl of soup and homemade bread smothered in butter. The aromas made his mouth water. Placing the chisel down, he picked up the cup. He caught the scent of something else and smiled.

"Well, it's cold out here. I put a tot of brandy in it. Got one in mine too." Janet sipped and moved around to look at his work. "Bit different this one. The others have all been standing up."

"Not always. I destroyed some." Seth had a feeling he would need to destroy this one when it was finished.

"Some folk would pay good money for them," Janet said. "You should let that dealer of yours have a look."

"No." Seth loved Janet's cooking but not her inquisitiveness. He finished the soup in a hurry, keen to get back to work. The shape was starting to become discernible. Janet's words broke into his thoughts. "So, where did you meet Cara?" Janet sat down on a stool near his workbench.

"She's one of those I watch over. I saw her in Bath with a young man I didn't know. I followed them to the bookshop. We both wanted the same book." Seth remembered how the young man had glared at him.

"So you did the gentlemanly thing and gave her yours. How sweet. I guessed she might be one of Rosie's descendants when I saw she had one blue and one green eye. I remember you telling me that about Rosie. Don't you always keep your distance?"

"Yes, I do." Seth hoped Janet would pick up this meant their conversation would go no further.

"Well, I'll go return to my emails. I'll be back with more sustenance later, whether you like it or not." Janet finished her coffee, picked up the tray and left.

The swords, the daggers, they were nothing. It was the statues that made his mind run wild. Maybe, they were trying to tell him something, but he was too stubborn to understand.

He chiseled away as the shape called to him. It waited to be released. It was a week after Rosie's funeral when he had started the first statue. At that time, it was just a big old lump of rock out in the yard. He'd been so angry and needed to hit something.

It had been in the image of Rosie but not as she appeared that night in the kitchen when she had been murdered. It was one of Rosie lying on her side, naked like the first time they had been together. It represented what he had lost and he had destroyed it.

Why did he bother? He knew this one would end up smashed like the others in the past. The same as his past loves, he thought. His love for Cara would end up crushed. It was dark outside now. Janet was coming up the path with a tray. Seth put down his tools and opened the door.

"Nice to see you haven't lost all your manners along with your common sense then. Here's food for those who don't know what's best for them." Her smiling face didn't match the statement.

"Thank you." He tipped his head in gratitude.

Seth sipped on the cocoa and grabbed a slice of the fruitcake. He found himself looking at the stone and the female form hidden there. She was naked and lying on her back. One hand cupped her head, the other arm draped across her abdomen. The legs were together and slightly bent to one side. Janet had been talking but he hadn't been listening.

"I told him I've never been to Paris. My friend went there once. Said the Seine stank. He said his gallery has a new exhibition next month. He wants me to come and help with the opening. It seems silly going off gallivanting. My late husband Bill never held with the French. Mind you, that might be a reason to go. What do you think?" Janet moved closer to the statue. "Will this one be holding a dagger or outstretched arms?"

"No." Seth answered, before he could contemplate the question. "She won't be holding anything." She would never hold him and that was the one thing he wanted.

"So should I go to Paris? I don't like to leave you on your own. You get broody."

"I went there once. I was looking for someone. Like all cities, it has its beauty, and its horror." Seth picked up his tools.

"Did you find her?" Janet asked packing up the supper things. "Or was it a man you hunted?"

"Who?" Seth wanted to get on with his work.

"The one you were seeking in Paris?"

"Yes. Both the person I was looking for and his friend were found deceased in the river."

"That's cheerful. I'm going back to my computer and then it's off to bed. If I go to Paris, I'll need my beauty sleep," Janet laughed. "Don't forget Robert Fetter's coming tomorrow. I don't know why you don't let him out the back. If he saw your statues, I'm sure he could find a buyer."

"All the more reason to keep him inside then." Seth started to chisel away at the stone. He heard the door close. His body relaxed back into the repetitive movement of his sculpturing. As he tapped the chisel, he thought back to his time in Paris.

———

IT WAS New Years and the turn of the century, 1900. Everyone was happy. Perhaps, many were just deluded. He had followed Nigel Farnborough from his hotel. He had the same group of hangers-on as the night before, young bucks with more money than sense. They would surely have been disillusioned to find the person they were carousing with was in fact seventy years old.

The Eiffel Tower rose into the dark sky above with thousands of revelers gathered around its base. Three young women had already kissed Seth. He wasn't interested in such things. Nigel and his friends were partaking of the joys being offered as well. There would be a few less virgins in Paris come the morning, but then again, Seth doubted there were that many anyway.

Paris was renowned for having more prostitutes than any other city in Europe. The taxes they paid the church in the past had made it possible for the Notre Dame Cathedral to be built, so they were not going to disappear anytime soon. Nigel's group made their way from hotel to brothel. Seth doubted with the amount of alcohol they had imbibed, they would last long. Nigel had left the brothel alone. It was the first time in the week since Seth had arrived that he had seen him away from the others. Seth followed Nigel for a short distance.

He appeared oblivious of Seth's presence as he nonchalantly strode along. They turned into an alley. Seth drew the dagger from inside his cloak and stared at it. It was identical to the one he had repaired so long ago.

The one that Rosie had made him push deeper into her chest.

Nigel was the only link to the dagger. James Rushton had eventually told him before he died that Nigel had been the one to order the repair. Seth had searched for him for so long that he was not going to turn away now. Two men approached. Seth moved back and hid in the shadows. Nigel shook the hand of one man before slapping the back of the other and turning to hug him. Seth saw something catch the light. He needed to move closer but now that there was more than one of them was hesitant.

"Why, Edgar?" Nigel yelled, as he fell to his knees.

"Because I'll live longer if you die."

The attacker moved away. Seth glimpsed the blade handle of the dagger impaled in Nigel's chest. It was a duplicate of the one in his coat pocket. Could it be the original? Was it the one he had repaired so long ago?

Nigel collapsed onto the cobblestones. His lifeblood seeping away. The attacker turned to the other man who had his back to Seth.

"Shouldn't I feel different?" He asked.

"You will. Take the dagger from his body. The power will be in it already."

Edgar pulled the blade from Nigel's body and held it up. It appeared dull in the moonlight. Then Edgar bent over clutching his own chest. He put his hand inside his coat. When he withdrew it, his fingertips were covered in blood.

"What's happening to me?"

"You're dying, just like he has. Did I forget to mention that whatever you inflict with the dagger on another immortal will then be your own fate? How remiss of me. His soul as well as yours are removed. The immortal Lord awaits you."

Seth went to move from the shadows but the man who had spoken whistled. Four more men came around the corner of the alley. The stranger whispered to them. Then, he bent down and picked up the dagger as the men dragged the bodies from the alley.

Seth followed them as they walked along, supporting the dead Nigel and Edgar. The two victims must appear to any passersby as nothing more than drunks who had celebrated too much bringing in the new century. The hirelings made their way under one of the bridges and finally tipped the bodies into the Seine.

Seth needed to find the other man to get his revenge and be free of this world. A woman's scream broke into his somber thoughts. He turned to see a coach hurtling towards her. Its driver slouched over, either dead or drunk.

Seth pushed the woman to the ground covering her with his body. The wheels narrowly missed them as water sprayed up from the gutter. The horses swerved causing the coach to crash into the wall of the bridge. Screams filled the air as people fought to get the horses under control. Seth helped the woman to her feet. She appeared unharmed as her partner rushed to her side.

Seth looked around for the man with the dagger. He was gone. He had saved one woman's life but still had to avenge another's. The man was alive. Seth would find him eventually. That night, Rosie came to him in his dreams. "Only the one left now my darling, and he's the worst."

---

SETH LOOKED at the stone in front of him. While he had been reminiscing of Paris so long ago, he had slowly chiseled away. It was her, Cara consumed him.

He stretched. It felt as if the muscles and ligaments in his neck would tear apart as he moved. *Why didn't you get immunity to pain with immortality?* It had been a thought he had pondered on many a time. He heard voices coming from the garden.

"So who does he have dealing with his statues? I know my thing is the weaponry. These would sell anywhere though."

Janet tried in vain to draw Robert back to the cottage. His agent's gaze devoured the statues, as he touched them. *That was why no one was allowed to see them,* Seth told himself. Each chip had been pain, trying to capture something he couldn't have anymore. Other people might want them, but they couldn't share his anguish. They had no right. Let them deal with their own. Seth glanced towards the new statue he'd worked on all night. He couldn't let Robert see it. He left the sanctuary of his forge.

He had worked all night and was hungry. "Janet is making breakfast for me. Come and join us." Seth took his agent's arm and guided him back to the cottage. "Now, I hear you're interested in selling these statues."

"Listen, Seth, I was going to talk to you about an idea I had. Seeing those statues in the garden crystallized the whole thing in my mind."

"What?" Seth asked with dread.

"A friend of mine is an editor of the magazine, Art U.K. He's looking for a new slant to the magazine. The previous editor was into stately homes and the like. He wants young people showing the country their work." Robert's eyes glowed with excitement.

"I'd hardly call myself young," Seth said dryly.

Janet laughed and he gave her a sideways glance.

"Rubbish, what are you? In your early thirties? Look, your work is crying out for someone to see it."

Seth was about to tell Robert how foolish he was when it occurred to him this might be a solution. He could bait Rosie's killer and draw him into the open. Then, he'd also be able to see Cara again. It was always an option to fool himself, to tell himself that he needed to see her again to create the statue.

It wasn't true. He knew her so well after all these years. Holding her in his arms earlier made it all seem so clear now. The touch of her was all he needed to make him be truly alive again.

"I will let you sell my statues, but I want to know who is going to buy them. I reserve the right not to sell."

Robert smiled, rubbing his hands together eagerly. "Artistic drama always makes the public want more and the prices go up."

## ELEVEN

Cara stretched her arms above her head to relieve the ache in her back. Maybe she could go to a physiotherapist and call it a work-related injury from leaning over her recipe books. It was a week since she had met the mysterious Mr. Scanlon. He kept cropping up in her mind. She accepted his explanation the dagger she'd noticed in his forge was a copy of an old one he had seen a long time ago. She still reckoned the thing looked like something medieval and gave her the creeps.

He must have thought her hysterical to go fainting on him the way she had. It was just as well she would never see him again. This schoolgirl crush had to stop. It was a pity. He was rough and yummy. A part of her wanted to know if he was as good in bed as her dream lover.

Last night had bought another dream about mutilation, but there had been nothing on the news. It was all rubbish. She couldn't foresee people's deaths. The stuff with Nanna and Aunty Eileen were coincidences. She had to keep believing that for her own sanity.

Mr. Perfect Peter Connor from *The Evening Post*

wanted them to do another dinner. This time he requested a particular meal. He had been informed there was a well-known Irish treat called Dingle Delight. The fact that she had never heard of it and couldn't find any reference to it in her books or online, made her think it didn't exist. Dingle was a beautiful little fishing port but she hadn't been there for a while. They did manage to get some of their fish and seafood from there and it was always excellent quality.

He was testing her, which was okay. He might not get the dish he was expecting. He would get something original and hopefully delightful. She was thinking along the lines of a rich chocolate orange cake with clotted cream and chocolate and cherry ganache on top. It could become her signature dish and make her famous.

Merlin rubbed up against her leg.

"I'm sorry darling. I'm ignoring you, aren't I?" The black and white bundle of fluff purred as she scratched under his chin. She loved Merlin so much. She had since she found him as a scrappy kitten fighting for survival on the streets. Sometimes he would have a mad five minutes and run around and around the flat.

Occasionally he had been known to run into a wall or door, which caused him to slow down and go cross-eyed. "You're right, it's bedtime. Come on. I'll let you out to do your thing. She would stand close by though he never usually went beyond the front yard. Plus she had the garden hose to squirt any other cat that got close.

Merlin followed her downstairs and out the front of the flats. It was only September, but it was already getting chilly at night. There had better not be any pretty felines around. It wouldn't do him any good anyway. He didn't have the equipment anymore, even though he pretended to spray everything in sight in her flat.

Cara peered up and down the street as she stomped her feet to keep them from freezing. A car crept down the street. She stiffened. Was it a taxi? No, it was a police car. It pulled in out the front of the flats, just as Merlin ran back and pressed up against her legs.

An elderly couple owned the flat on the bottom floor. She doubted the police were there for them. The two nurses renting the flat above were okay as well. They had some lively parties, but on the whole never caused any problems.

Cara eyed the officers warily as they approached. Policemen looked so young these days, or maybe she was getting older. Regardless, the car and the uniforms still made her heart race as if she was guilty, no matter how boyish their faces looked. They pressed her buzzer.

"That's my bell." Her stomach churned as she spoke the words. Even though the night air was cool, her skin burned as if their eyes were boring into her.

"Ms. Cara O'Donovan?" A policeman asked.

Cara nodded and led them inside. Merlin purred in her arms as they walked up the stairs to her flat. The stairs echoed with the clomp, clomp, clomp of the heavy-footed policemen. Once in her flat Merlin ran off to the bedroom to hide. Cara wanted to follow him. Turning back to the policeman she waited for what was to come next.

"Ms. O'Donovan, we're investigating the discovery of a body found earlier today. We feel you might have some involvement with the victim. You may be able to help us with the investigation."

Body. What on earth were they talking about? This was like some American cop show. How would she know someone who turned up as a mysterious body in some investigation? She felt sick and her hands were clammy.

"Your business card was found on the deceased. We're hoping you might be able to help with the identification."

"I've handed out hundreds of my business cards. Look, I'm sure there must be some mistake." Cara's breath caught in her throat. "Do you really want me to look at a dead body?" Having dreams about mutilated bodies was enough without anything else fueling her imagination. This sort of thing didn't happen to people like her.

"We understand this is stressful. Someone has died. Your card is the only connection we have. We would be very grateful if you could help."

As she rode off in the police car, she saw the curtains of the downstairs flat pulled back. What rumors would be flying by tomorrow? It started to rain as they drove through the city center. At this time of night there wasn't much traffic. It wasn't a good thing as they would get to their destination that much sooner.

The two policemen introduced her to Detective Seps as they walked into the morgue. He was short. However, the man reminded her of a terrier her parents had once owned that always gave the impression he was much bigger than he really was.

His gray suit was crumpled and matched his expression. It gave her the feeling she wasn't the only one who didn't want to be there. He looked sixty and tired. His beady eyes glanced at the two young policemen, perhaps with jealousy at their full heads of hair. It was against her better judgment but there was something about this man. He made her relax more than she had with the two young cops.

The smell assailed her nostrils. No amount of disinfectant could disguise the reek of old blood. She followed the detective along cream painted corridors. There were doors in front of her. Beyond them, was where the body waited. They stopped outside of plastic see-through doors.

All she could make out were vague shapes on the other side of the doors. Cara was pretty sure it would be a good thing to keep it that way. The detective opened the doors to let her through. A big room, more cream tiles and silver drawers. The doors closed with a flopping sound behind her bringing back reality. She pulled her jacket around her to keep out the chill.

Another face, someone called Dr. Pierce. He was polite. It didn't help her. She was frozen to the spot. The detective took her arm and guided her across the room to a gurney with a covered body lying on top.

"The body was found on the side of the motorway between here and Gloucester. She had no identification on her except your business card in her coat. I should warn you the body has been mutilated."

Cara wanted to run. Another part of her was compelled to look. Dr. Pierce took hold of the corners of the cover. Cara held her breath as he uncovered the face. She didn't want to believe what her gaze told her. It was Shona. Even with her brown hair all matted with blood and deep slashes across her forehead, Cara recognized her cousin.

The food she had eaten earlier started to rise up in her throat. Before she could stop herself, she vomited. She couldn't lift her head. She saw the splashes on the detective's shoes and pants and her empty stomach clenched again. Her body went cold and hot. She gripped the side of the gurney to steady herself.

Someone guided her to a chair. Her knees buckled beneath her as she sat down. Dr. Pierce cleaned away the pool of vomit. Detective Seps went to a desk nearby and brought back a glass of water for her. Cara sipped it, trying to rid herself of the bile that was burning her throat. It didn't work. This couldn't be real.

"I take it that you knew the deceased?" Taking some tissues from Dr. Pierce, Detective Seps started to clean the vomit splatter from his shoes. "Who is she?"

Cara stared at the glass in her hands, not wanting to look up at the covered body again. The words stuck in her throat. Eventually, they came out in a whisper. "Shona Williams."

"What was your relationship to the deceased?"

"We are... were cousins. She used to help out with the business when things got busy." Cara's nose began running. More tears streamed down her cheeks. Dr. Pierce handed her a box of tissues. He held out a waste-paper bin for her to discard the soggy mush. Her stomach twisted again. She couldn't vomit anymore. There was nothing left.

"I understand this is distressing for you," Detective Seps said. "It's important we get some information about another aspect of this case. I need you to take another look at her body."

"I can't." Cara blew her nose. "I'm sorry, but I can't."

"It may be important in finding out who did this to her. Look, my own daughter is about the same age. If someone did this to her, I'd want to know."

Cara nodded. "I'll try." She loved Shona so much she would do anything she could to help find the killer.

Detective Seps took her elbow and led her back across the room to the cart where Shona lay. There was a bucket on the floor. Cara accidentally kicked it, causing a metal clang to echo around the room. She gripped Detective Seps' arm as Pierce pulled back the sheet again.

Fresh tears flowed when she looked at the pale white face of her cousin. The only color was the maroon hue of blood from the deep cuts to the forehead. The sheet was drawn down to reveal Shona's torso. At that moment, the world darkened. Cara saw the floor rising up to meet her. And she passed out.

---

SHE HEARD VOICES. They sounded close, but she was too groggy to understand what they were saying. Whatever she was lying on was hard. Where was she? Opening her eyes, it all came flooding back. Shona's body as they pulled the sheet away. The marks were the same as those she'd viewed in the news photo and in her dreams, only worse.

A deep slash extended from her chin to her navel and another across her chest. They cut deep through the breast tissue. Then, they dissected each nipple in half. The bone showed through muscles that had been sheared off.

Another meandering cut had been made from the top of the breastbone to Shona's navel. It was so deep, some of the bowel had herniated through. There was one other mark Cara remembered. It was a dark hole just below Shona's heart.

Shona's covered body lay close by on a cart. Cara's nostrils flared. She could pick up the scent of who had lain on this cot before her. Detective Seps and Dr. Pierce came over to her.

"I'm sorry about that," Detective Seps said. "I think we should continue this discussion back at the station. You've probably had enough of this place. I know I have."

Cara wasn't sure her legs would hold out, but she was determined to leave, although she regretted leaving Shona here alone.

HOURS later she left the interview room. She all but fell into Jeff's and Daniel's waiting arms. Jeff was calm as usual. Daniel's face was red. Cara wanted to be home in her flat. She wanted to be safe and a world away from where people were getting up and going to work.

Opening the front door of the flat, Merlin ran across and circled around her legs. Cara wished she could be as oblivious to what had happened as well.

She allowed Daniel to guide her to the sofa. She wanted to cradle her knees against her chest and rock. She didn't have the energy. It was as if nothing could fill the void that had been Shona. Daniel placed a cup of tea in front of her. His hand touched her arm. As she looked at him, the tears welled up again.

"I'm so sorry, Cara. I've only known her these last few years. I loved her too. She was crazy. I've never known anyone else who could drink that much red wine and not have a hangover the next day. You know if it wasn't six in the morning, I'd have a glass now and I know she'd approve." Daniel wiped his eyes on the sleeve of his jumper.

For someone so particular about his clothing, it showed Cara the depths of his distress. Jeff came over and sat beside her for a moment.

"I've got to go to work, but I'll call back later. You should try and get some sleep." Jeff looked from her to Daniel. "You'll stay with her, won't you?"

"I don't think I can sleep. If I shut my eyes I'll see her again." Cara clasped her hands together. If they were apart, she couldn't stop them shaking. She wouldn't risk trying to hold a mug right now.

"Are you sure you don't want us to ring your doctor or your counselor?" Jeff asked.

"No. I'll only have to tell them about last night. I can't right now. I've enough sedatives in the bathroom to make a whale sleep for a year. I'll be fine, Jeff. You go to work. Daniel's here with me." Jeff kissed her forehead and walked to the door.

Daniel followed him and she could see the looks on their faces as they hugged and said goodbye. Shona had always been envious of them. She claimed she wanted to play the field. Deep down she longed to meet Mr. Right. Now, she never would. Unbidden tears started to fall again. Cara gasped for air between the sobs. Daniel came back to her side.

"If you're not going to drink that tea, then I'm going to run you a hot bath. I'll find those sedatives and make you get some rest." Daniel put on his best authoritative face.

It didn't really work with the red eyes and a nose with sniffles but she loved him.

VOICES, people talking and she was awake again. The sedatives had worked well. They hadn't lasted long enough. Then again, at the moment, how long would be long enough? Rubbing her eyes, she sat up. Her glance fell to her chaotic bedside table.

One of the things that stood out at this moment was the picture of Shona and herself when they went to Spain. They had been nineteen and having fun. Way too much fun involving young men, midnight strolls on beaches and booze.

They both looked so happy. How did she move on from

this? Cara peered at her bedside clock. It was three in the afternoon. What would she tell Daniel and Jeff? This morning they hadn't pushed her. They just knew Shona had been killed.

Detective Seps now knew Cara had seen the marks before. Once on a picture a reporter carried, and then on the front page of the paper. There would be no point in telling him about the dreams. He'd decide she was ready for a one-way ticket to the loony bin.

She started to shake. She pulled her legs up and hugged them to stop the tremors. Was this what it was like to go insane? Had she truly killed that other woman and Shona? If that was the case, why couldn't she remember doing it?

The bedroom door opened a crack. Daniel poked his head inside. "You're awake. I'll put on the kettle."

Her bladder needed emptying. Staying in bed forever wasn't an option anyway. Daniel was there with a cup of tea when she came out of the bathroom. An aroma of food cooking filled her flat. Daniel went back into the kitchen and stirred something on the stove.

"I've made some soup. It's almost ready and the bread will be done soon. I don't know about you, but I need comfort food at a time like this." He tried to smile, but it quickly faded. "Well, that and a large amount of alcohol."

His laptop was open on the coffee table. A glance showed a list of their upcoming bookings. It was crazy. She didn't think she would ever be able to leave this flat again, yet alone make meals. Daniel sat down beside her.

"We've nothing on till the weekend and I can manage with Matcher's help. If we get stuck, I'll arrange for a waiter from the agency."

"No, Daniel. I want to keep working, though at this

moment I'm not sure how." Her hands shook as she held her mug of tea.

"Are you sure you don't want to call Jessica? You've been through so much, and now this."

"I don't want to talk to her right now, maybe later." Merlin came and sat on her lap, digging in his claws. Cara scratched his neck. Shona had always loved him. When she had slept over, he would always end up sleeping on her. She would be sneezing by morning because of her allergy.

"Did the police say if they would want to talk to you again?"

"No."

Daniel looked dissatisfied with the answer, but it was all she could give right now.

"We received another booking today for next month. The Crescent in Bath, no less. He's in advertising or something and a friend gave him our card. Runs a magazine called *Art UK*."

Daniel was rambling on about what meal they would do. She let him keep talking, discussing menus and staff. The dinner was for ten. Jeff returned. From the look on his face as he frowned, Cara was sure she must look like crap. She certainly felt like it.

Daniel dished up the soup in the kitchen and whispered something to Jeff. She couldn't eat the food. It was wonderful, almost as good as hers, but her stomach rebelled.

"I'd like a drink, Jeff." Cara said, disrupting their conversation.

"Are you sure that's a good idea with the sedatives you took earlier?"

"It might not be a good idea. If I have to tell you about last night, it's what I'll need."

"Fair enough." Jeff went to the kitchen and returned with a bottle of red.

Cara sniffed the rich aroma.

"Shona would have approved of this one."

By the time they opened the second bottle, she had told them of the wounds on Shona's body. Daniel's fists clenched. Tears fell down his face. The phone rang and they all jumped. Then, they sat staring at it. They watched it ring on the kitchen wall. Cara was sure it was the police again. She had nothing left to tell them that they would believe.

In the end, Jeff got up. He answered the phone. He talked quietly for a while and then put the receiver down. "It was Matcher. He's on his way over. I hope you didn't mind me saying that was okay?"

"No, of course not," Cara told him. "Matcher can stay here and you two can go home. Tomorrow's another day, as Shona said when Nanna died. You have to celebrate them if you're alive."

Cara heard the words spouted by her own mouth, but at this moment didn't believe them. Her life was officially shit.

---

IF THERE HAD EVER BEEN a time Matcher had not wanted this gift, it was when he had turned up at Cara's flat. She was being so strong. All he wanted to do was wallow in the loss of losing his own Mum and then part of his body. His life was crazy with all these frigging people around him who were glowing like light bulbs with a happiness he didn't understand. Or had colors swirling with misery rotating at various areas of their bodies.

He loved the new people who had come into his life,

but were they enough to keep him from going under? Mum said he couldn't die yet. Until he got another message, he would stay and see what life would bring. Cara looked a mess. Her aura was strange to start with. Now, the dark swirls started taking over. Her head had been surrounded by a dark cloud. He had to change it. The others had gone so it was up to him. She was at rock bottom so he couldn't do much harm.

"Listen Cara, I know this sounds stupid, but when Mum was dying we used to play a game." From the look of shock on her face Matcher realized he had not told her about his mother.

"I'm so sorry."

"Hey, it was a long time ago. We talked about silly things. When I was four, I decided the lounge room carpet was boring, so I got her fabric paints and redesigned it. Mum took all my Ninja Turtle toys and locked them in her wardrobe for a month. I thought my world had come to an end. Fuck, I hated her so much then. I remember telling her she was the worse Mum in the world, but I still wanted her to read to me at bedtime." Matcher wondered what his aura was like as he spoke.

Cara smiled for the first time since he had walked in and started to talk. "I remember when Shona and I went to Spain and we both had a crush on the waiter at the hotel. He went for Shona, but said he would bring his friend along for a double date. His friend was so hot and really good in the sack. God, we laughed about that so much."

Matcher observed the change in her aura as they spoke. He would veer the conversation in whatever direction gave the best outcome. It was the first time since he got this crazy gift that he realized he could actually do some good.

"Mum said I use to be so funny when I was in the bath

as a toddler. I loved to splash and water would go every-where. Dad would get in the bath as well sometimes. I used to have these egg shaped strainers that I would drip water through. Dad had to start placing one over his privates as I whacked them on more than one occasion. Hey I suppose that's the bright side to my cancer. I've only got one ball that can be walloped if I ever have kids."

Cara laughed and her aura brightened except for that gray area closest to her body.

"Shona once managed to get us back stage at a concert when we were eighteen. I can't even remember the band now. It was at the Colston Hall. They asked if we wanted to go back to their hotel where they were having a pool party. I'd never driven in a stretch limo before. We played table tennis with a beach ball and I managed to whack the lead singer in the balls. That's what your story reminded me of. There was so much booze and pot there. You know I never smoked. I didn't try it. Shona disappeared with the lead singer. She swore to me she hadn't slept with him." Cara shook her head and sighed. "Now, I hope she did."

They drank and talked on for hours about everything and nothing. Cara eventually grew tired and wanted sleep. He walked her to her room and then went back to pull out the bed settee. It didn't change things, he couldn't bring Shona back, but he did feel as he had helped.

TWELVE

Sleep had come easily with the amount of wine she had consumed. Now, she lay awake in the darkness crying. It wasn't the hacking sobs of earlier, but a continual outpouring of tears. They flowed silently until the pillow was damp. Eventually, exhaustion took over and sleep returned. With the sleep came a dream.

She was on a bridge gazing down at a river. The people around her were speaking French and she could understand it.

"More bodies pulled from the Seine."

Cara looked at the person beside her who had spoken. They were dressed in costume as though they were from an old movie in the 1800's. Turning back to the riverbank, she watched the gendarmes drag the bodies from the water. They were dumped unceremoniously onto the walkway.

Someone nearby vomited into the river. The stench of regurgitated alcohol attacked her nostrils. Cara peered down at the river to see a reflection that was not her own. It was Seth Scanlon's face, but not the one she knew. This was the man from the past, the one with long hair. She felt her hand or rather Seth's go into the pocket of his coat. Hers, no Seth's fingers gripped the hilt of a knife. From the feel, it was the one from her dreams and his workshop. Was this her imagination or had those people really died in the past? Had Seth known them or possibly even killed them?

---

IT WAS MORNING. Another day but nothing was the same. Another loved one was gone from her life. She was too tired to even think what the dream might mean. It was probably too much booze and too many sedatives.

Matcher had the coffee machine going when she left her room. The aroma was comforting and normal. He wore black and white stripped pajamas, in complete contrast to her pink pajamas with yellow teddy bears. She smiled, despite herself.

"You look like crap," he offered.

She sipped on her super strong, super sweet coffee. "I know. I presume you mean my aura as well. Don't tell me. I don't want to know right now."

"You probably don't need this right now. Last night when I took Merlin down to do his thing, I think someone was watching. Did the police put someone to keep an eye on your flat?"

Cara looked around. She couldn't see Merlin anywhere in the kitchen. "If they did, they never told me."

"I probably just imagined it. I'm hungry. Do you want some toast?"

The toast tasted like cardboard. She swallowed it down. "Did you ever see anything strange in Shona's aura when you met her?"

"Not really. She was like most people. I saw colors in

layers with a few dull patches. The patches were brown as if she was dealing with an old pain." Matcher shook his head. "Shit, this is such a stupid gift. What's the point if I can't stop crap like this from happening?"

"I have crazy dreams. You see people differently. I don't know what any of it means, except I feel so terribly sad right now." The tears were coming back. She choked. Her body ached.

Matcher moved across the couch and hugged her.

The rest of the day passed in a blur due to the sedatives Daniel had insisted she take before he left again. He was worried. Letting others take control was what she needed right now.

Daniel came back later that day. He talked, Jeff comforted and even her mother turned up to offer what she believed was support. The problem was Cara kept seeing Shona's body in her mind again and again.

They all needed to go. First her mother and then everyone else. Cara knew it wasn't a good idea right now, but she desperately needed to be alone. Her mother was dealing with the relatives and making the arrangements for the funeral. They had not been told when the police would let the body go yet though. When they were all gone she took Merlin out for his evening constitutional.

A black and white fluff-ball ran past her and to the entrance door of the apartment block. He sat there meowing to be let inside.

"Don't you start whining at me. If you would use a kitty litter tray you wouldn't have to come out in the cold." Turning to go back inside, she stopped and glanced back into the darkness. Had she had heard something or some-one? There it was again. This time she heard it loud and clear. Her stomach churned. A stranger's voice called out her name.

"Cara."

Running back inside, she slammed the front door to her flat. Grabbing the phone she called the number Inspector Seps had given her. He promised he would send a patrol car around. If it happened again, she should let him know.

She ought to phone the others and get them to come back. There wasn't anything they could do. She wanted Seth here. She didn't know him, but he would be comforting if only because of his size.

———

A MONTH HAD GONE by since Shona's death. It seemed wrong that time could pass without her here. The police were nowhere nearer to finding the killer. Cara still shivered when she thought about the voice outside her flat. It hadn't happened again, and it was most likely just her over-active imagination. Considering what had happened in her life that was understandable.

The first couple of weeks had been the worst. The funeral had helped which had surprised her. So many people came and shared their love and stories of Shona that it had been beautiful. Mum had done a brilliant job since Aunty Jose couldn't cope. Dad had been aloof as always.

When the phone rang some days, Cara would think it was Shona. Then, the realization would come like a kick in the guts. Shona was gone. She'd never call or come by again. Jessica had phoned twice. Cara didn't want to talk about Shona's death with anyone, especially not someone who knew so much about her dreams.

The night they had done the meal for Peter Connor

from *The Evening Post* had been the worst so far. He knew she had been Shona's cousin. He spent all evening, trying to get information about the murder.

Matcher and Daniel had ended up forming a barrier every time Peter walked into the kitchen. There would be no more jobs from him for now. At least, it got them another article in the paper. Daniel was right. They were getting more bookings. The work kept her busy so the thoughts of what had happened didn't totally overwhelm her.

Tonight's booking was in Bath, at The Crescent. She had never been one to stand and admire architecture. It didn't matter as the semi-circle of beautiful Georgian houses would take anyone's breath away.

The apartment was beautiful. It looked like it came straight out of an interior design magazine. The kitchen had all new appliances. Daniel drooled with envy. The walls were painted cream, but the curtains were rich burgundies and navy that complimented the beautiful oak furniture.

The huge walnut table in the formal dining room was resplendent with a beautiful floral arrangement. The crisp white tablecloth could hardly be seen beneath the silver cutlery, bone china and crystal. Normally they provided the crockery and cutlery since most people's cupboards were filled with a hotchpotch of items, but not here.

The flowers were striking in their simplicity. Cara loved the way Blooms and Shoots came up with such personal concepts. She'd informed them tonight's booking was from an art editor. His magazine was planning on an article on swords and daggers. The centerpiece was made of red flowers in the shape of two hearts pierced with arrows. The client loved it. So had his new partner who was at least twenty years younger.

MATCHER CAME BACK in the kitchen and kept pacing. He was all twitchy for some reason. She'd thought she would be the one struggling tonight. The main course was served, so they could have a breather. It had been a new dish for her. She needed to challenge herself at the moment and it took her mind off of Shona's death.

The starter of seared scallops and Irish bacon served on a bed of fresh mint and baby spinach looked perfect with its blend of colors. The main of venison marinated in mead and served with creamy mashed potatoes and vegetable stacks had been equally as popular.

Dessert was in the fridge and was her Dingle Delight. It would take only minutes to finish. Daniel was in control anyway as always.

"Okay, what's bugging you?" Cara asked Matcher. "Since the guests arrived, you've been uptight about something?"

"He's here," Matcher mumbled.

"Who is here?"

"Think huge man. Shaved head. Get who I mean?"

She recognized Seth from the description. So, he was one of the guests.

"It's okay. I met him. Honestly, he looks scarier than he is. It's funny the last time I saw him was not long before..."

It was the week before Shona died. How long would this pain continue? Conversations kept bringing back memories, ones she couldn't face. Matcher folded his arms and looked at the floor. It wasn't that she doubted him. It was just so much had happened. Having to cope with anything else was too much right now. She just wanted everyone to be able to sort out their own stuff. Then, she could deal with hers in private.

"That's fine. You believe what you want. I'll believe what I see." Matcher turned and headed back out of the kitchen and down the hall.

Cara hoped if he was angry he wouldn't take it out on the crystal, the bone china, or the six-foot muscle-bound smithy.

The dessert was a success and now they could serve up the coffee and liquors. Daniel walked back into the kitchen beaming from ear to ear.

"They loved it. Four of them asked for our cards and sample menus. It's good, Cara. This is where we make our name. These are the sort of people who have contacts. This is the beginning of things going well for us." Daniel hugged her. "They want to meet you as well. You are the other half of the dynamic duo."

Her stomach turned at the thought of polite conversation. "I look a mess. I'm not sure tonight is the right time."

Daniel wasn't going to give in. "I hear excuses. I loved her too, Cara. You need to face people or you'll hide back here forever."

Cara stared at her reflection in the stainless steel fridge door. It was blurry but she could tell her hair was messed up and she looked red from cooking. Why did everyone think all cooks wanted to be chatty like Jamie Oliver? She didn't have a cute lisp to make her more endearing. Entering the room, she went cold. All the blood drained from her face, when she heard what they were discussing.

"I find it amazing no one has a clue about who did it. If the person kills so horrendously, how can it be no one has ever seen bloodstained clothes at least?" The comment came from a man dressed casually in a blue polo shirt.

"I can assure you once you're dealing with a killer of this nature, a quick slash and cut is not what it's about. They're meticulous in their planning. It's like an art form to them, perfect in every way. The disposal of necessary items will have been planned in advance."

Cara knew the speaker this time. It was Curtis Spencer, the solicitor who had hired them. His wife spoke next. She was perfect with manicured nails, glamorous hair and designer clothes.

"I used to feel safe in Bath. I'm not so sure I do anymore. I mean sometimes you think people have made bad choices. They might be walking down dark alleys or letting strangers into their home. From what I've heard she was last seen walking to her car with lots of people around. We frequently finish late. If Curtis wants to work on, I make my own way home. I really don't want to have to change my life because of what happened."

Curtis reached across and squeezed his wife's hand and then glanced towards Seth.

Cara wanted to talk to Seth. Somehow, she knew he would understand what she was going through. She paused when she saw Curtis approach Seth. Goosebumps broke out on her skin as she listened.

"You make blades. Does it ever cross your mind they might be used for something unlawful?"

Seth's jaw tightened as he pursed his lips. His stare became even more intense, if that was possible.

"I've made many blades. More than you can imagine. I cannot control what's done with the knife or dagger once it leaves my possession." Seth sipped his wine.

"I understand that it's not the weapon. It's the person using it that makes it evil. However, you can't deny the weapons you create, although beautiful are created for killing or fencing. That's the sport of playing at killing." Curtis Spencer smiled, knowing he had everyone's attention.

"A long time ago one of the blades I had worked on was used to kill someone close to me. Unless you have experienced the grief of losing someone like that, you shouldn't ask the question." Seth drained his glass. Then, he stared at everyone around the table as if daring them to make another comment.

Silence. Grabbing the bottle of Glayva from the buffet, Cara went up to Curtis. She coughed quietly at his shoulder and asked if he would like a refill.

"That would be lovely. I believe you are the mysterious Cara who's been hiding from us all evening." He picked up the glass she had just filled and took a large gulp.

"I thought it would be interesting for you to know the combination of herbs and whiskey in this drink." Cara amazed herself as she spouted off. It wasn't that she knew these things about the herbs, the whiskey and her culture.

It was more the fact she could discuss the ingredients after the guests had talked about Shona so dispassionately. She behaved like a robot. Only once did she catch Seth's gaze. He smiled. It was the first time she had ever seen him smile. It gave her the courage to continue.

Looking at Daniel, his wink told her it was all right to leave. The clients were most likely relieved as well. She kept up the façade until she reached the kitchen, but she couldn't stay inside anymore. It felt as if the walls were closing in on her.

She needed some air. No matter how deeply she tried to breathe, her chest fought against her. "I'm going out the back balcony to get some air."

"Do you want me to come with you?" Daniel asked, as he was about to head back to the dining room.

"No, I just need some time on my own. I'll be all right, honestly."

Once alone in the dark she stared out at the garden. She shivered as an invisible hand twisted in her gut again. Her eyes started to water. The tears came. She tried to be silent. Gasps escaped her lips, and her shoulders shook.

"Here, take this."

Cara jumped when she saw Seth standing there. He offered her a handkerchief. She had been so wrapped in her own grief that she hadn't heard him come out.

"Thank you." Cara wiped her eyes. The tears kept coming. He just stood there next to her. He didn't speak. Even though he appeared as dark and threatening as before, she was glad he was there.

"I'm sorry. I didn't mean to spoil your evening. Please, I'll be fine. You can go back to the others." Cara struggled to control her breathing.

"You haven't spoiled anything. I was glad to get away. Something has upset you."

Cara took a deep breath and spoke. "The woman they talked about. The one who was killed. She was my cousin and my best friend."

"I'm sorry for your grief."

Those simple words started the tears falling again. Her shoulders heaved. Strong secure arms wrapped around her. Cara turned her head against his chest and bawled. He was going to have a wet patch on his jacket, but she didn't care. She just wanted to stand there, enfolded in his silent strength.

Eventually the tears subsided, but he didn't move. He smelt so good, a mixture of Glayva and cologne. She stared up at him. It was too dark to make out what he might be thinking. His head bent down to hers, their faces so close, she could feel the warmth of his breath on her lips.

She wanted him to kiss her. This man she hardly knew. This man she had dreamt about for so long. She wanted him to make her forget life with a kiss, even if for only a moment. His mouth touched hers so gently. Her lips parted. She tasted the whiskey on his tongue as it entered her mouth.

His arms pulled her closer. Her heart beat fast as she pressed against his chest. She never wanted this kiss to stop. Their bodies melded together as time passed. Her arms went up around his neck as she tiptoed so she could kiss him back with equal passion. There was so much need in both of them. Her whole body yearned to be closer to him. He was hard for her and the thought made her ache inside.

The balcony door opened and Cara sprang back.

"The guests are leaving. Daniel asked if you could come back." Matcher said.

"Of course."

Turning back to Seth, Cara began to return his handkerchief. She thought better of it. "Thank you."

Walking away, she glanced back. He wasn't staring longingly after her. He had his hands on the balcony rail as he peered out into the dark unlit void of the gardens below.

# THIRTEEN

As they headed toward her flat a short time later, Cara wished Daniel had offered to take Matcher home. Anger began to replace her sadness. Matcher barely spoke and only in monosyllabic answers. If he huffed once more, she'd hit him.

"Okay, I've had enough of the silent treatment. Out with it." Big drops of rain started to plop on the windscreen.

"Look, I like working for you. If you don't believe me, I can't stand around and watch you get hurt." Matcher glared out the front windscreen.

"The people were talking about Shona. I got upset. Seth provided a shoulder to cry on."

"You weren't crying on his shoulder when I walked out."

That was fair enough but she didn't regret what had happened. "I know you think he's evil or something, but he's always been polite. I don't want to lose your friendship, Matcher. I've lost enough recently. If Seth and I meet again which is very unlikely, I promise you can be there to defend my honor."

The rain was getting so heavy; the windscreen wipers could hardly keep the window clear. She peered ahead.

"Now you're being stupid. He's twice my size and fucking scary." Matcher hesitated before he continued. "You do believe me about him, don't you?"

"Yes, I think he's different. Look, we'll all get through this but we have to be there for each other." Cara pulled up to her flat. Thankfully the rain had eased. They didn't have too much to unload. Unlocking the boot, she heard music coming from the top floor flat. She'd forgotten her neighbors were having a party tonight. They'd promised to turn the music down at one and it was twelve thirty.

"Did you leave your lights on in the flat?" Matcher asked.

"No. My electric bill is big enough as it is."

He was right. All the lights were on and the curtains wide open. Making their way up the stairs, partygoers from the top flat going out to have a cigarette greeted them. Cara thought her flat door was locked. As she put the key in the lock, the door moved inwards.

"Okay, so you left the lights on, and the door unlocked. I don't think so." Matcher stepped in front of her.

"Don't be ridiculous, we can go in together. You know as much as you think he's odd, this would be a good time to have Seth here."

They placed the boxes inside the door and looked around. Everything looked the same as always. Tables weren't turned over and curtains weren't ripped. Then, Cara noticed something. The picture of her and Shona on the coffee table lay flat.

Someone had moved the cushions on the couch. They were all at one end, as though a guest had been leaning on them. The more she looked around, the more she discovered. With each little thing the knots in her stomach got worse as cold and dread wafted over her. Other small items had been shifted to new places. Removed from her jewelry box, a necklace lay on the nightstand beside her bed.

Her hairbrush was on the bedclothes. Come to think of it she remembered pulling up the sheets and blankets. Now, they were pulled to the foot of the bed. Oh my God, someone had been lying on her bed. What else had they done? She thought she was going to be sick as all the blood drained from her face and she started to shake in fear.

"I think you should phone the police, Cara."

She nodded agreement as she fumbled in her purse for her mobile phone. "What the hell is happening, Matcher? Who would want to do this?" Her hands shook as she dialed for the police.

DETECTIVE SEPS WANDERED around the flat as Cara made coffee. He scrutinized her bookcase. Good luck to him if he could work out anything from her eclectic mess of reading material, except that she liked cooking and medieval romances.

Placing the mugs of coffee on the table, Cara offered some cake. He finished it so quickly she wasn't sure if he liked it or he was just famished. He wore the same crumpled suit she'd seen him in before. He made her think of a wise old owl with its feathers all ruffled.

"After seeing the report this morning, I thought I'd look in on you. I read the door wasn't tampered with and the windows were closed."

"Yes, but I know I locked the door. The lights were all off when I left too."

"You're certain things were moved though?"

"Yes." Did he think she would make it up? Why would she want to bring more chaos into her life? "My cat was stuck in the office as well and he was on the sofa when I left."

"Of course it's difficult for us to know who was around. The front door of the building was open so the people upstairs could go and smoke. I noticed the lock on your flat isn't a very secure one." He eyed the rest of the cake.

"I always thought the intercom would be enough." Cara watched when Detective Seps picked up the photo of her with Shona.

"I was looking at this picture of Shona Williams. It appears to be a more recent than the one we have. Could I possibly have it?"

Cara snatched it out of his hand. "I'm sorry. It's the last photo taken of us together. I've a scanner in the office. I'll do you a copy."

"I understand. That would be fine."

Cara got the computer going, willing it to hurry up. With the scanned copy in hand, she walked out to find him going through her booking diary. She had left it on the breakfast bar. Well, she had nothing to hide. That wasn't completely true but he wouldn't want to know about witchcraft.

"Here you are and thank you again for calling in. You'll let me know straightaway if you hear anything new."

"Of course and in the meantime you'll get that lock changed, won't you? Perhaps, you might add a deadbolt."

She nodded. "Yes, I will. Thank you, Detective."

As soon as he was gone, Cara went back to her appointment book. It was open to the week of Shona's death. No surprise there. Cara went through all the names on the two pages. Suppliers, florists, Mum, Dad, Matcher and Daniel. There were also names and addresses of five clients and other people she needed to see about a variety of things. The two names she wasn't happy about Detective Seps seeing were her counselor and Seth.

If he went and saw Jessica, he might find out about the dreams. Then again, wasn't there such a thing as patient confidentiality? Cara decided that her therapist would respect her privacy. As for Seth, he was a stranger. She had no right to involve him in her crazy life even if they had kissed. She felt desperate and lonely. He seemed like someone steady, who could keep her safe. The problem was there were too many secrets as far as he was concerned as well. She still wasn't sure about his connection to the dagger.

THREE DAYS LATER, Cara couldn't delay going to see her mother any longer. When she pulled up outside of her parent's block of flats, she noticed a van unloading furniture at the house next door. It was such a beautiful house. It must have been built about a hundred years ago. It sat on at least half an acre looking out onto The Downs, the beautiful grassed area that stretched over to the Avon Gorge where the famous suspension bridge by Brunel still stood. At night though, the street lighting wasn't good and a dangerous place for a person alone.

Someone touched her arm. Cara jumped. It was her mother.

"Oh you are edgy, darling. I didn't mean to surprise you. It's Vincent's place," Anne said. "Remember, he was at our last dinner party and I think he liked you. I might try and have another little get-together."

"Please don't, not on my account anyway." Cara knew she had been abrupt but her mother always got her on the defensive.

"But, you're never going to meet anyone stuck in a kitchen all day."

"I don't remember saying I wanted to meet anyone." Cara gritted her teeth.

"I see, dear. Come inside. It's so tragic about Shona. She seemed such a nice girl though your father has not really had much to do with his sister's in-laws family. I'm glad I was able to help with the funeral. They all seemed so distressed. It was the least I could do."

Cara followed silently. She knew her own tongue would be bitten through by the time she left. Why did she put herself through this? After a few hours of her mother droning on about her friends, Cara knew she had to go or there would be bloodshed.

As an only child they had very specific expectations for her. Preferably to marry a lawyer like Dad, then raise children and bring them up good little Catholics. The fact that her mother was always complaining about someone hardly seemed very Christian to Cara. She had given up long ago trying to be the perfect daughter.

It was only three in the afternoon. Clouds rimmed the horizon. She wanted to get home before dark, but didn't want to tell her mother about the break-in. Her parents would probably want her to move back in with them. That would prove that she really had gone insane if she was contemplating it.

Unlocking the van, she heard someone call her name. She turned and saw Vincent walking out his front gate. He looked distinguished in a black designer business suit. Cara tugged at her old coat. It was a lovely vintage duffle from the 1960's but had seen better days.

"I'm so glad I caught you," Vincent said. "Do you have a moment?"

She longed to say no, not really. *Some weirdo's stalking me and breaking into my flat. I want to be home while the sun is up in case he's a vampire.* That was right. She remembered she didn't tell people things like that because they would think she was odd.

"No, that would be fine." At least she would get to see inside the house.

"Anne must have told you I purchased this property a while back?"

"Yes she did."

"I'd like to celebrate with a house-warming party."

Cara followed him through the front door. She hoped she didn't look like a hound dog with its mouth hanging open. Although the furniture was not adorned with any personal pieces, everything fitted exactly as though it had been made for the house. Vincent had exquisite taste. Then again, he could afford to buy what he liked.

They went into what was going to be his office. It was at the front of the house. The windows looked out on the garden and the rolling grass of The Downs beyond. The large room had mahogany bookshelves on three walls, from floor to ceiling. From the number of boxes on the floor Cara had no doubt Vincent would be able to fill the shelves. She wondered what Detective Seps would make of his collection?

Vincent moved over to his desk where his laptop was open. He obviously functioned appropriately in this century, not like she did. She'd bet he never left his books open for anyone to peruse.

"I know this is short notice. The Sunday after next is the date I want. I'd like to have about fifty guests. I prefer simple but impressive food that allows people to talk and mingle. I planned on using the conservatory, but I'll see what you think."

Cara followed as he walked through the house. He had taken off his jacket. His butt looked good in the expensive pants he was wearing. Mother would be pleased she had noticed, Cara thought. Hopefully, he didn't notice her looking down as he stopped and turned.

They walked into the conservatory. Cara adored it. The enormous area stretched the width of the rear of the house. It opened onto manicured gardens. At the moment, it was empty. She could imagine it with elegant palms in large containers.

"I know you usually do dinners and lunches, but I've a few collectors coming from Ireland. If you showcased produce from their part of the world, it might impress them." He laughed. "They might sell me some of their collections more cheaply."

"I think you overestimate the persuasive power of my cooking. It would give us an opportunity to try something new though." Cara was already thinking about salmon, lobsters and oysters.

"Don't worry about the cost," Vincent said. "I know this will be a rush job, but I want the best."

"I'll draw up a menu and fax it to you. Then you can approve what I want to serve. Of course, I'll need to double check and be certain we're not already booked."

"I'm so glad I saw you, Cara. I'll be busy enough trying to sort the house out without trying to organize functions. My PA, Stephan, will help you with everything."

"I'll look forward to working with him," Cara said politely.

They started to walk back through the house. Vincent smiled at her. "Would you like a tour of the place?"

"Yes, that would be lovely."

Each room was immaculately furnished. It wasn't her taste. The drapes and the furnishings were all so dark. She wanted to open the windows, let some air and light into the place for a while.

Vincent led her into yet another of the upstairs rooms. This one was not made up as a bedroom, but as a studio. Paintings of women adorned each wall and at least three easels were set up with works in progress.

"Did you do all of these paintings?"

"These paintings are of women who've all been important to me. It's my way of honoring their memories."

Beside each picture was a small glass case. Each case had an item inside. A bracelet or hair comb or earrings.

"I've been lucky that each woman I painted let me have a little keepsake to remind me of her."

"Could I see one of your latest projects?"

"No." He answered abruptly. "I'm sure you wouldn't want someone to eat one of your meals if it hadn't been cooked properly. Did I tell you the house even has a wine cellar? I managed to purchase some of the wine."

Cara followed Vincent out of the studio room. She was glad. The room gave her the creeps with his paintings of all his old girlfriends. It was like the dead wives of Bluebeard locked in the cellar.

"I always loved this house," Cara said. "I dread to think what you had to pay for it."

"It's worth paying any price if you want something enough. I hope you don't think I'm forward, but Anne said you had lost a relative recently. I wanted to offer my condolences."

"Thank you."

"Death is such a final thing. I'm sure we'd all avoid it if we could. Please let me know if there's anything I can do."

"Thank you. That's very kind." Cara put out her hand to shake his. He held it slightly longer than was necessary. For some reason the hair on the back of her neck stood on end.

Maybe he was interested in her. Mother would be pleased since he was a good catch. Not bad looking and a great house. After all, love had gotten her nowhere in the past. *No,* she thought. *I don't want to be another of his paintings hanging in his studio when he calls it quits.*

Seth's face came into her mind at that moment, providing a conundrum she didn't want to think about. She couldn't forget him or that wonderful kiss.

---

WHEN SHE TEXTED HIM, Daniel loved the idea of the booking. She wasn't so sure, but what the heck? It would keep her mind busy. There was a message on her phone when she arrived home. It was Seth. Her stomach jumped up to her throat when she heard his deep voice. Every time she spoke to him her world went into overdrive as her heart sped up.

"Cara, this is Seth Scanlon. I was just phoning to see how you were. I'd like to talk to you about a booking. I hope to hear from you soon."

The memory of his kiss the night at The Crescent made

her hot all over again. She was being irrational. He was dark and scary. He had hardly spoken two words both times she had met him. He had a dagger in his forge that was identical to the one in her dreams.

Her cousin was dead, probably killed by a knife similar to Seth's. Then there was the strange dream of him in Paris. All in all, he was definitely the last person she should be thinking of right now.

That was it. She was fed up of things just happening to her. From now on, she would start to take control and see where it led. No more spells and dreams, but action. Tomorrow she would phone Seth. She needed to find out why he had a dagger like the one in her dream.

As she dozed off to sleep, she thought back to his strong arms around her, the smell of him and the way his mouth tasted. No matter what fears she had about him the thoughts of him as a lover always took over and made her body heat up.

## FOURTEEN

Matcher felt he should be thinking of Cara now as he lay on his bed. Instead his mind kept going back to the other night and the girl he had met. Darren and Andy from the flat had been going down to the local pub. Matcher was more than happy to join them after having another session with Jessica.

He liked his flat mates. Darren was a mechanic, which was handy as he kept both their old cars from dying completely. Andy was working at the local supermarket. Night supervisor. He had a night off so it was pub time for all. The Three Bells was just around the corner and they had some decent real ale. The money he was getting from Cara and Daniel didn't go that far, but you could still get drunk enough. Darren was telling them about the girl who had brought her VW in and had asked him out.

"Shit, that's the first time the job has ever thrown up any fringe benefits." Darren said.

"So when ya seeing her?" Andy asked.

"She's invited me and my mates to a party at her place next Saturday."

"That's cool with me. Its Jack's weekend on," Darren replied.

They both looked to Matcher.

"Saturday isn't good for me. That's when they have most of their big meals."

"Shit, they can do without you for one night, can't they?" Darren looked annoyed.

"Sure. I'll be there," Matcher answered.

"Bloody right you will."

"My round." Matcher stood and walked over to the bar. Someone bumped his arm.

"Sorry I didn't mean to..." He turned to see a girl smile at him as she walked past back to her friend's table by the door. Her aura showed fear and yet she smiled. He got their beers and went back to his table.

"Looks like you've caught someone's eye, Matcher my man. Go and chat to her and then get them to come over." Andy said taking a gulp of his beer.

"What?" Matcher asked.

"She hasn't taken her eyes off you. Probably short sighted."

"What, cause she should fancy your ugly mug instead," Darren replied.

They all laughed. Matcher glanced across and she was still looking, but then reddened and turned away. He had only had a couple of girlfriends since the cancer. He didn't like telling people about it. They always felt sorry for him. She wasn't his type, but then again what was his type? Well, recently he'd gone for girls wearing black clothes and lots of mascara.

Looking over again, he noticed that she was chatting with her friends. Her hair was fair and cut short around her shoulders and looked a bit messed up. He liked it. There was something written on the front of her bright red top. He couldn't make out from this angle what it was.

"Stop staring at her tits, man and go and ask her out. Looks like she's got a good rack though." Andy offered.

"More an ass man myself. Saw her mate on the way back from the gents and she bent down to pick up her bag before she sat down. I could see her G. Damn I love seeing the old floss." Darren said.

"Shut up. Shit, you're assholes." Matcher shook his head.

"That may be true, but go and do your stuff so we all might get laid tonight." Andy said.

Matcher walked over and stood behind the girl he had bumped into. One of her friends winked at him. That was the floss girl. He put his hand on the girl's shoulder. She jumped and squeaked.

"I'm sorry." Her friends were giggling.

"God, Rachel, the guy is trying to say, hello. He's not trying to scare you to death. Hi I'm Rita, and this is Liz, and that's Rachel who you just caused to spill half her drink."

"I'm sorry. We were wondering if you wanted to come over and have a drink."

"Yeh that would be nice." Rachel answered as she looked up at him.

That was the hard bit done. Darren and Andy would take over and keep the girls amused.

"So, how do you know each other?" Matcher asked Rachel as she sat down next to him.

"We all work at a fast food outlet that won't be named but sounds as though a Scotsman thought of it. Rita is my boss, and Liz works the late shift with me."

She was talking quietly. Her friends were chatting and laughing. Matcher liked her. She wore no makeup. It was nice and open. Her aura had swirls showing disturbance in her emotions but as they talked she started to even out.

"You okay?"

Rachel was staring at him. He must have phased out.

"Long day, work and everything. I'm in catering too. The company I work for does dinners and stuff."

They talked on and he couldn't remember anything the guys had said to him. Walking back to the flat, he held her hand. It was good. Simple, good aura and no stress. When the other guys drifted off to their rooms with the girls, he saw the tension in Rachel's aura.

"What's wrong?"

"Rita was supposed to be giving me a lift. I'll have to go soon. I live at home and my step-dad gets real mad if I'm late in."

"Look, I know you were down at the pub, but how old are you?"

"I'm seventeen."

"Where do you live?" Matcher didn't want her to go.

"Southmead, near the hospital and they expect me home by eleven."

"That's only fifteen minutes away. I'll give you a lift. Be warned though my car is a mess, but it works." Matcher took her hand and she gripped it back.

"I'd really like that."

Pulling up outside her house, Matcher noticed how she was screwing her hands together. He wanted to kiss her but perhaps not. In the dark he couldn't see her aura so clearly.

"I'd like to see you again." He waited for the brush-off.

"I'd like that too."

"We could go to the movies tomorrow night if you're not working."

"No my next shifts are Friday and Saturday night."

"I'll pick you up at seven."

She leaned forward and flicked his fringe back behind his ear.

"Why'd you do that?"

"I just thought it would be nice to see both your eyes when you kissed me."

He didn't need any more prompting. He had wanted to part those lips for the last hour. She didn't resist when his tongue started to probe and discover every corner of her mouth. He was finding it hard not to let his hands wander when a light went on and the front door of her house opened. A large man stood in the doorway.

"I'd better go."

With that, she ran up the path and was gone. The door slammed behind her. Matcher decided he liked her. He liked her a lot and aside from that she was a bloody good kisser.

FIFTEEN

Seth grabbed the towel he had thrown aside earlier and wiped his face. The air was cool, but he was sweating. Looking up, he could see light coming through the window of the forge. He'd been awake all night. He'd lost any sense of time yet again. Glancing at the statue, he could no longer pretend it was just any female form. It was Cara. Why was he doing this again?

After all this time, he should be in control of his feelings and reactions, but no. Seth's hand touched the mallet. For a split second, he contemplated destroying the statue. The phone rang. He let it ring twice. Then, he remembered Janet was away. He picked up the receiver. "Hello."

"Hi, Seth. This is Cara from Celtic Dinners."

He instantly regretted his abruptness at the sound of her voice.

"I got your message about the booking. I'm sorry. Have I called at an inconvenient time?"

"No. How are you?"

She went silent.

It was selfish. A part of him wanted her to be in pain so

she would need him. The feeling of her in his arms had been intoxicating. He wanted it again. He had watched her at Shona's funeral and the weeks following. He'd wanted to comfort her, but her friends were there for her. He was just a stranger.

He had known her company was catering the meal at The Crescent. In fact he had suggested them to Robert, hoping to see her that night. It was unforgivable that he had kissed her when she was so lost and vulnerable. Holding her in his arms Seth knew he'd lost all his common sense.

"I'm getting there," Cara said. "One step forward, two steps back. It takes time like you said. So, what is the date for the booking?"

"It's this Friday night. I know it's short notice, but it's just a dinner for two. Here at the cottage." Silence again. What was she thinking?

"That sounds lovely. You're lucky. I've had a cancellation. If you don't mind me asking, why aren't you using Janet? From what I sampled, she's a great cook. Not that I'm trying to do myself out of a job." Cara's laugh was a little too high-pitched.

Obviously, he was making her nervous. "Janet has gone to Paris."

His throat tightened, causing another awkward silence. He wanted to see the lips that were talking to him. He couldn't tell her that no matter how much he wanted to.

"I'll fax through an idea for the dinner. If there's anything you'd like to change, just let me know. The price will be on the bottom of the fax."

They continued discussing the menu and cost. He wanted her to keep talking. He could listen to her for hours, even if the conversation was only about what vegetables he liked. Perhaps he could tell her the truth. If he did, she would never come though.

---

HE STOOD at his bedroom window waiting. She turned up promptly at seven, in preparation for the meal to start at eight. Unloading the car, she'd been polite. He wanted to stay in the kitchen and just watch her. One look had sent him from the room. Like the forge for him, this was her area. In the front parlor, he took out his mobile and dialed his home number. The phone rang in the front parlor. He answered it and pretended to have a conversation with someone.

"I'm sorry, Cara. I've wasted your time. I will of course pay you what we discussed." Cara smiled, as he explained. The way she placed utensils down with added force showed her true feelings.

"It's not your fault. I'm sure he couldn't help his flight being delayed. Oh well, your fridge will be full."

"It was a dinner for two and you're here. Please, why don't you stay?"

She hesitated staring at the empty plates in front of her. Then, she turned and smiled at him.

"That would be wonderful. The lamb is one of my favorites. The gravy is a special concoction and will make you smile when you taste it. It's just a lot of effort to make it just for myself."

Had she seen through his ruse of a delayed dinner guest? Possibly. He didn't care. She was staying. That was all that mattered.

"I need to check on a piece of work in the forge. I'll leave you for a while to finish your preparations."

When he returned, Cara had set up the small round table in the dining room at the front of the cottage. She'd put out a plain white cloth with deep red placemats and white napkins. Two silver candlesticks held red candles. The centerpiece was a white camellia with dark rich foliage floating in a bowl. She grinned at his reaction when he bit into the lamb.

"It's good, isn't it? Even if I do say so myself."

"This is the second time I've tasted your food Cara. I haven't been disappointed on either occasion. I think it was very wise of me to have you cook while Janet is away or she would be jealous." Seth poured himself a glass of water. He had removed the wine glasses. If she wouldn't drink, neither would he.

"Trust me if I can find Janet's recipe book, I wouldn't be so nice. I'd love the recipe for her cookies. By the way, please don't let me stop you having some wine. It's just I have to drive back to Bristol. I don't like to drink while I'm working." Cara sipped on her tonic water.

He needed to break the silence. He wanted her to feel comfortable with him but knew his presence didn't engender calm in most people. "Have you always wanted to cook?"

"Yes, I made the kitchen a mess from an early age. My mother always hoped I'd grow out of it. I think she still does."

He wanted her to tell him everything about herself. Then, he knew there would be no escape from caring about her. Perhaps it was too late already.

"I was always a blacksmith. I started as a farrier. After that, I made swords or scythes or daggers, anything people would buy. When my wife died, I needed the money. I liked to drink." He was saying too much.

"I'm sorry I mentioned the wine."

"I still enjoy the odd glass. Then again, it was a long time ago. I have discovered there are worse demons than the bottle, though it is bad enough."

Seth stood up when she did to help with the dishes. Following her into the kitchen, he wanted to touch her. He wanted to carry her upstairs to his room and slowly remove her clothes and caress her. To discover things about every inch of her body. He wanted to know how she would react to him. To hear her groan with pleasure.

He left her to serve dessert. It was a homemade blackberry and strawberry ice cream with thin caramel flavored wafers. As he went back and sat down. She placed his plate down and smiled at him. He wondered if she had any idea what she was doing to him. He was hard for her again. He only had to think about her and all he could imagine was being inside her. He needed to get his mind onto something else.

"So did you inherit your culinary skill?"

"Yes, from my grandmother. My family was originally from Ireland. My Nanna had a cookbook published earlier this year. Unfortunately she passed away not long after. I was sick for a while last year and couldn't eat. My partner, Daniel came in with this wonderful crème caramel. I don't think I had realized how important food was till then."

She was biting her bottom lip. Did she feel she was saying too much? Seth knew she had been in hospital a year ago, but was unaware of the cause. She would tell him in her own good time if she wanted to. She appeared so full of health. Had he found her only to lose her? She took the occasional deep breath and held it. "Are you well now?"

"Yes. Look I'm sorry. I shouldn't be boring you with my medical history."

The color rose to her cheeks with her honesty. He almost reached over to touch the soft skin. Instead, he ate the wonderful food. The ice cream melted in his mouth as the wafer crumbled on his tongue. He should be telling her how delicious it tasted. He couldn't look up for fear his feelings of desire would show in his eyes.

"Seth, there's something I wanted to ask you?"

"Yes."

"It's about a dagger I saw in your forge the last time I was here. I know this sounds ridiculous. I dreamed of one that looked the same. It was the knife with two snake's heads on it."

"I fixed a dagger like that a long time ago. The one you saw was just a copy." This was definitely a mistake. He should never have asked her. He had been a fool to think she wanted to stay to be with him. She just wanted to get information.

"I know it's an odd question. It's just I've been trying to make some sense of Shona's death. I know the dreams most likely have nothing to do with it. I'm just trying to think of anything that might help."

"I lost a close friend once to murder," Seth said, slowly. "They never found out who did it. For a long time, I tried to make some sense of it. You must move on." It would not be prudent to mention he had never taken his own advice.

"I'm sorry. It's funny, but I knew the other night that you'd lost someone too and understood my pain. You're right though. I have to move on. I just hope the police get the bastard. Sorry about the language."

"Don't be. It's been a very long time since my friend died. I think they'll be able to help you now in ways that they couldn't help me then."

The darkness of the night surrounded him and

increased his emptiness as she drove off a short time later. The world somehow appeared more complete when she was near, as if she had filled the cottage with her presence.

A car pulled out from under the trees on the other side of the main road. Seth watched as the taillights disappeared into the distance. It seemed like two red eyes following their prey. Few cars stopped near the cottage and even less at eleven o clock at night.

As he walked through the front door, the smell of the food still lingered. The car was probably just a couple of kids kissing in the dark on a lonely road. Touching the camellia, he picked up the lovely flower. Just the lightest touch bruised the petals.

He had promised to protect her. What if she was being followed? He headed for the garage.

Seth revved the bike, as he stopped at red lights entering Bath. The car next to him was full of loud music and laughter. The music continued, but the laughter stopped as he lifted his visor and glared. Frightened eyes stared back at him.

The lights changed and they were gone. He couldn't move. Rage like this had overpowered him before. He had to control it. She was not his woman. All they had shared was a kiss, but he knew Rosie's killer was still out there. He would really go insane this time if he lost another woman he loved.

---

HE WALKED down the street disappearing into the shadows of a tree across from her flat. She lived on the second floor. The lights shone. No one screamed for help.

Cara walked out the front door and picked up a basket

from the back of the van. She walked back into the building. The door closed behind her. Looking up to her flat, he saw someone pull back the curtain and gaze down. She couldn't have gotten there that quickly. Seth had to get inside, but how? Not through the front door with the intercom link, he thought. He would try the back garden.

He made his way up the alley at the side of the house. The rear door had a simple lock. Reaching for the handle, it turned. Damn, it was unlocked.

Seth crept past the door to the downstairs flat. If he was wrong, then Cara would never want to have anything to do with him again. He saw himself as her protector, but stalking was what it was called these days. He knocked on her door. Why was she taking so long? Maybe, the person at the window was her lover. He was a strong man but at this moment he was unsure how this would all play out. The door opened.

"Yes, what is it? Seth? What the hell?"

He thought it a good sign that she looked more confused than frightened to see him.

"When you drove off, I believe you were followed." She went to shut the door. He put his foot in the way.

Her eyes widened but not in fear. It looked more like anger. "I don't know what you're trying to do, Seth. To tell the truth, having you turn up like this is freaking me out. I can't believe you followed me here. How do you know where I live? I should call the police."

She still pressed against the door blocking his entry. "I found your address when you dropped your bag at the forge. I'm not trying to scare you. When I pulled up outside, I thought I saw someone at your window. Please let me check. If there's no one here, then I will leave. I won't come back. I promise."

Cara hesitated but eventually opened the door.

"You know I didn't think my life could get anymore peculiar. I guess I was wrong." She stood back to let him pass.

He walked past the kitchen where she had placed the boxes and basket from her van and into a cozy living room.

"How many rooms do you have?"

"The kitchen lounge here, my bedroom, the bathroom and the second bedroom that's used as an office." Cara answered with her arms folded across her chest.

"Show me." He didn't mean it to come out as an order, but knew it sounded like one. Cara raised an eyebrow and frowned at him. Then, she turned towards one of the doors. The bathroom was empty. So was the office. Cara stopped outside of what he assumed was her bedroom. She was blocking him and so was the black and white cat at her feet. Its tail flicked back and forth in warning.

"This is stupid. Last time I noticed when someone had been here. Nothing has been touched."

"There was a last time? You mean you've had someone break in before?" Seth knew he had raised his voice from the way Cara crossed her arms across her chest again and glared at him.

"Seth, who the hell do you think you are coming in here and talking to me like that? You hardly know me."

"I'm sorry, you're right. Please let me check everywhere. Your safety is my only concern."

Cara shook her head at him, but opened the bedroom door and switched on the light. The room was empty. The bed was made. There were clothes on the two cane chairs and shoes on the floor. Knickknacks, cosmetics, jewelry or picture frames covered every surface. It was chaotic, but real. The room showed the other side of Cara's character. It was a complete contrast from the neat appearance of the business side of the flat.

"I don't know what you're playing at, Seth. This isn't funny. You've scared me. With what's happened in my life recently, I don't need anything else strange going on."

"It appears I've made a mistake. I'm so sorry." Seth ran his hand over his head. How could he have been so wrong? He had wanted to be in Cara's life. Instead, he had come in and tried to take over.

"I think you should go now. By the way, how did you get inside?"

"The back door was unlocked." Seth walked towards the front door of the flat. He was about to leave when a noise came from the bedroom. Reopening the bedroom door, a yowling cat ran between his legs.

The wardrobe door stood ajar. A man was getting up from the floor. Seth didn't bother to ask questions. He just grabbed him around the neck and dragged him from the room.

"Tony? What the hell are you doing here?" Cara yelled.

SIXTEEN

Seth's deadpan expression and silence were more terrifying than if he had been screaming abuse while he held Tony around the neck. If she didn't do something soon, Seth would hurt her ex-lover. This was bizarre.

First, there was Seth's arrival. That wasn't good. She had been having unladylike thoughts all the way home. What the hell was going on? Tony's lips were turning blue. Why was he even here?

"Let him go, Seth. Trust me, he's harmless."

Seth released his grip. Tony coughed. Then, he took a deep breath. As he rubbed his throat he glanced toward the door. Seth moved to block his way.

Tony's shoulders slumped as he flopped into the chair. Leaning forward, he placed his hands against his forehead.

She couldn't see his face. "That's it, I've officially had enough," Cara said. "You can both stay there while I put on some coffee."

She peered across at the two men as she got out the mugs. Talk about chalk and cheese. Seth stood in his motorcycle boots, bike pants and a black top. His muscles bulged.

The shaved head and unshaven face added to the menacing appearance.

Then there was Tony. She had always thought he had a good appearance. Against Seth, he looked scrawny. In the past, Tony had always taken pride in the immaculate exterior he portrayed to the world. His suit was creased. Laura would never have let him go out like that. It meant one thing. They'd separated.

Cara put down the tray and sat down opposite Tony. She glanced up at Seth. He took the hint and sat next to her.

"As I'm the only one who has the slightest idea of what is happening here, I'll take charge." Her breathing was steady and her heart wasn't racing, this was good so far. "Why did you come, Tony?"

"I..." His voice cracked, but there were no tears in his eyes.

"You're going to talk. If you don't, I'll phone the police and have you arrested. Don't think I won't with all that's been happening to me."

Tony's hound-dog face and beautiful blue eyes showed themselves as usual. Using guilt to manipulate her might have worked in the past. In fact it had, but not now. She wasn't that person anymore. She had loved him or so she had thought. The feelings in the past involving him had been so intense. Now she felt nothing. It was strange.

"Laura's thrown me out."

"I don't mean to sound cruel but what did you expect. It doesn't explain why you broke into my flat." Cara watched, as both men picked up their coffees and drank. "I'm waiting for an answer."

"You remembered. Two sugars." Tony smiled at her.

"I'm a chef. I remember things like that. It's business. Now, talk." There was no way she was taking Tony back into her life. Their times together had been wonderful, but pain always followed. Even seeing him sitting here in a chair pushed her to an area she didn't want to go. It was not just him she had lost, but her unborn baby.

"I just want to be near you, Cara."

Tony and his needs had a way of making her feel so indispensable. In the past, she'd found it endearing. Tonight, it sounded desperate. In truth, that was what it had been all along.

"Stop waffling. What really happened, Tony?"

"It was a business trip to London. I didn't mean anything to happen."

"You never did. I'm surprised she kept taking you back. What I don't understand is why you came here. You can't believe I'd have a sympathetic shoulder to cry on."

"I didn't know where else to go. I turned up earlier. You were driving off so I followed you. I'm sorry. I waited for you to come back. The rear door was open, so I came in while you emptied the van. I just wanted to talk."

"People usually ring a doorbell and ask. You're probably right. I wouldn't have let you inside." Cara thought back to the other break-ins. "This isn't the first time you've been here, is it? Have you been stalking me for weeks" She stared him straight in the eyes.

"I've been staying at a motel. She wouldn't talk to me. I wanted to be somewhere that felt like a home. I never meant to scare you."

"Well, you did. We tried twice and it didn't work. Go back to Laura. If she'll have you, don't ever be stupid again. You need some help and I'm not the one to give it to you." Cara hoped he would take the hint and go. He didn't. Her heart was in her throat dealing with this. She didn't want him to say anything else and bring back more memories of her time in hospital.

"I'm sorry I wasn't there for you. I only found out later. You have to be believe me I didn't know about the baby."

Her stomach turned at the way the conversation was going. Why would he do this to her? She took a deep breath. "That's the past. You can't change what's done. I've moved on and so should you."

"Have you?"

"Yes." Cara reached over and took Seth's hand in hers. She hoped he would go along with the pretense. He did more than that. He lifted her hand and kissed it. He looked straight at Tony and she could see the smaller man flinch under the gaze.

"I think you should leave," Seth stated.

Tony started to add something, but must have thought better of it. They all stood and made their way to the front door.

"Cara. I've never meant to hurt you."

"I know you believe that, but you did, Tony."

Seth put his arm around her waist. He pulled her closer. Her body tingled in a good way where he touched. Tony looked at the two of them once more and was gone.

Seth took his arm away and walked back to the lounge. He crossed to the window and drew back the curtain. "I should go too. I'll wait a little while for him to drive off."

"No, don't go. It's late. You can sleep on the bed settee. What I mean is. I'd feel better if someone was here." *How desperate did that sound?* Half an hour ago she yelled at him for turning up unannounced.

"You'd really feel better if I stayed?" He came back and towered above her. The question seemed so much more than that from intense look in his eyes and taut stance.

"Yes. Yes I would." She might be an utter mess but she would hold it together for a bit longer. "I'm going to have a nightcap. I need one after all that's gone on." Cara went to the dresser in the lounge. She found a bottle of brandy and poured each of them large drinks. "Thanks for pretending and for following me. When I first saw you at the door, I was freaked out to say the least. Obviously I'm glad you picked up something was wrong."

"If I'd been wrong about someone being here, you would be having me escorted away by the police." Seth placed the glass down.

Silence. She wanted to break the ice between them.

"I need to tell you something about Tony." Cara took a deep breath.

"There's no need. Your past is your own. I've intruded on your present enough."

He fidgeted and she wanted to grab his hand. She was making him uncomfortable and she wanted to do anything but that. "I want to tell you, Seth. I know we've only met recently. For some reason and I'm really not sure why, I would like you to know the real me."

He smiled and sat back on the couch. His smile made her heart ache with need. Merlin jumped up on the couch next to Seth. Both of them peered at her. She took a deep breath.

"I was very young when I met Tony the first time. He was the older brother of a school friend. I was sixteen. He was twenty-two. I thought I was cool having an older boyfriend." She took another sip of brandy. "I wasn't the first one of my friends to have sex, but I was the first to get pregnant."

Cara shook her head. Seth's smile faded. His hands clenched into fists. "That's when I found out he was engaged to Laura. Funny thing, she was pregnant too. The main difference was she was twenty-one. Both sets of parents adored her. They didn't know about me. Shona came with me when I had the termination."

"He came back into your life again?" Seth took her hand in his.

"Two years ago. His marriage was on the rocks. I thought we could make it work where we hadn't the first time. I'm not proud of what I did. I knew I wasn't his only indiscretion. His marriage was living on borrowed time. It didn't make it right. The week he went back to Laura, I was admitted to hospital with an ectopic pregnancy. They removed my right tube and ovary. I lost a lot of blood and nearly died on the operating table. Tonight's the first time I've seen him since then."

Seth's dark gray eyes watched her intently as he listened. Why was she telling him all of this? They hardly knew each other. She took another sip of brandy. She felt tears well up and she didn't want to cry. Sometimes the thought that she had lost two children and might never have any more was too much.

As the tears started to flow, he pulled her into his arms, strong arms that could be so gentle. As she cried, he stroked her hair. Warmth spread through her body at the feeling of safety in his arms. Finally, her tears stopped. Why was this stranger she had let into her home being so kind?

"I feel like I'm losing so many things. There was Nanna, my Aunty Eileen and Shona. I can't take much more. I'm sorry. I shouldn't be telling you all my problems." She was sniveling like a blubbering child. Her face was probably red and blotchy. Her nose running.

"I'd like to think things are going to change. Your life

will improve from now on." He took her chin in his hand and turned her face towards him.

"How? I attract disaster and pain like a magnet." She sniffed.

"You attracted me. I hope I'm neither of those."

Grabbing a tissue from the box on the table in front of them, he gently dabbed her tears away. He pulled another tissue from the box and handed it to her.

"Blow." He raised one eyebrow as he looked at her.

Cara blew her nose. This wasn't romantic. It was definitely not like any of the dreams involving him. She wanted him so much. She wanted comfort and solace. She wanted something, anything that wasn't pain. She suddenly realized what he had said. He was attracted to her.

"You're attracted to me?" Cara's mouth hung open.

"I'm sorry. I've been too forward."

"No, not at all. I've wanted to kiss you again since the dinner party. Oh hell, now I'm being forward." Her lips quivered at the old-fashioned term and she tried not to laugh.

"I took advantage of your sadness that night. This time I was going to ask for a kiss. You answered my question."

Leaning closer, his lips touched hers. It was so delicate at first, the sensation tickled. She kept her eyes open. She wanted to see him. She needed to believe he was really here. He was actually kissing her. She had thought about it, dreamed it so much.

He moved away. He touched her lips with his fingers, tracing their outline. His fingertips were rough, but touched so lightly it didn't matter. He ran his fingers across her cheek. Then he moved away. She wanted more.

"What is it?" Cara asked, worried he regretted what had happened.

"I know you asked me to spend the night on the couch, but..."

Before he said anything else she interrupted, "I don't want you to." He would have no doubt how keen she was now.

Seth stood and pulled her up from the chair with both hands. His expression one of pure lust and she was drowning in it. A light kiss was all they had shared and yet she could tell from his leather bike pants he was aroused. The thought she was causing it made her hot between her legs.

Now, he kissed her passionately. His hands ran up and down her back as he pushed her body gently against his. His tongue searched the moist and welcoming interior of her mouth. She closed her eyes and lost herself in the passion of his kisses. Was this really happening?

It had been so long. What the hell was she doing? She pushed the thoughts away. He drew back from her and looked at her through half closed lids. She felt heady and intoxicated by him. From his appearance she was having the same effect. She took his hand and led him to her room. She took a deep breath, then bit her lower lip as they stood beside the bed silently looking at each other. Neither of them said a thing but savored the moment, anticipating what they were about to do.

He leaned forward and kissed her again, just a gentle brush across her lips that caused her to lean into him. He pulled away. One by one, he undid the buttons of her blouse and slipped it from her shoulders. He leant forward and placed a kiss on each shoulder. His hands went around her back. He pulled her close.

His mouth touched her neck. His tongue swirled around sending a sensation through her body causing her to shiver. The ache inside her so strong she knew only one thing would take it away. She nibbled on his earlobe. He let out a low groan. He pushed her away.

"If you do that again, this is going to be over a lot sooner than either of us would like." His smoldering gaze met hers.

"I don't want it to be over quickly," she replied in a breathy voice that didn't even sound like her.

"I was hoping you were going to say that." He laughed. It was a beautiful sound. Now it was her turn to tower over him as he sat down and removed his motorcycle boots. She wanted to rip off his black t-shirt. Before she had a chance, he reached out and pulled her close so she was between his legs. His kisses meandered across her abdomen sending fluttering sensations throughout her body. His unshaven face tickled her sensitive skin. She ran her fingers over his head and loved the feel of his short hair.

Moving back, his hands went to the belt on her pants. He unbuckled it and pulled it free. Then he looked up at her as he slowly unzipped her zipper. She nodded as he slid her brown work pants over her hips. The slacks fell to the floor and she kicked them away. Looking across the room she caught a glimpse in the dressing table mirror of her comfy work knickers and a sensible bra. Suddenly the reality of what she looked like overwhelmed her. She hadn't been naked with a man for so long.

She folded her arms across her chest and stared at the floor, embarrassed.

He stood and tilted up her chin. His eyes filled with concern as if he'd done something to upset her. "What's wrong?"

"My scar from my operation, my body, and me in general. That's it, I'm going to ban mirrors from my bedroom." She shook her head and for a moment considered this had been a foolish idea.

He pulled his t-shirt over his head. She gasped. His chest was criss-crossed with scars. There was also a nasty red mark on his left shoulder. Her fingers touched the marks. He trembled.

She bit her bottom lip thinking of the pain he must have endured. "How did you get hurt?"

"It doesn't matter now but you need to know your scar doesn't matter to me. I only wish I could've helped you with your pain."

Her hands traced the scars till her fingers touched the waist of his bike-pants.

"I want you, Cara."

He could have no idea what effect those three words would have on her. Feeling emboldened by his statement, she pushed him back on the bed and unzipped the pants. She pulled them off, pulling his boxers with them.

"I'm sorry." She tried to stifle a giggle but it didn't work. He was aroused and he was magnificent.

He sat up and smirked. "I had this image of us having a slow intense experience. From the way you undressed me, you can see I'm eager. Don't just stand there. Please."

He sat on the edge of her bed, naked and incredible. His eyes looked like those of a carnivore about to devour its prey as he stared at her. What was holding her back? *If he goes in the morning at least you will have had sex. From the look and size of him, it will be great.*

Her track record of choosing the right man wasn't good. She didn't know that much about him. She had a few one-night stands over the years, men that she had known even less about. Was she afraid he wouldn't match the dream lover she knew so well? She really needed to stop thinking and act.

He reached out and took her hand. "That day you came to my home something came alive in me again. I won't hurt you. I promise." He lay down on the bed.

Her breath was rapid. She stretched out on the bed beside him. He took her hand and kissed the palm, then her wrist, and slowly made his way up her arm. Each kiss, each touch sent little sparks of excitement through her. Easing her onto her back, he lay on top of her and she reveled in the way his body felt so right with hers. Her stomach turned to jelly at the thought that he was naked and on top of her at long last.

Feeling him hard against her, she opened her legs and wrapped them around his thighs. His hands eased around her back and undid her bra, flinging it across the room. He stared at her breasts as he supported himself on his arms. It had been so long since anyone had looked at her that way. It was wonderful.

His tongue gently explored from her neck to her left nipple making her sigh with contentment. His lips closed on the nipple and nibbled. Shivers rippled through her. She ran her hands up and down his back with a feather light touch. When she found a spot that made his skin turn to goose bumps, he arched his back and pressed against her. His kisses returned to her mouth parting her lips and his tongue fought passionately with hers.

"You're so beautiful," he whispered huskily against her skin. Rolling to her side, he hooked his finger in one side of her knickers and edged them down. Cara's hand instinctively went to her scar just above her hair.

"Let me see."

The dark pink line ran across her lower abdomen. He

traced it with his finger. Then he bent and kissed her scar from one side to the other. "There is nothing you need to hide. I want you in front of me so I can see all of you."

As his finger entered her, she let out a gasp. .

"Cara you're so wet, so ready for me." He caressed each fold and gently moved his finger in and out of her as she moved with him. Meanwhile, his kisses continued across her face, her eyelids, and her neck. Her hands roamed his body. When she encircled his shaft and squeezed gently, he groaned.

She moved her hand slowly back and forth as he massaged her clitoris and caused tiny sensations until she caught her breath. She needed him inside her.

He sat up and pulled her to him. She sat on his thighs with her legs circling him. He leaned forward and kissed her neck and breasts. She moved. His hardness pressed against her tummy. She smiled as she watched his face as his hands explored her body. He looked as if he was drugged on her. His lids almost closed. Leaning forward he sucked hard on one nipple, then the other. It caused the ache at her core to intensify. He trailed kisses back to her lips.

Feeling him hard between her legs, she couldn't wait anymore, she lifted up until she kneeled on him. She leaned slightly forward so she could feel the head of his shaft press against her opening. She yearned for him. He slid in easily. Both of them groaned. The more she moved, the more intense the sensations became. She wanted to become part of him, to be lost in him.

Then he reached down. He touched her clitoris. Sensations wracked her body. The feeling of power and energy flowed through her. She arched her back and screamed in release. He kissed her, staking a passionate claim.

Withdrawing from her, he gently rolled her onto her back. He kissed her neck and mouth and lay on top of her. When she nodded, he entered her again. He might be holding his body off of her because of his size but it didn't stop him as he thrust forward until the complete length of him was inside her. It was the most glorious thing that had ever happened to her. To be so completely connected felt perfect. She'd been waiting all her life for this.

She ran her hands down his back and placed them on his buttocks. He needed no encouragement. His movements before had been slow. Now, he didn't hesitate. He plunged deeply inside her again and again. She curled her legs about him, drawing him deeper. He groaned in release. His movements slowed.

Finally, they lay still, wrapped around each other. She didn't move. She didn't want the moment to end as he pulsed inside of her. Breathing heavily, their chests rose and fell in unison. If sex was like this every time, she'd be constantly exhausted. But oh my God, it would be worth it.

He rolled off her and leaned on one elbow. His face wasn't filled with passion or laughter. He looked sad. It wasn't the expression she had expected after what they had just done.

"What's wrong, Seth?"

"I lost myself, Cara. I thought I'd hurt you."

She giggled. "I don't mean to laugh, but I have no complaints. You were magnificent."

"Thank you for the compliment. I don't want you to feel that I underestimate the gift you've given me."

"You made me feel beautiful for the first time in a long time. If this is where my life is taking me, it's a marvelous place."

"If you get some sleep, maybe we can go back there again."

"I'll keep you to that."

It was easy to fall asleep with him curled behind her. His strong naked body felt warm and comforting. She didn't care if this was love or lust. At this moment, everything felt safe and good. Her queen size bed was full for the first time in a long time. His arm draped over her waist and she took his hand in hers.

She felt his warm breath on her neck. She listened to the steady sound of his breathing as it lulled her toward sleep. She wouldn't dream about him tonight. In fact, the dreams were nothing in comparison to reality.

## SEVENTEEN

Nanna had always said that the best way to a man's heart was through his stomach. Cara decided she would cook Seth breakfast. Did she want his heart? That was too big a question to contend with right now. She certainly wanted his body.

Easing out of bed, she pulled on her undies and grabbed her dressing gown. Merlin ignored her and refused to eat breakfast when she measured cat food into his dish. He stalked out of the kitchen to the front room. He really didn't like her sharing her bed with another male.

The coffee had finished brewing. She stirred the pancake batter and glanced at the bedroom when the door opened. Seth wore his bike pants and t-shirt. Her heart sank.

"You're going? I was making pancakes." How pathetic did she sound?

He walked over and put his arms around her waist. He pulled her close. She loved having his body next to her.

"I'm not going anywhere, except down to my bike. I've

got some clean clothes in the top box. I didn't think your neighbors would appreciate me walking out naked."

"No, but I would." Cara giggled. "Hang on. If you brought a spare set of clothes, it sounds as though you were pretty sure about getting lucky. I'm not sure I approve." She pulled a snooty expression and pursed her lips.

"I won't lie. I hoped. The clothes are there because of Janet. She has a thing about not leaving home without a set of clean underwear. You know she's probably reorganized the whole gallery of that poor man in Paris."

"I'll let you off then, but somehow I don't think he was poor."

It was wonderful to have someone to share breakfast. She enjoyed watching him eat. She wanted to go back to bed with him. Why did it have to be Saturday? It was always their busiest night.

Opening her business diary she saw they had a dinner party at eight for twelve guests. Tomorrow was worse with a lunch and dinner. She would have to start preparing soon.

"I'll clean this up. You go and have your shower." She wanted to join him. Maybe she would. As she went to turn the handle of the bathroom door, the intercom buzzed. Cara thumped the button. "Yes." She tried to keep the frustration out of her voice.

"It's Matcher."

Opening her flat door, she saw him coming up the stairs. He was dressed in black as usual. His hair covered half of his face.

"Want some coffee?" She wanted to send him away. It seemed childish but the short time with Seth had been a break from reality.

"Sure. Thanks." Matcher glanced towards the bathroom as he answered. "Did you leave the shower going?"

"No, I had someone stay over." She knew Matcher cared about her, but she wanted this time with Seth. He wasn't really as frightening as he looked. Anyway she was an adult. She could choose who shared her bed.

"Why are you here so early?" Cara inquired.

"I was on my way into town. I wanted to ask a favor. Daniel told me that you have this big housewarming party coming up and you're looking for extra staff. Well…"

Matcher started fidgeting. He bit one of his nails.

"I met someone. I wondered if she could get some work. She wants to move out of home and needs some extra cash." Matcher went red. The shower stopped running.

"I'll have to meet her, but if you vouch for her, it will probably be okay. I'll need a couple of references."

"I didn't give you any."

"That's true enough, but if the silverware goes missing, you pay."

Matcher didn't smile at the weak joke. He stared towards the bathroom. "It's him, isn't it?"

Matcher didn't wait for an answer. He tapped on the bench top with his fingers. "You did a meal for two for him last night. What did he do? Dump her and follow you home."

"Back off, Matcher. It was a business dinner. His guest couldn't make it. Why did she bother? Matcher didn't act as if he was listening. Instead, he watched Seth leave the bathroom. "Anyway, it was good Seth followed me home because the intruder showed up again."

"Did you call the cops?" Matcher turned back towards Cara.

"Seth dealt with him. It was actually somebody I knew a while back. He won't return," Cara replied.

Seth walked over. "Hello, I'm Seth Scanlon." He held out his hand, but Matcher didn't take up the offer.

"This is Matcher. You'll have seen him at the function at The Crescent. I'm going to have a shower. Try to be nice to each other." Cara shook her head as she walked away.

The hot water coursing down her back made her feel refreshed. If Matcher hadn't been there, she'd want to get sweaty all over again. If she walked out after her shower and Seth was gone, she knew she would be hurt and angry. She didn't care what Matcher saw in Seth's aura. She wanted that feeling from last night back again. It made all the other pain in her life bearable.

She hadn't heard the intercom while she was in the shower. Daniel was there when she walked in the front room. He looked a mess. Had he slept in his jeans and T-shirt? His hair was all over the place. When he glanced her way, she saw dark circles under his eyes.

"What happened?" Cara asked. "What's wrong?"

Seth was pouring a mug of coffee for Daniel. Matcher eyed Seth as if he had put poison in the cup instead of cream. Daniel hugged her. She felt him shaking.

"Jeff's in hospital. He got sick last night. I called for help. The ambulance came. They thought his appendix had exploded."

"Is he all right now?" Cara asked. If there was one thing she knew about, it was hospitals.

"They said he arrived just in time. He looked so bad. He even looked sort of pale, which was odd for a black guy. Oh God, I thought I was going to lose him. I don't know what I'd do if I did."

"He's going to be fine. You have us here. He's where he needs to be right now." Cara pushed Daniel into a chair.

"But what about the dinner?"

"I can deal with that. You need to go home. Get some rest. Then, you can come back and help me get ready. Matcher and I will do the party. He has been helping with the plating up recently. Matcher has a friend who will help with the serving. You can go back and spend the evening with Jeff at the hospital. He'll probably be out of it for most of the day anyway. Matcher will go back with you. Won't you?"

Matcher nodded. Cara looked around. Seth was no longer there. "I'm going to get dressed. I'll be back in a second."

As she walked into the bedroom, she saw Seth pulling on his leather jacket.

"You're leaving?" She heard the lost puppy sound in her voice. He smiled. He walked over and pulled her close, his arms around her waist. Every time they came around her, the world seemed solid. His lips were on hers encouraging her to open to him which she did willingly. She was breathless when he broke off the kiss.

"Trust me, I want you in bed all day. At the moment, you have friends that need you and a business to run. I want to see you again, don't doubt that."

"I'll call you when things are calmer. Knowing my life, it might be a while."

Seth grabbed his bag and shoved his clothing inside. "Matcher doesn't like me, does he?" He sat on the edge of the bed and pulled on his boots.

"He worries about me. He doesn't see you in the same way I do, but he'll come around." Cara hoped her statement sounded convincing.

"I'm rather glad he's not seen me in the way you have." Seth chuckled.

With a quick kiss farewell, he headed back to the main

room. He nodded, said goodbye to the others and left. Cara missed him already.

Daniel came over and hugged her. "He scares the shit out of me every time I look at him. He's brought a smile to your face. After last night I appreciate that. Matcher thinks he's in league with the devil. That's if Matcher believes in the devil. I'm not sure if he does. Do you?"

"I know you both think I'm crazy with my aura stuff," Matcher said, indignantly, "but he's not right."

"That's an understatement. He's like Vin Diesel on a bad day. I like my men big and dark, but not like that." Daniel laughed. It was a weak, unconvincing sound of amusement.

"I understand what you say about him. When he's around, I feel safe." Cara said. "I'm going to brush my teeth. Matcher, tell Daniel about your friend. Didn't you say that her name was Rachel?"

There was nothing like someone being in a new relationship to get Daniel going. It might stop him worrying. If his attention was off Seth and her, it could only be for the better. Was she being stupid? She didn't really know Seth. Her feelings when she was with him were so intense. Lately, there had only been bad things happening in her life. Being with him felt so good. The sex last night should have been illegal.

She walked back out of the bathroom ready to work. Daniel was loading the mugs and plates in the dishwasher while Matcher wiped down the counters. She'd trained them well. Now, she had to get on with everything else.

SATURDAY PASSED IN A BLUR. At midnight while she put the away the crockery, she thought about ringing Seth. The mind was so willing. She knew she would be asleep by the time he arrived.

Sunday wasn't much better. Daniel helped with the preparation. Then, he headed off to the Bristol Royal Infirmary. If Seth were in hospital instead of Jeff, she would be by his bedside. She was starting to fall for Seth way too quickly. Yet, she couldn't stop thinking about him. How many people had a dream lover come to life?

<hr>

IT WAS MONDAY MORNING. If Seth said he was too busy for her, she would sit down with a glass of chardonnay and cry. Touching his business card and phoning his number made her breath quicken. It was an answer machine.

"Hi, it's Cara. By the way, I hate these machines. I'm free tonight. Life's been a bit hectic over the weekend as you can imagine. If you're free, call me."

If he didn't phone back, then she knew where she stood. She really did believe that he was as keen on her as she was on him. She had made that mistake in the past, but she didn't think she was this time. Sipping her coffee, she willed the phone to ring.

It didn't but she nearly jumped off the couch when the intercom buzzed. It was the postman. The package he held looked heavy from the grimace on his face. Carrying the parcel upstairs, she noticed the stamps had Eire on them. Putting the package on the breakfast bar, she tried to see the return address. It was Nanna's solicitors in Killarney. Her stomach did a little flip at what it might contain.

She got scissors and opened the cardboard box. Inside, she found a wooden chest and an envelope. The solicitor's letter apologized for the delay in sending her the chest. The will had held up things. Her hand went to the necklace she wore all the time now. She needed to look for the stag necklace again. She would never forgive herself if she lost it. She placed the chest on the coffee table in the lounge room.

*I won't cry*, she told herself. She felt the tears coming anyway. For once she managed to keep them under control. The chest was about two feet long by eighteen inches wide and high. Its curved top, brass corners and lock made her think of a scaled-down version of a pirate's chest. Cara turned the key. The lock clicked. She peered inside, feeling an ache in her heart. The woman who packed away these keepsakes was gone.

First, Cara found a pile of fine embroidered handkerchiefs. She picked up one. She smelled the lavender Nanna always put on them. Cara removed the handkerchiefs. Next, she found two frames holding old black and white photographs of Nanna and Pops, then a picture of their wedding. He looked so handsome in his suit and her dress simple yet so pretty.

Something big wrapped in tissue paper filled the next layer. Cara gasped when she opened it to discover Nanna's wedding dress. It was no longer white, but a cream color. The lace and silk were still beautiful.

Finally, the box contained a small leather-bound notebook. Cara turned to the first page and started to read. The italic writing was beautiful.

*'My name is Margaret Turner. This is for those who'll come after me. This isn't just about me, but my sister Rosie who was murdered. I was born in 1825, she was born in*

*1823. Mother took in laundry. We helped out. Father was a chimney sweep and my brother worked with him.*

*It was a hard life but we all got by. Then Rosie married and moved away. I couldn't blame her for getting out. I would have if I could. When I was sixteen our father died and my brother followed not long after. The soot made them cough up blood. We had to find more money so I started to work the streets.*

*It was hard the first time, but then I saw my mother's smiling face when I gave her the money. She spent it all on grog and died in the gutter. Rosie didn't know what I was doing. When she found out, she took me to live with her.*

*She was special. She had the healing touch. People would come and see her, but she never charged them. I think it gave her happiness. There was never much love between Rosie and her man. He was just her way out.*

*She used to smile though when she spoke of the man she did love. He was a blacksmith. They met too late. She was married and then when her man died, the smith was wed. When his wife died in childbirth, Rosie was blamed because she helped at the delivery. It wasn't her fault the woman and her baby both passed.*

*After Rosie's husband died, the local landowner took a shine to her. He used to beat her up a bit. She said it didn't matter as long as we had a roof over our heads. He beat her so badly one night that she stabbed and killed him. I knew nothing but the streets. It was all I had to offer as a way to survive.*

*We escaped to Bath. When the peelers were around, Rosie sank into the shadows. She would put up with the customers roughing her up a bit for the money. She always said we would get away from this and start again. Then things got worse.*

*Our first customer that last night was a posh bloke. Him and his friends wanted her to stay until dawn. Hours later, she came to me as a ghost and said they'd killed her. She told me to run away. She had terrible wounds. Her head was sliced up and so was her body.*

*She said it was a ritual. They'd taken her power to extend their lives. She couldn't stop them, but she managed to give some of her power to the man she loved to avenge her death. I assumed she meant the blacksmith. She also said that with the power shared they will not be immortal. Her killers will fade unless they can obtain power from another, like she was. A witch.*

*What was left of her was found the next day floating in the weir. I fled to Ireland. I always worried they'd come after me. I'm an old woman now and will not be around much longer. My daughter Nell has the odd colored eyes, one blue, one green like Rosie. I think she has the power. She has tried some spells over the years and has helped some of the folk nearby when she lays her hands on them. I worry someone will come for her when I'm gone.*

*I sent a letter to Seth, the blacksmith. He came and visited me. It was true. Sixty years have passed and he is unchanged. He's promised to watch over those who come after me. I've done what I can and hope you will all be safe.*

*Margaret.*

Cara didn't have time to think about the contents of the journal before the phone rang. The book fell to the floor. When she answered the call, she heard Seth's voice.

"Cara, I'm sorry I missed you. I was at the airport picking up Janet. I'll be there at five. Is that all right?"

"Uh, yes."

"Is something wrong? Is your friend well?"

"No everything's fine. Jeff's improving. I'm going to see him this afternoon, but I should be back by four."

"I was wondering if you would mind if I cooked for you."

That took her off guard. "You don't have to. Most people don't want to cook for a chef."

"I know, but I want to."

A couple of hours ago Cara had wanted Seth to bash her door down and ravish her. Now, she wasn't sure what she wanted. She hung the phone up and sat down by the chest again. The story of her great, great-aunt Rosie was so sad. Cara shuddered at the description of the murder. It was so unbelievable. How could someone over one hundred and fifty years old who had been told to protect her be out there? It also meant someone of an equal age might want to kill her.

It was a bit freaky that Rosie's love was a blacksmith and his name was Seth. Her Seth wasn't immortal. He was just an everyday guy. That wasn't entirely true. He was a big, muscled, strong, incredibly sexy and frightening guy. Cara allowed herself a grin thinking of him naked. He wanted to see her again. He was even prepared to cook for her, a brave thing to do. She should tidy the bedroom and get some candles.

She started to pack away the contents of the chest. Putting the book back, she realized she had missed something. There was a photograph inside. It was an old sepia picture. It had two women in it. They were dressed in old-fashioned clothing from the 1800's and smiling. Cara turned the photograph over. On the back was written Rosie and Margaret. 19 September 1846.

She hated to admit it, but the one she assumed was Aunt Rosie looked very much like her.

CARA HATED HOSPITALS. There were too many memories. She grimaced at the odor, a certain smell which could only be described as disinfectant mixed with fear. Jeff was doing well. He looked as if he'd lost weight. She could just see Daniel devoting all his time to fattening him up.

"So when are you seeing Vin Diesel's evil twin again?" Daniel asked.

Jeff tried to turn over in bed to look at her. The movement caused him to screw up his face and clutch his side.

"What's this? I get sick and for the first time in years and you find a man."

"She mixed business with pleasure."

"It wasn't like that." Cara explained all about Tony and how Seth had helped.

"She did a meal for two, only they ended up being the two. Matcher can't stand him. It's that aura stuff he goes on about. He says Seth has a bad one. I wouldn't be surprised. He scares the shit out of me." Daniel did a mock shiver.

"I can't wait to meet him, Cara. The doctor says I may be able to go home tomorrow. Don't finish your relationship until I get a look."

"I don't know about him. He gets sick and now he doesn't trust my opinion. Seth is six foot, muscle-bound with a shaved head." Daniel winked, then added. "He has a good butt in bike leathers."

"I thought you were distressed the other day." Cara shook her head. "All you were doing was staring at Seth's butt." She paused, "I had a small chest arrive from Nanna's solicitors this morning."

Daniel turned toward her wide-eyed. "So what was in it?"

"Most of it was mementoes. It's strange. I still think if I catch a plane, she'll be waiting for me at the farmhouse. It's the same with Shona. So I'm bloody glad that appendix of yours didn't explode." Cara waved her finger at Jeff. "I refuse to lose anyone else."

"I'll second that." Jeff looked at Daniel, then back at her. "You'd better get him a tissue Cara. He's going to blubber on us."

"Was there anything else in this box of your Nanna's?" Daniel asked.

"There was a book." Cara reached in her purse. She handed the journal to Daniel. While she talked to Jeff about the jobs she had done that weekend, Daniel skimmed the book. When he finished, he handed the diary to Jeff to read. She tried to tell herself it didn't matter what they thought but she found herself wringing her hands.

"Don't just sit there looking at me with a blank expression. Say something." Cara frowned at her partner.

Daniel bit his bottom lip. "Cara, what do you want me to say? It sounds great if I was watching *Supernatural*, but sitting here in the Bristol Royal Infirmary, it sounds like she lost her mind. I reckon it's true that your ancestor was killed and all of that stuff. I don't believe the ritual thing and people living forever."

"She believed it. That makes it sort of sad."

"I must admit the guy being called Seth was a coincidence. She didn't mention he was six foot and scary. I think you're safe. You don't actually believe this stuff, do you?" Daniel shook his head as Jeff put down the book. "What do you think?"

"As you said, it's an amazing story, That's all it is." Jeff moved and winced.

It was time she left, Cara thought. He needed rest, not her jabbering on about her crazy family.

---

CARA SAT on the other side of the breakfast bar. She sipped a glass of Riesling as Seth cooked. She smiled. No bike leathers this time. He'd driven Janet's car. He wore jeans and a shirt. Daniel was right. Seth did have a great butt.

He had walked into the flat with flowers, a bunch of roses no less. She could have ripped his clothes off right there and then. No one ever gave her flowers before unless she was sick. As soon as she put the roses down he had pulled her into his arms and kissed her. Their lips melded together as though they couldn't get enough of each other. She had felt his erection hard against her so she was disappointed when he returned to cooking. She felt hungry, but not for food.

He glanced at her. "What are you thinking this time?" He stopped stirring and picked up his own glass.

Cara felt warmth flood her face. She must be bright red. She didn't answer right away.

He went back to the cooker and switched it off. Walking back around to her, he held her face in his strong hands. He kissed her eyelids, forehead, cheeks and then her lips. Pulling away, he whispered, "We can eat later."

Cara nodded. She wanted to forget everything and lose herself in him. She'd removed her blouse and he'd dropped his shirt on the hall floor by the time they reached the bedroom. Collapsing on the bed, she drew him to her. She wanted him naked and inside her. Her hands went down to his jeans and unzipped them.

She felt him straining for release. His hands slipped around her back and unfastened her bra. He tossed it across the room. She laughed when it landed on the wardrobe doorknob this time.

Rolling her onto her back, he caressed one breast with his hand. His lips and tongue toyed with her other nipple. The man made her crazy with the sensations he caused. He had only just started and she had tingles all over her body.

She clutched his shoulders. His fingers left her breast. He stroked down her leg and beneath her skirt. Cara wasn't sure if she was hot or his fingers were when they slid inside her.

"Oh my God. You're so ready. And wet."

The words slipped from his lips in a breathy gasp. That was it. She was in the palm of his hand, literally. This lust overpowered her. They were a tangle of hands as the rest of their clothes came off.

Just touching his body was beyond what she could bear. It sent her mind spiraling into a glorious oblivion. They lay alongside each other, caressing shoulders, hips and inner thighs. Lips touching lips, necks, breasts, his wide chest.

Seth trailed kisses down her body stopping at her scar. He placed tiny kisses along the scar before his head descended lower. She was no virgin, but never before had a man made her feel so wonderful. His tongue swirled on her and flicked against her clitoris.

It sent her mind into spirals of ecstasy. Then, he was delving inside her. She pushed against him to get closer. The action spurred him on even more. She appreciated being a woman more than she had in ages. She couldn't remember how long. The thought brought tears to her eyes.

Seth stopped and moved next to her.

"What's wrong?" His hand cupped her face. He looked at her with concern.

Damn it, this man touched her far too deeply. She had just gone way beyond lust.

"I thought after the operation I'd never feel like a complete woman again." She tried to stop her tears. "You make me feel sexy. No, you make me feel sex."

His pupils dilated. Her heartbeat sped up.

"Cara, you're everything and more it takes to be a woman. I can't get enough of you."

"You can try."

She laughed as she pushed him onto his back and sat across him. She felt his hardness between her legs as she moved. Leaning forward, he took her right breast in his mouth and sucked her nipple hard. He nipped her, but the pain caused the ache inside to increase. She put her hand down, guiding him into her moistness. A groan escaped her lips.

He bit harder on her nipple. She moved slowly at first. When he put his hands on her hips, she increased the momentum. How long could she cope with the intensity of feelings arising from her body? She moaned with delight as each new sensation hit.

She heard him groan. His face contorted as his whole body shuddered in release. At this moment, she never wanted to sleep another night in this bed without him.

He smiled at her. "Cara, how could you possibly think you're not all woman?"

---

HER SHOWER WAS TOO SMALL. It meant they were extremely close as he washed her. It was strange after the closeness of sex that she could feel shy. As he lathered her breasts and then moved his hand lower so he made his way through her tangle of curls washed between her legs. She closed her eyes unable to look at him.

"It's your turn."

She soaped his back, his glorious buttocks and legs. God, she wanted him again. The ache inside was almost painful. He turned around to face her. She started to giggle as she tried to wash his privates.

"You find this amusing."

"No, it's just I feel useless at it."

"You are doing very well, trust me."

She started to wash his chest. The scars grew more livid due to the hot water. The red mark on his shoulder didn't look so angry anymore. Without thinking, she had been massaging the spot. She glanced up at him and met his gaze.

"Don't ask me, not yet."

"Well then, let's eat," she said. "I have an appetite and someone said they were cooking for me."

THEY SAT on the couch eating pasta. Cara had lit candles. The sex and the wine made her feel mellow. "I want the recipe, unless it's a trade secret."

"It's no secret. I chuck in things." Seth took her empty dish to the kitchen. As he sat back down, he hit something with his foot. He refilled their glasses. He reached down and picked up Nanna's chest.

"This looks old."

"It's my grandmother's. Her solicitors sent it to me. I got it today. You can open it if you want." Cara watched as Seth went through the contents. He touched each item slowly with reverence.

"You should cherish these things. You'll always have part of her here with you, now that you have this."

Cara bit her bottom lip at his comment but then decided to tell more.

"I loved Nanna, but she didn't get along with Mum. To be honest, I think Mum had a point. Nanna did have some strange ideas. There was a book in the box also written by my great, great whatever grandmother. It's in my bag. I'll show it to you. It's a bit out there, but I'd like to see what you think."

Cara reached over the side of the couch. She picked up her bag while Seth sipped wine. As she pulled out the book, the photograph of Margaret and Rosie fell face upwards on the floor. Seth picked it up.

He said one word as he stared at the image in front of him. One word that made Cara's heart stand still and her blood run cold.

"Rosie."

## EIGHTEEN

Cara didn't bother sipping. She took a big gulp of wine. Her stomach clenched in a tight knot as she sat and watched Seth read the book. He hadn't seen the back of the photograph. He'd paled at the sight of Rosie though. That rat was gnawing at her insides again. He wasn't the sort of person who looked or acted shocked by anything. How the hell did he know the people in the picture?

It was just the ramblings of an old woman, Cara told herself. She took another gulp of wine. Why wasn't he saying something? *I don't want to know*, she thought, but she did. She also wanted him to stay, no matter what. The thought of a life without him was too much to bare.

Seth placed the book down on the coffee table. He glanced up and then looked away.

"I never knew Margaret well, but that is Rosie. I loved her. What the book says is true." Seth spoke quietly.

She was sitting next to a stranger. Okay, so she'd just had sex with him, but this was insane. Surely he didn't expect her to believe he was the Seth from the book. He would be getting on for nearly two hundred years old.

"What the hell is that supposed to mean?" Cara gave a strained laugh. She had never been afraid of his size but she was afraid of what he was saying.

"I'm not going to lie to you. No matter how strange what I might say may sound, I'm telling you the truth. I don't want to leave your side unless you ask me to go."

This time he looked straight at her and she couldn't cope with the piercing stare.

"I haven't asked you to go." Cara bit her bottom lip. She should kick him out. Making the right decisions in life had never been one of her strong points.

"Your face shows fear since I saw the picture of Rosie. We've just shared our bodies. Now, you sit at the far end of the couch clutching your knees. You've never feared me until tonight, until this moment."

"Yes, but this doesn't make any sense." For the first time in ages, Cara would have liked Jessica there. "I don't know what game you're playing, but I'm prepared to listen." She looked at the wine glass on the table, but didn't pick it up again. She needed to be sober enough to understand.

Seth didn't touch his wine either as he placed the picture down. "I lived in the cottage you visited. My father was a blacksmith. He was also a drunk who beat my mother. I don't remember her. She died when I was small. My father taught me his skill and I was a quick learner with a natural ability. One day he was so drunk, he fell in the forge. He lasted four days screaming in agony from the burns."

Seth stood up and paced. He looked everywhere but straight at her. "I developed a reputation for making fine ceremonial swords and was living well. I met Rosie and fell in love. Like Margaret says, Rosie was already married but she never cheated on her husband. Then Annie said she was with child and it was mine. I had no reason to doubt her. A spring fair, too much drink and a mild evening had been our undoing. We married. There was no child. We deserved better than what we were to each other."

Seth stood next to the table and looked down at the picture. His story seemed to have elements of her own with Tony. If she believed it.

"Rosie was wild and beautiful." Seth paced again lost in thought.

"What happened then?" He looked her way and ran his hand behind his neck as he struggled to speak.

"I became my father. I drank too much. I rarely touched Annie, which suited her. Rosie always said if I laid a hand on her the way the local gentry did, she would kill herself. I loved her. Annie died in childbirth after eight years of marriage. We finally had the child that brought us together, but it died. People blamed Rosie because they said she had the touch. It's wrong, but when my wife died, all I could think of was Rosie. I was going to sober up and ask her to be mine. I was too late. She disappeared after the local landowner was found dead in her house." Seth sat down again.

Cara looked at him. His hands were shaking. He wasn't painting a good picture of himself. She didn't know if he really was the man in the book. In an odd way what he was saying made sense.

"Go on," Cara encouraged.

"You know what happened to Rosie. When they found her body, she'd been stabbed to death through the heart. The killers mutilated her."

"What did he do?" Cara unclenched her arms from around her knees and leaned forward. Her heart pounded in her chest. Her hands became clammy and cold.

"You don't want to know." He shook his head as if the action would help him forget the scene.

"Tell me." She touched his hand.

He looked at her. Tears filled his eyes at the memory. "She had cuts across her forehead. They slashed her abdomen and stabbed her through the heart. The night she died, she came to me in a vision. She had the markings on her and a knife in her chest. I tried to help her. She pushed the knife deeper. An amazing heat and light surrounded me. It was only later when I tried to kill myself that I understood I couldn't die. I wanted to, but I couldn't. She needed me to avenge her death."

Cara fiddled with her necklace. There were too many coincidences. She wanted to be rational and tell him he was insane. She couldn't. Her hands trembled. What did he mean, he couldn't die?

"The dagger in the vision was the same as the copy you saw in my forge. I fixed the weapon that killed Rosie. I tried to find the man who had brought it to me. He died before I could get all the information I wanted from him. I found two of the other killers in Paris. I couldn't stop their deaths." He clenched his hands in frustration.

"I still have to find the mastermind, but I don't even know a name. Then forty years after Rosie died, bodies started being found with the same markings. It stopped for a while. Forty years after that it began again. And now, he's back. I've been so close. That's why I scarred myself each time to remind me how I've failed."

Cara remembered the night in the morgue. Seeing Shona cold and dead was one of the worst events in her life. Tears flowed down her cheeks at the memory. Seth picked up one of the handkerchiefs from Nanna's chest and handed it to her.

"Shona was cut like that. I had to identify her." The words caught in her throat.

"I'm so sorry." Seth started to take her hand, but hesitated.

"I'd told Shona about my dream. I'd drawn a picture of a dagger," Cara said. "She told me someone had come in and was interested in the drawing."

"The police think it's someone copying a killer from the past," Seth said. "I believe it's the same person. He's long lived like me."

"Now, you're asking me to believe there's someone else as old as you. That's if you're telling the truth and you are so old. I'm not saying I believe you yet. This is all mad, so unreal. I feel like I'm listening to someone in a dream and I will wake up."

He knelt in front of her, looking into her eyes with such sincerity. Her heart ached with feelings for him despite what he was saying. "What Margaret said was true. I know you'll find this hard to accept, but you of all people must believe me."

"Why?" She folded her arms against her chest to stop herself from hugging him.

"Because I stopped wanting to live a long time ago. Rosie wanted me to avenge her death. I was so tired, tired of trying to stop myself getting attached to people around me. Then I found you. I've watched over your relatives for so long. None of them have meant anything to me, but I ensured their safety. If money was a problem I made sure they were provided for. Then I saw you with your parents. You'd just moved to Bristol from Ireland. As I watched you that day, something real and human started to live in me again, something I had no right to feel. When Kathleen died, I could no longer keep that distance. Please forgive me."

"Go on."

"At the funeral I picked you up. When you turned up at my home and I touched you, I knew there was no point in trying to stay away any longer. I offer no excuses for what I've done. Let me ask you this, Cara. Do you want to believe me?"

She did, but why? That was easy, she loved him. "Yes, but this is ridiculous. People don't live that long. It means you're lying and that hurts me. I can't imagine my life without you. You've been in my dreams for so long. I just never believed you were real." She wanted to hold him so much but had to keep her distance for now.

"My Nanna told me she was a witch and said I'm one too. I've done spells. You keep showing up in them. I have dreams where bodies get chopped up. Another female would be calling the cops right now. I think you can answer my questions more than anyone else. I know it's stupid and illogical, but I want you to be telling the truth." Cara took a deep breath.

"It's important you believe me because I want you to care for me, and there's only one way to prove this to you." Seth stood up and walked to the kitchen.

He opened one of the drawers and pulled out a knife. As he walked back to the couch, he sliced his hand across his palm and then from his wrist to his elbow.

Cara screamed, clutching her hair. "What the fuck do you think you're doing?"

As she jumped forward, the edges of the wounds sealed together. In a moment, there was only a slight scar. He held his arm in front of her to touch.

Cara pushed herself back into the chair. "Don't come

near me. Telling me you can live a long time is one thing. Doing that's another. What the hell are you?"

He sat down and placed the knife on the table. He turned to her. Her heart was still pounding at what she had just seen. "I'm just a man. Rosie did something to me. I've read every book I could. I've visited every website. Nothing has explained what happened. I didn't ask for this. I believe I was meant to meet you though."

Cara sat on the far end of the couch.

"I've something else I need to show you." Reaching into his jeans pocket he pulled out the chain with a stag on it.

"You have it." Cara reached for the necklace.

Seth placed it in her hands. "It fell out of your bag in the forge. I should've given it back but I wanted something of yours. I'd made a doorknocker once that was a stag's head. I wanted to believe it connected us."

So, Seth was her protector. He was strong. He scared most people. Why couldn't she get a muscle-builder or black belt in karate, instead of an immortal? This was crazy. What was more insane was she actually was starting to believe it. After all she could do spells so why wouldn't somebody be able to live for a long time?

"Okay. Maybe, I believe what you said. After you freaked me out, I'm more inclined to do so. What are you protecting me from? If it's Tony, he won't be back." Cara laughed nervously.

"As always, I watch to make sure the killer won't come back again."

Cara glanced down at her hands that were still shaking and took a deep breath. "This is most likely the stupidest thing I've ever done. I'm going to tell you something about why I think you're telling the truth. First, I need another glass of wine after what you just did."

Cara stayed at the end of the couch but told him everything. He sat there and listened. She almost laughed at one point, listening to how crazy she sounded. They were suited to each other. They were both insane. When she finished, the tight band around her head had disappeared.

"So where do we go from here? The loony bin?" Cara bit a nail.

"It's up to you. I won't bother you again if that's what you want. I'll return to watching over from a distance."

Cara gazed down at the necklace in the palm of her hand. She wasn't shaking anymore. When she looked up, she knew he was right. There was some special connection. They just hadn't worked it all out yet. His gaze searched her face for a sign.

She leaned over and put the necklace on him. Cupping his face with her hands, she touched his lips with hers. Even after all that had been said, she still yearned for him. "I want you to stay." Cara stood up and took his hand.

---

SETH HAD BEEN GONE two hours. She missed him. It was as if the place was totally empty. She hadn't fallen in love since Tony. Now that she had, it was with an immortal that was a hundred and fifty odd years old. Perhaps, it wouldn't be such a good idea to go to her counselor right now.

Nobody else could understand the dreams and visions. Seth made sense. She had seen how he had healed. He said he would be back later. She would just have to wait. Anyway, she needed to knuckle down and do some work.

Vincent had sent her a fax saying he liked one of the menus. She needed to do the costing. It was a large number of people. They would have to hire extra staff since it was mostly finger food. She ought to give Matcher a call. Perhaps, his friend Rachel might be available. Cara hoped he wouldn't give her the tenth degree about Seth. She didn't have a clue what she would say that could stop him from telling her, "I told you so."

When she had gone through the numbers, she rang Vincent. His personal assistant, Stephan answered the phone.

Pulling up outside Vincent's house, Cara rang the doorbell. Stephan answered. He looked down his nose at her. Vincent appeared behind him. He smiled his perfect smile. Maybe, that was it. He was too perfect. Could that be why she hadn't fancied him? She had gone for the shaved head, well-muscled, bike-riding immortal that was brilliant in bed instead. Insane but ruggedly sexy was her type then.

Cara followed Vincent to the library. All the boxes were gone. Books had been placed around the room. One of the walls held a display of daggers and swords. Two comfortable leather chairs were at one end of the room and a beautiful old-fashioned desk at the other end. The light from the window made the room look bright but it smelled dark as if the old books emitted a sinister feeling. She shivered.

"I've a guest list on my desk. There are a few people who have special needs when it comes to food. They're good clients. I'd like to pander to them if possible." Vincent directed her towards his desk. The sound of the French National Anthem filled the room from Vincent's mobile. "Please excuse me."

"No, that's fine. I'll check the list." Cara watched him walk from the room.

Vincent's desk was extremely tidy like everywhere else. There was an in-box, out-box, pens and pencils, the guest list and a pile of books. Cara scanned the list. As she expected, mother and father were there. There were also a few well-known people from about town on the list. They would have to make sure they brought plenty of business cards and sample menus with them. As Daniel pointed out, it was a smart way to round up more customers.

She wondered if she could get a copy of the list. Vincent was still talking outside the door. His voice rose, but then he moved away.

The special requirements wouldn't be too difficult, except for one. He'd better be worth it, because they would have to do a completely different meal for him. What did he live on? He was allergic to milk products, animal proteins and required a gluten free diet.

She would try and make him see that he could still enjoy food. Maybe, there was another string to her bow. People with special dietary needs probably thought companies like hers couldn't be bothered with them. It was a niche market, but could be added to their existing format. It wouldn't take much to adjust the menus.

She tapped her fingers on the desk. There were about six books piled there. The bottom two had modern covers with garish scenes. Cara read the blurb. *Ritual Killings, Their Meaning in Today's World.* Well that's a nice bedtime reader.

Cara picked up the next volume, Anne Rice's *Interview with a Vampire.* The third book was a copy of *Grey's Anatomy.* The next two books were something about artifacts from the past.

Then, there was a little black book with nothing written on its spine. Its leather cover was damaged and scratched. Cara reckoned it was old. Most of the stuff in this house was except the owner. Cara opened it. The pages inside were yellowed with age.

*The title page said. "This is the True account of Mr. Robert Middleton's Life. 1744..."*

Cara flicked through a few pages. As she read, her stomach clenched in a knot. Vincent's steps echoed in the hallway. She slammed the book shut before he entered the room. He walked in calmly. Her hands were clammy.

"I'm so sorry. That took longer than I expected. Have you had enough time to work out if you'll be able to accommodate the needs of my guests?"

"Yes. I wonder would it be all right if I had a copy of the guest list?"

"Of course." He printed out the list for her. When he turned back to her, she could see he was watching her closely. "Are you all right? You've gone extremely pale."

'I've a bit of a headache coming on. I'm so sorry. I believe we've covered most things though."

"Of course. Please fax me if you have any concerns."

Cara was glad he didn't follow her out to the van. The open air outside was refreshing. She gasped for breath. The house had almost suffocated her.

"Cara."

She didn't need to turn to know who was calling her. It was her mother.

"I just received my invitation. I think this is going to be a wonderful opportunity for you. There'll be lots of big names there. You'll be able to branch out and then you will be able to get someone else to do the cooking.'

"Don't you think that kind of defeats the concept? I do this because I like to cook." She should have bitten her tongue.

"I'm so glad I introduced you to Vincent. He would be an excellent catch."

"As far as Vincent is concerned, he is a client, Mum. I don't mix business and pleasure. I can find myself a boyfriend. In fact, I have a new man in my life."

Cara wanted to kick herself. Now came the Spanish Inquisition. When her mother met Seth with his shaved head and bike leathers, there would be a ritual burning at the stake.

Anne pursed her lips. "You must bring him round. Your father and I would love to meet him. What did you say his name was?"

Cara had the distinct impression her mother thought she was making it all up. "I didn't say, but his name is Seth. Mum, I have to go. I've a headache coming on."

Cara breathed out a long sigh of relief when she drove off. Her mother had gone inside already. No parental wave to be seen in the rear view mirror. Cara's mind went back to what she had seen. The knot returned to her gut. She peered across at the book on the seat next to her. It would be okay, she thought. She'd return it on the night of the party. He wouldn't even miss it.

# NINETEEN

Cara picked up the book she had stolen from Vincent. What she had read had freaked her out, which was something for a person coping with being in love with an immortal. She needed to read it again though.

She passed over the first twenty pages or so, which talked of Robert's trysts with one of his housemaids called, Lillie and his nights of drunken debauchery with his friends.

---

ROBERT MIDDLETON WROTE, *I have retold everything that led up to the events of the night in question. Now, I will tell what happened to Lillie. My friend William's manservant came not long after dark with a message for me. My friends had decided to go to his estate, Basset Manor instead. It was no surprise. His father's wine cellar was something to be envied. William intended on draining it, if that was possible for one person to do.*

*I will not excuse my actions where Lillie was concerned.*

My friends were wrong in what they did. I was young and thought nothing of the consequences. I wanted to drink, fornicate and hunt until my father said I had to marry. Arriving at Basset Manor, I was taken to the drawing room. William burst in, smartly dressed as always. He might not have the looks. He had the money to make himself appear superior. He held what looked like an old yellowed piece of paper.

"We've been waiting for you, Robert. You cannot believe what we're about to do. Harry found this parchment at his uncle's estate. It appears the old man had been on travels in Eastern Europe and unearthed knowledge on this cult. They believed this ceremony could give immortality to those that undertook the deed."

"What are you talking about?" I asked though I was not sure I wanted to know.

"Read it, Robert. Then join us in the cellar."

It was ridiculous that they could believe this. The paper explained that a female was to be copulated with and then murdered as the men spoke sacred words. Cuts were to be made across her brow and her abdomen.

The knife was described and illustrated. Its two-headed snake design caused me to shiver with distaste. If William had a body ready in the cellar for killing, then I would watch. Life would be tedious soon enough when my father expected me to take over the estate.

I continued to read the parchment. It rambled on about a Lord Valselef from some obscure Croatian province that discovered some ancient texts and a dagger. He had believed a demon had made the dagger and inscribed it with words of power. It would grant immortality if the killers of the innocents performed the act and willingly offered him a part of their souls. One day, the demon Kocshie would be able to join his followers when he had a complete human soul.

There was a picture of the way the body should be cut. Also there were foreign words, I did not understand. I read that they were to be recited at the time of death. For the briefest moment I thought about who the poor unfortunate was, but the thought was fleeting as I drank and read on.

Lord Valself wrote how his attempt at immortality had failed because the girl he killed was pregnant. The demon could not take or alter power from an untouched soul. The victim had to be impure and the unborn child was an inno- cent. Valself had misunderstood and had paid the cost. He had written these words before he lost himself to madness.

I poured myself another glass of wine and made my way to the cellar. On the floor in the middle of the room, William moved on top of the woman they had acquired. The other young bucks cheered him on loudly. The cellar was dimly lit with candles. As I walked closer, William groaned his release.

The girl was still in her underclothing with her petticoat pulled up around her waist. She wore a mask of silver, which hid her real face. The mask was cherubic and somewhat grotesque. Somehow, I did not think the wearer would be wearing such a smile.

What little I could see of her eyes were glazed over and she didn't move. She was drunk or drugged, most likely both. William would want her subdued. He would not want to get his countenance scratched. Standing, he pulled up his trousers, turned and smiled.

"So glad you decided to join us. Now, we can get on with the deed in hand."

I helped myself to a bottle of claret. As I sipped, I watched as my friends ripped the young woman's clothing apart. I took the blade when offered and sliced across her abdomen. The others did the same. The blood flowed down her sides and soaked into her shift. She did not respond as we cut her, possibly due to laudanum.

"We need to remove her mask and make cuts to her forehead before the final stab," William said.

I drank too fast and was going to vomit. Maybe, it was all the blood. Perhaps I was not as strong as I thought. I headed for a bucket in the corner of the room and emptied the contents of my stomach. When I returned to the table, they had removed the young woman's mask. They had sliced through her forehead three times with the knife. Her face was a bloody mess. There was something familiar about her hair. It was a rich auburn color.

I joined them. I placed my hand around the hilt of the blade along with the others as they held it above her heart. William started to recite the words from the parchment. As they pushed the blade under the skin, something caught my eye.

In the folds of the material of her shift was a shiny object. I watched mesmerized as the blood from her wound welled and trickled down the side of her body. The object sat in a pool of congealing blood. It was my mother's broach. I had given it to Lillie to pay her to rid herself of our child.

"What's wrong, Robert? You'll not turn squeamish on us now the deed's almost done," William asked.

"You'll not succeed," I said.

"You mean that immortality rubbish. It does not matter. We were here for the kill. Why would we not succeed? What do you know, Robert?"

"She carries an innocent."

"You bedded the bitch. Well, this is a good night's entertainment that we've rid you of a problem as well."

*I have watched over the past two years as they all went insane. One drowned himself. Another threw himself in front of a coach. William locked himself in the cellar and set himself on fire.*

*Five years have gone by since that night. I often wonder why I still live. Maybe, it was because the innocent was my own blood or maybe because I took the time to make sure she had a decent burial. Whatever the reason, I took the broach and sold it. The money I gave to her family. They took it and asked no questions. It was one less mouth to feed. I do not deserve any sympathy and have never asked for any. I know I wasted my own and other's lives.*

*I have arranged a hunt this afternoon. My horse will take a start and run towards Cradle Bluff. They will find him wandering at the top and my body at the bottom.*

---

AS CARA PUT down the book, her hands shook. This wasn't a work of fiction. It was clearly a man's account of what had happened to him. The thought chilled her. There were too many similarities to everything else in her life to dismiss it. She was scared. She needed to talk to Seth. This book and its events may have taken place a hundred years before he was born but he would know something.

---

JANET WALKED into the forge and placed a tray with coffee and homemade cookies on the workbench. Seth kept working on the statue. It was almost finished.

"I hope you like this coffee. Henri told me about these beans. Life's too short to drink instant coffee, he said, and

I'm inclined to agree with him." She sipped the steaming brew.

Seth loved the aroma filling the air, but didn't want anyone here right now, not even Janet.

"It's beautiful."

She walked around the sculpture. He felt naked. His skin prickled as if this piece had gone too far and he revealed too much of his feelings. He was a fool to put himself on display this way. The truth was if it hadn't been for the sculptures he would have been locked away years ago.

"It's Cara from the catering company, isn't it?" Janet smiled, as she reached out to touch the head of the sculpture. Her hand stopped.

He shut his eyes and lifted the coffee to his lips. Why did he feel such intense anger that Janet, or anyone else would touch his creations? Cara knew his secret now. She accepted him. He had loved others who were prepared to accept this madness. He had lost them when he lived on. This time he didn't want to lose what he had found. In his long life, he never felt the intensity he had when making love to Cara. He couldn't give it up.

"I'm sorry. I know how you don't like having your things touched. It's just this sculpture's different. It draws you in and makes you want to touch it." Janet offered him a cookie.

Seth shook his head. "It is Cara."

Janet smiled. "I go away for a week and look what happens. She seems a nice young woman. I sense pain in her past. My husband always thought I was crazy when I came out with things like that. I've been right enough times now though to realize there's something in it. You could do with a bit of happiness. Don't fight it. I'm glad I'm not the only one, who got lucky last week," Janet laughed.

Seth joined in. He hoped this Frenchman knew what he was letting himself in for, but doubted it very much.

Janet gazed back at the sculpture. "Take care, Seth. I've accepted you'll see me die and many others after me. You've already experienced living long and losing love. By your own admission you don't deal with it well." Janet reached out and touched his arm.

"She knows what I am, Janet. Like others before her, she accepts it. Like others before her, I'll lose her. All I want is to live a life with her and die when we're old. I can't." He walked past his table with knives and absently touched them as he spoke.

"You may live a lot longer, Seth, but you still only live each moment the same as the rest of us. Just try and enjoy the moments."

"It's easy to enjoy the moments with her, which makes it harder."

"I'm an older woman who has made enough mistakes to be able to give advice. You're rough and ready, Seth. I'd have been tempted by you a long time ago. You're a decent, honest and troubled man. My man in France is probably less trouble, even with his neighbors. It sounds to me like you're in love, which means you've only one choice. Enjoy it. Accept the pain when you lose her or get out now." Janet picked up the coffee mugs and left.

Seth stared at the sculpture. Janet was right. He would end up in pain. She would be the one dragging him home from the police station where he ended up drunk and disorderly again.

He would fire up the forge and keep himself busy. Heating the metal, he shaped it to his will. It was about the only thing he could control. He wanted her, and wanted to be at her apartment, making her want him now. He wanted to draw her to him, to be on top of her. He'd make her yell his name as he drove his body into hers.

The blade was good. It wasn't his best, but it would sell. He placed it alongside the others. Heat, sweat, hammering. It did nothing to lessen the anguish, the anger, the wanting. Someone should die for this pain. Strolling across to the window, he saw the light on in Janet's room. She would be on the Internet to Henri.

Seth stared at his watch. It was only six o'clock, but it was already dark. He hated winter with its evenings that drew in and got dark so early. He turned back to the sculpture. He'd made it well. The face had that come-hither smile. The breasts were those a man could lose himself in, he had lost himself in them.

He was lying to himself. There was only one reason he had told Cara everything. It was revenge and freedom from this curse. He was getting close. Looking at the sculpture, he knew he couldn't let other feelings stand in the way. He couldn't afford to love her. He picked up his mallet. He had to stop the insanity that would only end in pain for everyone. He would become her protector from a distance again.

The first blow was the hardest as he smashed into the side of the face. He had to do this and destroy what he loved. He had made a promise long ago. He brought the hammer down again and again. The pain he felt in his muscles was nothing to the ache in his heart and mind at his action.

"What are you doing?"

The mallet was in his hands, hands that were shaking uncontrollably. A voice, someone had said something. A question drawing him back. The anger withdrew to be replaced by the usual numbness his life contained. He viewed the pile of smashed stone; a remnant of a shape that might have been an elbow was present, or a piece of smooth inner thigh. The mallet dropped from his fingers. He fell to his knees by the rubble. He wanted to weep, but he couldn't. Any tears he would shed had disappeared years ago when he lost the ability to cry. Why couldn't he just die?

"Rosie. Why did you do this to me?" The words ripped from his throat. Arms came around him.

"It's all right my darling."

Soothing words whispered in his ear, ones he didn't deserve. Of all the people in the world, what was she doing here? Didn't she know she deserved so much better? If he had any sense, he would send her away.

Cara knelt before him, looking into his eyes. She kissed his lips. She kissed his cheeks. She kissed his eyelids and then returned to his mouth. He knew at that moment, he was a person who would continue to hurt and cause others pain for eternity, just for the love he felt at this moment. Her lips were warm and soft and he wanted them again. "Cara."

"It's all right."

"You don't understand. You shouldn't be here." Seth said. "You shouldn't be with me. I'll hurt you. You need to leave."

## TWENTY

Cara leaned forward to brush his mouth with hers. He was obviously in so much pain. All she wanted to do was comfort him. "Then make me go, because I'm not leaving you like this."

"I keep telling myself you're different. When I don't age the pain of losing you will be bearable, but it won't. I'll want to die." Seth laughed wryly.

He broke her heart to hear the way the sound caught in his throat.

He turned back to the pile of rubble and laughed again. "And I'll know I can't. I've controlled the anger and frustration so far. I'm afraid at some point I'll hurt people. Kill people. What will they do, put me in prison, for how long?"

Cara's fingers touched his elbow. She didn't caress but needed to let him know she was there for him. She picked up the broken stone that had once been a part of her head. One side of the face was smashed in, but the other side was more intact. For some reason she felt incredibly calm as she stared across at him. She truly felt no fear, which might show foolishness rather than common sense. "Was it me?"

Seth nodded.

"I hope you made my hips smaller. I always liked the idea of artistic license." Cara kissed his cheek.

He shivered beneath her fingers.

"Why are you here? Why are you smiling? I just smashed you to pieces."

"Many reasons," Cara said, a blush seeping into her cheeks. "Some of them I'm too embarrassed to say. The main reason is because I can't seem to stay away from you."

She touched his cheek gently, a feather light touch and then went on, "Secondly I saw something today which may help us get closer to finding Rosie's and Shona's killer. Apart from you and your body, that's something I want more than anything. I want to stop the killing and get the bastard."

"Come with me." Seth took her hand and led her from the forge. The night air caused her to shiver but he put his arm around her and pulled her close. "I don't want to be near this anymore."

When they were inside the cottage, she heard Janet moving around upstairs. Seth went to the stairs and called her. He poured three glasses of wine and sat down at the kitchen table. "Let's wait for her to join us. Then, you'll only have to tell the story once."

---

HE WATCHED Cara breathing as she lay snuggled up against him. The warmth of having her there intoxicated him. She slept peacefully after they made love. His mind couldn't let sleep take over. He had another chance to find out something about what happened so long ago.

She deserved more than this. Touching her hair, he knew he loved her. This need for closure had gone on so long though. He couldn't give it up and he hated a part of himself for that. He had loved and lost before. He was tired of fighting and losing. It was too late for such thoughts.

The sun was coming up and a beam of light shone in illuminating his beloved. Cara stretched and turned over. The sheet fell back revealing her breasts. The cool morning air made her nipples harden. She was still asleep, but he could see the goose bumps on her areola. She was so beautiful and she wanted him. How did he deserve this?

Leaning forward he closed his lips around her nipple. It was so hard, cold and firm. He moved across to the other nipple sucking on its taut peak. His hand moved slowly down the smooth skin of her abdomen until he threaded his fingers through her tight curls. His fingers slipped into her as she groaned. He had lived so long and touched so many women, but this was different.

Wherever their naked bodies touched felt like life being lived. He wanted to remember each fold, each movement she made when he touched her. She was wet and he was hard. Opening her eyes, she yawned and blinked at him. Then she smiled.

He was losing himself in her again. Moving on top of her, her legs encircled his waist as he entered her. This was a place he was content to lose himself.

She gasped. He worried he hurt her with his impatience. He no longer felt the sensation of moving in and out of her body. They flowed together as one. This wasn't enough. He needed to be even more a part of her.

Looking her in the face, he plunged deeper and harder. He couldn't stop now. His fingers felt for her clitoris gently massaging. He felt himself entering and withdrawing from her. Her muscles tightened around him, matching the shudder that went through his body. She groaned. She yelled. He gloried in the sound he would remember forever.

"I don't care how long you've lived, Seth." She smiled up at him. "I have to say that was the best orgasm I've ever had."

"So far." Seth watched her eyes crinkle up as she giggled. He wondered yet again why he deserved this, deserved her. "Janet's a light sleeper. I want to watch you go red when she says something, which I know she will."

"She won't be angry at me. I think she likes me. She probably thinks I'm going to steal her recipes, which I would, if I could. She will be angrier at you for the pile of rubble in the forge that she has to clean up." Cara bit her bottom lip.

Seth leaned on one elbow and gazed at her. "Are you frightened of me?"

She hesitated before answering. "You look scary sometimes. You're huge in more than one way. I like that, as was just witnessed. When you found Tony hiding in my apartment, I thought you would kill him. I mean literally kill him. I don't know anyone else in my life that is as intense as you. That's intimidating. It's taking me somewhere I haven't been before, but no, you don't scare me."

"I know what I did to the statue. You must believe I would never hurt you."

She touched his cheek. "I'm not frightened at all when I'm with you. I was frightened of dying when I lost the baby. I was frightened of living without love again. I'm frightened of the fact I may never have a child. To be honest at the moment, the only thing that really frightens me is that I might die like Shona and Rosie."

"I won't let that happen." He took her hand and kissed her palm.

"I know you won't."

---

SETH ENJOYED the laughter as he stood outside the kitchen. The cottage needed this sense of happiness. Too many years of sadness and anger had dwelled here. He smelled bacon and eggs as he entered the room and the two women turned to look at him.

"Well, it's about time. Cara and I thought you'd left the country. You better have the decency to show your face as you woke me up earlier." Janet waved a whisk at him.

"I think I was the one who woke you up, Janet." Cara giggled.

Seth realized he was the one going red. These women were ganging up on him. Janet had obviously not been out to the forge. If she'd seen the mess he'd made, she would be giving him a much harder time.

"You know when I was in Paris, the same thing happened to me. On the way out of Henri's apartment, this woman swore at me in French. From the splattering of English, I knew she was on about us making noise the night before. I've decided to do an evening class in French. If someone's swearing about the sex I've had, I want to know what they're saying." Janet piled food onto a plate.

Seth realized he was hungry.

"So Cara, you accept this extended life of Seth's. Why?" Janet asked.

"When he sliced himself open and it immediately healed, I was freaked out. It convinced me at the same time. It may sound crazy but it made the other things happening to me make sense."

"I dread to think what other things that could be, for him to make sense."

Cara's hand came across and touched his. Janet listened while Cara explained. She told about Shona's death, her dreams, her Nanna and witchcraft and how much she cared for him. Seth sat back and watched them talk.

"You come over so levelheaded, Cara. Now, I realize you're as mad as the rest of us. Welcome, dear. We're a very select club. I'm not sure how I'll introduce Henri to it." Janet went around to Cara's side of the table and hugged her.

This felt good. He had lived long enough to know that. He had also lived long enough to know it wouldn't last. A taste of bile entered his throat. He couldn't join in with the laughter. He knew one thing for sure as he smiled and watched Janet and Cara talk. This was the end. He would not live to remember these two people as distant memories. There had to be some way he could avenge Rosie's death and still live to be with Cara.

———

HE PULLED up down the street from the address Cara had mentioned. He turned off the engine to his bike. She was not joking when she said the house was impressive. No lights were on. Should he risk breaking in? The security system was probably connected to the local police station.

He hated the idea, but he would have to let Cara deal with this. He had a feeling she wasn't telling him everything. Maybe he could find out for himself.

A car came along the street, a Mercedes. The gates at the end of the driveway opened and the vehicle disappeared inside. It stopped outside of the house. Unfortunately the windows on the car were tinted. He hadn't been able to see what the driver looked like.

Cara said he was an antiques dealer with a love for weaponry. Seth wondered if a call to his agent might get him an invite to this party.

## TWENTY-ONE

No sooner had Vincent placed the champagne flute next to the bath then Melanie picked it up and drained it. She burped and screwed up her nose. Why was he wasting good champagne on her? He just needed her dead.

She held out the glass for more alcohol. "It's a bit dry, isn't it?"

"The best always is." He refilled the flute. It always worked to get them going, Champagne, bubbles and a Jacuzzi. The fact that there were medications in the drink couldn't hurt. While she drank, he let his bathrobe fall and stepped into the bath. He wanted to make sure she was clean before he copulated with her.

As it was, she had been half drunk when he picked her up at a public house in Fishponds. He reassured her he would cover her payment for the whole night. Plus he had offered a bit extra if she wouldn't mind a bit of roughing up. She said she was okay with it. He had even bought a cheap car for cash and would take it to the crushers tomorrow. It would not do to have someone notice his Mercedes in such an area. She cuddled up next to him as the bubbles floated around them. He needed to get this over and done with.

Once out of the bath and clean, she sauntered to his bed. She lay down and indicated for him to come over by patting the sheet. He would burn the sheets later. His nostril flared in disgust. He wouldn't want the smell of her to linger. Kissing her, he felt nothing. It was always the same. Pressing his naked body against hers, he closed his eyes and thought of blood. In his mind, his hand held a knife. He pushed it into her chest and imagining the warm sensation of blood flowing over his skin.

"What do you want to do next?" She asked in invitation.

He turned her over and pushed a pillow beneath her hips as she giggled. He grabbed the condom packet from his bedside table. His body would cure him of any disease. The last time he had contracted syphilis, it made him sick for too long. He couldn't afford such delays right now.

Pulling her buttocks slightly apart, he plunged from behind. In his mind, he ripped her to shreds. Her blood flowed over his groin and down his thighs. The fantasy made him plunge deeper. Expelling his seed, he withdrew quickly. He was glad she would never be able to live to have his child.

He ignored Melanie as she sprawled on the bed drunk. Damn it. The pain in his shoulder consumed him. The dark mark ached despite the drugs he had taken.

Damn Shona for breaking his dagger. No relief had come from the pain when he killed her. When he looked at the knife afterwards, he'd seen the fine line breaking the words inscribed on the blade. He had heard of a new sword-smith in the area. He would get Stephan to contact him.

Black spider veins spread from the mark down his arm.

He would not allow this to happen. He would not become mortal again.

A hand touched his shoulder. Melanie smiled at him. He needed to kill her now. It was the only way the pain would ease. He thought back as always to Rosie. If he had her here now, he would kill her so slowly. He had been too rash, too young back then. If only he had gotten it right the first time, he wouldn't need to kill Cara.

It wasn't just the immortality though. He enjoyed the cat and mouse game he played as he made friends with his victims. He would kill even if he hadn't needed to.

Melanie didn't take much prompting to visit the cellar and his extensive wine collection. It wasn't as if he would let her touch anything. The drugs he had given her should have been working better. There were no tram tracks on her arms so she was not a user, but she had offered him pills.

Perhaps a fight would make things more interesting and take his mind off the pain. Melanie touched his arm. He flinched.

"I've a special bottle of wine I think would be appropriate after such a wonderful evening," Vincent said, leading the way further into the room. Wine racks covered two walls. The stairs crossed another. A large table was pushed up against the last wall. There was a bottle of red wine already opened. Next to it were two old wooden chairs. Vincent led Melanie to one of the chairs.

"I want you to experience how special this wine is. Will you let me blindfold you?"

Melanie smiled and nodded. Vincent placed the scarf from his pocket around her head, covering her eyes. Pouring the wine he added another ampoule to the liquid.

"I want you to breathe in the fragrance. Tell me what you smell."

"It smells fruity." She giggled.

He frowned. "Now drink it. There's not that much in the glass."

Melanie downed the contents. Taking off the blindfold he refilled her glass. Two glasses later, she was unconscious.

He usually liked them to squirm when he killed. Tonight though he needed to get on with this. He lifted her onto the table and undid her robe. Walking over to one of the wine racks, he removed the special bottle. He took the dagger from its hiding place. It was still cracked but he had no choice. A slight relief from the pain would be better than no relief at all.

She barely moved when he made the slits to her forehead. The other drugs and the added alcohol had finally kicked in. With her abdomen sliced up, Vincent plunged the knife into her heart.

Nothing happened. Before, there was always a surge of energy. Pain would be relieved. Even with Shona, he had gained some relief. Pulling open his robe, he noticed there wasn't any change. The mark on his shoulder was as livid as ever. The pain throbbed. This wasn't meant to happen.

Grabbing the dagger, he stabbed her again and again. He slashed her abdomen open, so the bowel protruded. Throwing the dagger aside, he plunged his hands into the warm bloody mess of flesh.

Again nothing happened. Grabbing the empty wine bottle he bought it down on her head with a thud. He smashed repeatedly until Melanie's face looked like a bloodied pulp. He would not wait for mortality to catch up with him.

He would kill Cara and soon. If he didn't, all these years would be for nothing. Teasing and tempting her with her own death had been stimulating. Playing her parents for fools as they offered up their daughter on a platter for him was satisfying. He needed her power now and nothing would stop him.

# TWENTY-TWO

Cara's stomach knotted when she pulled up outside Vincent's house. It wasn't the prospect of the party being a disaster. She knew they would do a good job and the guests would enjoy the food. At some point this evening, she would have to slip into the library and replace the book. If Seth read it, he would rip Vincent limb from limb to find out more. Robert Middleton might have lived a hundred years before Seth, but she was sure that they were connected. The ritual that had killed Rosie would have been the same as the one on Lillie.

Vincent had to know who the killer was. What she needed was more proof to get the police involved. The book didn't mean anything on its own. Vincent was allowed to collect old books. It was part of his job. The fact that the killings in this volume were repeated now in detail on victims could be attributed to a copy-cat murderer. It wasn't a comforting thought.

Telling Seth about the picture of the dagger, the cults, and murders was enough. In retrospect, she had been crazy to tell him that much, but she needed a reason for being there that night. Apart from wanting to jump into his bed again.

———

SO FAR THE evening was going incredibly well. The food disappeared from platters almost faster than they could fill them. Even Vincent's friend who was allergic to everything sent a special thanks to the kitchen. Thankfully, as the evening wore on, the numbers started dwindling, and then a message came through that a small group would be staying longer. There was still enough food left to set up a few platters in the front parlor as Stephan called it.

Cara would drop off one of the platters. Afterwards, she'd make her way to the library to replace the book. It was the perfect opportunity, as long as Daniel and Matcher weren't stalking her. As she walked into the parlor, her jaw dropped. Seth sat in one of the chairs next to a beautiful blond woman. Why hadn't he told her he was coming?

Stephan came over and took the platter. He even smiled at her, which had to be a first.

"Ah, here is the elusive Cara," Vincent said. He came across and took her hand. "You'll come and join us, won't you? The seafood from Dingle was wonderful and the turkey pate from Dunmanway made me sigh."

"Just for a moment, Vincent. Duty calls." Cara wanted out, but that wasn't going to happen.

Vincent introduced everyone including Seth, and Robert Fetter, his agent. She also met Craig, who had to be one of the world's fussiest eaters. He was so excited about his food he gave her a hug. He had their card in his hand. It was wonderful and nothing to do with dead bodies and magical powers. Someone just liked her food.

She struggled not to gape like a fool when she was introduced to Jane Purcell, one of the BBC presenters from the Ten o'clock news. She felt tongue tied before a woman who could make a Prime Minister stutter.

It was stupid to be impressed by someone like that when she had an immortal lover and he wanted her. Of course said lover was sitting next to a blonde goddess on the other side of the room at the moment.

Where was Daniel when she needed him, Cara wondered? She breathed a sigh of relief when he walked in.

She was a happy to let him take over. Anyway, he was in his element. All in all, it was the perfect function. Death and insanity revolved around her. Yet she still wanted to be seen as a thorough professional.

"I need to deal with a few final things in the kitchen. It's been wonderful meeting you," Cara said. She wasn't sure who was more relieved, her or the guests. Daniel was more than happy to take on the social challenge.

As soon as she was out of the room and in the hallway, she let out a deep breath. Leaning back against the wall, she put her hand to her chest. Her heart pounded away. This had to be done. She hurried down the hall.

The library was dark. Her eyes took a while to adjust. Making her way over to the desk she stubbed her toe, but managed not to yell out. Pulling the book out of her apron pocket, she placed it back on the pile. This room gave her the creeps. At any moment, she thought books would fly off the shelves and attack her. She turned and fled back to the safety of the kitchen.

ALTHOUGH THEY RETURNED to her flat by twelve, it took forever to sort out everything. The office was full of equipment. She couldn't have swung a cat in there. Merlin was probably glad about that as he curled up on the couch.

Daniel had gone and picked up Jeff. It was two weeks since the operation. He was doing well, though he still moved a bit stiffly at times. She was glad they had only been doing the food at Vincent's tonight. Organizing the drinks and glasses would have sent her over the edge.

"We have no jobs tomorrow. Who's up for wine and nibbles?" Cara asked.

All hands went up. Matcher sat in the beanbag, with Rachel cuddled up next to him. Daniel was in the kitchen making nachos. Jeff lounged on the couch. Cara grabbed some dips and a bottle of red. It was half past twelve. They needed to chill. Daniel always liked this time. She usually did too, except tonight she kept thinking about the book and Seth.

"I'm not so sure about weddings after dealing with sixty ravenous drinkers. They devoured food like they'd never eat again." Daniel poured the wine and sat down.

Cara grabbed her glass and took a sip. "Yeah, but we did it with class. We really need to look at what we want for the future, especially if any bookings come in from this."

"I want new feet." Rachel chimed in, taking a big swig of wine.

Cara tried to remember how old Rachel was. She didn't relish the idea of angry parents at the door. From what Matcher said, they wouldn't care.

"I'd like to say you get used to it, but you don't. Your feet, your back, they can kill but you keep going all night on the adrenaline," Cara replied, massaging her own feet. She straightened, fighting the urge to yawn.

"Did you see Peter from *The Post* was there?" Daniel asked.

"Yes. I still can't stand him," Cara said. She still remembered how he tried to grill her for information about Shona at the dinner party at his house.

Jeff rubbed the back of Daniel's neck and he relaxed back on the couch. "Daniel told me about him. I see his sort all the time. When they look at you, their eyes are working out whether you'll make them money or not. As tonight went well, he'll watch where you're going. If it's good, he'll claim he helped. If not, he'll say he saw you were flawed from the start." Jeff turned around slowly. He stretched out and stuck his feet on Daniel's lap.

Daniel didn't say anything but started massaging them. Not delicately but methodically pressing and sensing where his partner was holding pain.

Jeff yawned and relaxed even more. "I should be doing yours."

"You can, when they don't stink from standing on them all night." Daniel laughed.

Cara knew what she was witnessing was a basic relief of tension. Yet, she also saw closeness and love. She wanted it too. Was she fooling herself with Seth? He could be with the blonde now. No he wouldn't do that. No book, no man, no answers. That was her life right now. Feeling pathetic, she went to the kitchen and got out some Camembert and crackers. She'd distract herself by taking care of her guests and being a good hostess. She was just being silly because she was tired.

Matcher followed her. "Do you remember me saying Vincent's aura was odd?"

"Sort of. Wasn't there something about him being weird at my mother's dinner?" Cara nibbled on a cracker.

"Tonight, I realized his aura reminds me of Seth's. I don't know what it is, but there's something wrong with both of them. Those guys are really fucked up. I know you don't want to hear that, but be careful." Matcher hugged her.

Daniel called out, "Who's totally fucked up? I want to know. I'm jealous. Not that I've the energy right now."

Cara grabbed another bottle of wine and headed back. "I'm not saying a thing. This is your area, Matcher, you go on." Cara sat down and sipped on her glass of red.

Matcher walked back and settled next to Rachel in the big bean bag. "You all know I see auras. I get that some of you think I'm full of crap. It really doesn't matter. I see them whether you believe in them or not." He raised his glass to Cara.

Jeff leaned forward. "I know you mentioned it. To be honest, I sort of see it like reading your stars. You'll believe it, if it says something good,"

"What's mine like?" Daniel asked enthusiastically.

"See what I mean?" Jeff replied, shaking his head.

"Daniel, you have an aura that's bright and full of energy. When you and Jeff are together it's like your auras meld. There are some dark patches on Jeff, but that's understandable because of his operation."

"What about me?" Rachel asked eagerly. Cara was surprised he hadn't mentioned his talent to Rachel. Perhaps, Matcher worried he might scare her off.

"The red shows you're sensitive and caring, but your blue layer has some dark spots. When we're together they almost disappear. When you talk about your family they get bigger."

"I'll just have to stay close to you to keep the dark spots away then, won't I?" Rachel leaned in and kissed him.

"Sounds great." Matcher put his arm around her.

"So, who were you talking about earlier?" Jeff asked, glancing at Cara.

What could she say? How much would she tell them before they thought her mad, or rather, more mad? "He's talking about Vincent. The last time Matcher saw him, he said he could see his aura was different. Tonight when he saw Seth, he says his aura is strange as well. That's not a good thing. I know why Seth's is different." Cara took a gulp of wine.

She had gone this far, she might as well go the whole way. Matcher kept watching her and nodded. He had never liked Seth. What would he think now? She took a deep breath. Then, she told them everything and no one interrupted. They just sat there absorbing the information. When she finished, she expected someone to start laughing at how absurd it all was. Daniel just looked at Jeff and shook his head.

Matcher smiled with an, "I told you so" look on his face. "I knew it would be something like that. It makes sense. From what I've seen, most people's auras are constantly changing. Those two are stuck."

Daniel leaned forward, ready to give his five pennies worth. "Come on, Matcher. You don't really believe this. Your aura stuff is harmless, but this is mad. People don't live that long. I can understand how you might be taken in by this, Cara. You've been through so much recently. I know you really like the guy. This is crazy. It's goofy like the stuff in your grandmother's book."

"Enough, Daniel." Cara doubted this would cause their business to go down the drain but she had to say something. She loved Seth. She really did. "Look, you don't have to accept this. You're probably sane. I may not be. I do believe it though. From what Matcher's said, we're finding out a bit more that will lead us to who killed Shona. If Vincent murdered her, I want him to rot in hell."

"Does Seth know about the book? Is that why he was there?" Matcher asked.

"I haven't told him what I've found out. He would attack Vincent, beat the information out of him, or kill him. I want to find some way the police can deal with this. I just haven't figured out how to go back and get more evidence."

"That's nuts. Why would you go in there when you think he kills people? I can't believe I just said that." Daniel shook his head.

"The book said if Seth tries to kill whoever killed Rosie, then he'll die himself. I can't risk that. If I die, he'll live. Without me, he won't control the anger. He's already told me he's afraid of what he will do."

Silence. No one spoke and she couldn't blame them. The door buzzer broke the silence and they all jumped.

"Cara. It's Seth. Can I come up?"

Cara didn't look at any of them. She stood up and pressed the intercom button.

"Yes, Seth. I'm not alone." If she had to choose between her friends and him, it would be him. She went to greet him at the apartment door. Silence greeted them as they walked into the lounge room.

Everyone stared at Seth. He turned. His gaze searching hers. Cara drew a deep breath. "I've told them about you."

Seth nodded. He smiled at her and then looked to the others. "And do you believe her?"

"I do. I've always known you were different. Now, I know I'm not barmy," Matcher said. "Still don't know if you're good or bad shit though."

"That's a question I ask myself regularly. If you find the answer out before I do, let me know," Seth said, smiling.

Daniel stood up with his arms crossed. It was like David and Goliath, Seth with his huge frame and Daniel with his fit but slight one.

"I think this is a load of crap. Come on Cara. You don't really accept this rubbish he's telling you. Look, Seth. I don't know what your game is, or why you're trying to hurt her with this rubbish story, but she's been through enough."

"Daniel, stop it. He isn't hurting me." Cara said as she held Seth's hand.

Seth turned to her. "How important is it to you that they accept this?"

"I want them to, but if they don't, it won't make me change what I know." Cara sat down and so did Daniel. He was on the couch with Jeff. Matcher and Rachel were at the end of the coffee table on the beanbag. It felt as if she was facing off against her friend and she didn't want that.

Seth went to the kitchen. He took a knife from the drawer and then walked over to the couch. She thought he was going to cut himself again, but instead he handed the knife to Daniel. The action did not reassure her.

"What the hell do you expect me to do with this?" Daniel started to place the knife on the coffee table.

Seth stopped him. He grabbed the hand holding the knife and pulled Daniel towards him. It all happened so fast. Daniel couldn't stop Seth. The knife was embedded in Seth's abdomen up to the hilt. Rachel screamed. Matcher leaped out of the bean bag. Jeff tried to move, but winced and sat back down. Seth let go of Daniel's hand.

"You're fucking mad," Daniel yelled, as he stared at the knife.

Blood oozed around the hilt of the knife and stained the

front of Seth's shirt. He pulled out the knife. Matcher had returned from the kitchen with a towel to press against the wound. Then, Seth lifted up his shirt. As they watched, the wound healed. The blood was still there as evidence of what had occurred but the skin edges joined leaving nothing but a smooth line. Then he sliced across his palm and up his arm to the elbow. The cut went so deep that the muscle bone and sinews could be seen. Again it closed. Each layer slowly reaching out and pulling its opposite edge until the wound was healed

"Do you want more?" Seth offered the knife to anyone who wanted it.

Daniel and Matcher sat down, shaking their heads. Daniel trembled. Jeff placed an arm around his partner's shoulders. Seth sat down next to Cara. He took her hand in his; entwining their fingers. If what he had done had hurt him he didn't show it. At that moment she realized he would do whatever he had to if it meant being with her.

"I love Cara. I'd never hurt her. I am who I say I am and I can't change that." Seth looked at her, his gaze obviously searching her face for a glimmer of what she might be feeling. She hoped her care for him showed through.

"I love Seth too. I also want to find out what happened to Shona." Cara squeezed his hand.

Seth leaned over and kissed her gently on the lips. Her heart swelled. She couldn't keep the smile from her face.

Jeff shook his head. "I think we're all going mad and having a joint hallucination. If that's not the case, we'll help in any way we can," Jeff said. "Right, Daniel?"

After a moment, Daniel nodded reluctantly. "I need a drink and a big one." He went to the kitchen and came back with a bottle of whiskey and six glasses.

"So, what did you find out, Seth?" Cara asked.

"His collection is impressive. He even has some of my earlier pieces. I haven't seen a few of those for over one hundred years. He's commissioned a piece from me for a friend. He also gave me a dagger to repair." Seth pulled a package from inside his jacket and handed it to Cara. "He might be able to help us find the killer."

Her stomach clenched in a knot when she unwrapped the item. Horrified, she found the dagger she had seen so many times in her dreams. If she had ever doubted being a witch in the past the thought was gone. The dagger held power and she could feel its evil influence. It was reaching out like a suffocating vine to grab her. Her body went cold and her hands clammy and if she didn't put the thing down she would pass out. She placed it back on the table.

Seth reached across and squeezed her hand. "Are you all right? You look pale."

"I'll be fine. What are you going to do?" Cara sipped her drink. The whiskey burned the back of her throat. She never wanted to feel that clawing darkness again.

"I'll fix it. I made it a long time ago and it led to Rosie's death. I won't make that mistake again. I'll go back and find out who asked him to have it repaired. If he won't tell me, then I'll beat it out of him," Seth replied.

"You had a copy at the forge. Couldn't you just give him that?" Cara asked.

"I destroyed it."

Cara wondered why he would have done such a thing. Was there something else he wasn't telling her?

"I'll go back to the forge in the morning to start the repair."

"Promise me you'll let me know when you're going back to Vincent's." Cara caught his hand with hers.

"I promise," Seth said.

JEFF AND DANIEL had gone home. Rachel and Matcher were on the pull-out sofa in the living room. After Seth had made love to her, he slept but Cara couldn't. Was she right not to tell him everything about the book and that she suspected Vincent was the killer?

After all Seth had lost someone too. Didn't he have a right to know? Cara hesitated. She couldn't lose him. Someone loved her, and for the first time in her life she was starting to like herself. She would go back tomorrow and find something that would make Detective Seps accept Vincent was the killer.

As Seth slept beside her she considered that none of this made sense. What did make sense was that she wouldn't let Seth die. This way she might have thirty or forty years with him rather than two days.

Seth turned over and opened his eyes. "You're awake. What's wrong?"

"Nothing, nothing at all." Cara pulled back the blankets and moved on top of him.

# TWENTY-THREE

Before Seth left, Cara made him promise again not to go to Vincent's alone. To keep her mind occupied, she made Matcher and Rachel pancakes. Why couldn't everything be like cooking? It was simple and made sense. If you added the wrong ingredient things turned out differently? Sometimes it worked sometimes it didn't. She wasn't prepared to take that chance with Seth's life. Matcher turned on the television to watch breakfast news.

"Do you want lemon juice or maple syrup?" Cara called from the kitchen. They ignored her as they stared at the television screen. Hearing the words the newsman spouted brought bile to her throat.

"The woman's body was found at Avonmouth. Police suspect the victim was thrown from the Coronation Road footbridge. The perpetrator must have hoped it would go out to sea on the strong tides. Police have not clarified yet. It is believed the body was mutilated in a similar way to the other recent slasher murders. It is thought she might have been there at least three days."

The newscast continued with news on a by-election in

the area. Cara mechanically placed the serving dish of pancakes down on the table. Rachel looked pale and didn't touch them. Matcher loaded his plate and topped it with syrup.

Rachel kicked him in the shin. "How can you eat?"

"What?"

Rachel shook her head. "Guys. I'll never understand them."

"He's a killer, you know that. I'm sorry, Cara. It's months since Shona died. Any evidence would be long gone. With this recent murder, he may have left some clues. You have to work out some way you can convince the police he's involved." Matcher shoved pancakes in his mouth, syrup running down his chin.

"We left some platters behind." Cara's hands shook. Suddenly, she didn't feel so brave anymore. Will you come with me, Matcher?"

"Sure. I'll take Rachel home and then I'll be back."

It wasn't lost on Cara how Rachel stiffened at the mention of home. From what she had heard her mother and stepfather were fighting and she was caught in the middle.

THEY PARKED OUTSIDE of Vincent's and sat. If they were going to do something, they needed to do it now.

"What you gonna do then?" Matcher said biting his nails. His fringe was back over his face. "Go home?"

"No, we have to do this today." Cara took a deep breath. "Okay, let's move."

Stephan answered the door. Some people spent their lives looking down their noses at others. This man was one of them.

"We were passing, and thought we could pick up the platters. I know Vincent said he would have them returned, but I thought we would save you the hassle."

"Mr. Blatchford is not in at present, but I suppose it would be acceptable. They're in the kitchen. Follow me."

Cara had expected Vincent, but Stephan might be easier to handle. She could keep him talking while Matcher went searching on the pretense of using the loo. When she listened to the conversation last night, she discovered that Stephan thought he was a worldwide authority on wine.

"Are these some of the special wines you mentioned? There were quite a few people appreciative of a good drop. When I was leaving the platters in the sitting room, several faces lit up when you said you planned to open a bottle of red."

Cara knew she had hit the right spot with the grin on Stephan's face. She didn't miss the fact he looked towards the kitchen door.

"I'm sure Matcher will be back in a minute. He's on one of those organic vegetarian high fiber diets. New age stuff. As a cook, I know all you need to eat is a good range of decent food, but he won't listen."

Stephan screwed up his nose, but his attention soon went back to the wine in front of him. "That would be the Grange Hermitage you heard everyone discussing. It's an Australian wine but some people are so insular and refuse to look outside of Europe."

"I love Australian wine."

Matcher walked back in and Stephan gave him the appropriate look of distaste. She noticed the almost imperceptible shake of the head from Matcher.

"I presume you're ready to go then," Stephan said, picking up a case of the wine.

"Do you need some help to take these back to the cellar? We could help before we go."

"Thank you."

He looked at Matcher's hands as he touched one of the cases. He probably thought the wine was contaminated forever. Cara followed him and Matcher down the stairs to the cellar.

She didn't like the smell. It might have been faint but as a cook she could pick up the slight odor of blood. There was so much wine. Racks covering most walls of the room. Down one side was a table on which she placed her two bottles. Her head spun. Her bag fell to the floor as if in slow motion. Her vision blurred.

THE BLOOD ENTICED her to another level of ecstasy. Her nostrils flared at the stimulation. Staring at her hands, she saw blood coating them with a red hue. She gazed down at a dressing gown.

She was in Vincent's mind reliving the murder. The body of the woman in front of her was already mutilated, but she felt the frenzy build. She had to rip the woman apart. Rings, a necklace and bracelets were torn off and thrown aside.

This filth shouldn't be adorned by such precious metals. She grabbed the blade and stabbed repeatedly. Slashing the abdomen with such force the dead body jolted with each stab and thrust.

"Cara? Are you all right?"

Matcher's voice brought her back to reality. She knelt on the floor, her bag's contents strewn nearby. She couldn't stop shaking at what she had seen in Vincent's mind. She never wanted to go there again.

"You look pale." Matcher's face was full of concern.

"I'm fine, just a bit dizzy. Skipping breakfast will do it every time."

Stephan ushered them up the stairs, to the kitchen for their platters and out the front door. Cara took in a deep breath of fresh air as soon as they were out of the house.

"Okay, what the hell was that all about?" Matcher said the words under his breath as they walked to the gate.

"I'll tell you in the car."

"So?" Matcher folded his arms across his chest as he scowled at her. "You scared the shit out of me."

"I had one of the visions I told you about. In this one, I was in Vincent's mind. He was in that cellar killing a young woman. She had a bracelet with the name Melanie engraved on it."

"You need to tell the police what you saw. They can go in there and find DNA or something, and he'll be locked up."

"The only reason I know it's possibly the dead woman from the river, is because of my vision. The police aren't going to raid Vincent's house because of that. It's the same as before. You see that his aura is different. That won't stand up in court either. I see him killing people and believe he's as long lived as Seth. The police will just think we're mad."

"Maybe they'll identify her."

"I doubt it. Before my vision stopped, I was cutting off fingers and her face was so badly beaten." Cara's hand went to her mouth to stop herself vomiting.

"You're sick having things like that going through your head. You've been watching too much CSI. If you go back there, you'll end up chopped up like everyone else. By the way, can you explain to me why I'm talking about chopped up bodies so calmly?"

"Do you think I like this? Maybe the police can match any blood in there to her DNA. If Vincent had touched it too, then his DNA will be on it as well. It would give Seps a reason to go in there and hopefully find something else."

"Do these guys have different DNA than the rest of us?"

"I don't know. It's not a subject I happen to have discussed with Seth. The thing is the police wouldn't have Vincent's DNA on record. Unless I can convince them he's involved this is going nowhere. All I have is our visions and auras to get them interested." Cara paused. "They'll decide we're new-age nut-jobs."

"We need something more," Matcher said.

"Wait a minute," Cara said. "Remember the paintings. I bet they are of the women he has killed. He was painting another one, which he wouldn't let me see. It must be Shona. When I saw her at the morgue, she wasn't wearing her butterfly ring. She never took it off. I bet he took it as one of his mementoes." She couldn't keep the anger out of her voice.

Cara pulled up outside Matcher's flat. Rachel waited on the front steps, a big bag at her feet. She was crying.

"It looks like she has left home. I'll call you later." Matcher got out of the van. "Don't do anything." He rushed over and hugged Rachel.

Cara struggled to pull her thoughts together. She managed to remain calm driving home, but as soon as she got into her flat, she started to shake. Vincent really was the killer. She had no doubt of that now. He had killed Shona. Cara shuddered. Somehow, she had to make him pay.

The phone rang when she walked in the door. The

sound made her jump. She didn't answer it. It was Seth. A part of her wanted to pick the receiver up so much. To talk to him was to be near him. Instead, she opted to let the machine take the call and just listened.

"Cara. It's Seth. I've finished fixing the dagger. I will pick you up at five to go to Vincent's. I reckon we're close. I truly believe he knows who killed Shona and Rosie." Click.

The phone rang again. This time she hurried to answer, but it wasn't Seth. Cara shivered when she heard Vincent's voice.

"Cara, I'm so sorry I missed you earlier. Stephan said you were unwell. I hope you're feeling better now?"

"Yes, I'm much better now. I hope you were pleased with the food and service last night."

"I was more than pleased. I've a few people coming this evening about seven. Some are thinking of employing your company, especially one of my associates. I wondered if you could pop in and talk to her."

"Yes, that would be fine. Can I ask who?"

"Patricia Palmer. A few of my friends phoned her after last night. She wants to meet you. You know what these movie stars are like about their privacy."

"I'd love to come."

"I'm expecting them to arrive around seven, so I'll see you at six then."

"That will be fine." She was proud of her calm tone and grateful he couldn't see how scared she felt as her hands shook.

---

AS SOON AS she replaced the receiver, she collapsed on the sofa. Merlin came and sat next to her and head-butted her arm. She scratched him. He flopped on her and started purring. His life was so simple. Hers was anything but.

Last night Seth had said he loved her in front of all of her friends. She believed him, but she also knew he had been driven by vengeance for over a hundred years. He needed to find Rosie's killer and avenge her death.

Cara drew a ragged breath. She had been in his life for such a short space of time. She wanted to believe that love could cut out the past, but it wouldn't. Seth could not let Rosie's killer live on, no matter how much he loved her. He was determined to protect society from people like Vincent. And she was just like him, Cara thought. She would not let Shona's killer live on either. She knew what she needed to do.

CARA DIDN'T HAVE any nails left by the time she got through to Inspector Seps. She was becoming like Matcher chewing on her nails.

"Ms. O'Donovan, how can I help you?"

"I need to talk to you. I think I may have a lead on who killed Shona. He may also have had something to do with the body you found in the river."

"If you'd like to come down to the station, then we can take your information."

"I can't do that. What I know you can't put down on an official statement."

"You're being very cryptic."

"All I ask is that you trust me. You may find the killer. If you come to my house at five thirty, I'll take you to him."

SHE WATCHED out the window when Seth pulled up on his bike. It felt like an invisible hand squeezed her heart. It seemed to take forever for him to arrive at her apartment door. When he walked inside, she ran into his arms. The touch of his body against hers almost made her break down and tell him everything. She couldn't. She had to be strong for both of them.

"If I'd known you were going to miss me this much, I would have come back sooner."

He gazed down at her. Cara knew that look. It was the one he had when he tried to work out what she was thinking. Maybe, there was a reason she had so many sessions with Jessica. Here he was in front of her, no longer a dream, but all man and all hers. Looking at his face as he gazed into her eyes, she melted. His lips touched hers. The rest of the world drifted away, but it didn't last.

Seth walked over to the breakfast bar. He put down a cloth wrapped item, the dagger. He wouldn't be distracted tonight.

"Well, show me then." She feigned eagerness.

Seth slowly peeled back the cloth, revealing the dagger. He eyed it with such reverence. He was right. It was beautiful but evil. The blade shone where he had polished it and she could make out words etched into it in a foreign language. She shivered as the sense of malevolence reached out for her once again. She would not touch it again if she didn't have to.

"You're an artist, like Rembrandt," Cara said. She didn't dare touch it. Instead, she stepped closer and stared at the knife again. Her eyes watered at the thought that Vincent would have killed Shona with this. She had to make him pay.

Seth smiled. "He wasn't appreciated until after he died.

I just fixed this, that's all." Seth wrapped up the dagger. Leaving it, he picked up the coffee mug Cara placed next to him. He sipped the hot liquid as he walked over to the couch.

Cara sat down next to him. She placed her mug on the table. "How are you going to get him to tell you who ordered the repair?"

Seth laughed, but didn't answer. It wasn't reassuring. He stared at the wrapped dagger on the coffee table in front of them. He didn't speak. How could she know what it must be like to suffer so long? She had to take control.

He might not see it now, but he would later. She did what she had to do because she cared. He finished his coffee, placing the empty mug on the table.

"Seth, how will you make him talk?" Cara asked again.

"I'm not going to risk our lives by going in there and slaughtering him to find out who killed Rosie. He's my clue. I just need to make him talk." Seth's head flopped back on the couch. He looked sideways at her and grinned. "I love your eyes. Have I told you that?"

"No." She smiled back at him. She hoped he couldn't see the tears forming.

"I lose myself in your eyes. You make me forget the pain that has lasted too long." He shook his head and tried to lift it, but failed. "Cara? What have you done?"

He grabbed her hand. His grip weakened as he stared at her. Cara's eyes watered as she watched a tear flow down his cheek. His eyes closed as he fell asleep.

She snuggled close to him and held on tight as she shook. That was one silver lining to having been depressed and sick. When she couldn't sleep because of the pain, the doctors prescribed strong sedatives. She had crushed up enough to put an elephant to sleep. It was lucky that he liked sugar so she could cover the bitterness.

She leaned closer, kissing his cheek. "I love you so much, Seth. I didn't think I could feel this about anyone again. I know you want to find a way to be like the rest of us, but that way I'd lose you forever. You think you need me so much, but I wasn't really alive until you came along. I know you'll live on after I go, and I'm being selfish. I'm sorry. Please don't hate me."

# TWENTY-FOUR

Inspector Seps waited outside her flat. Fifteen minutes later when she finished her story, he shook his head at her and glanced at his watch.

"Ms. O'Donovan, Cara. I know you've been through a rough time recently with the family deaths, and then Shona's murder. You can't expect me to believe this. I've been up since two this morning dealing with the body we found yesterday. At this moment, my team thinks I've gone home to see my sick wife."

Cara clenched her fists. "I know some bad things have happened but I'm not lying." This wasn't going well, surprise, surprise!

"You're having counseling, aren't you?" Inspector Seps raised an eyebrow. "Are you taking any drugs that could cause hallucinations?"

*"No." Okay, snapping at the cop isn't such a good idea right now either.*

"So you want me to go in this man's house and accuse him of being a murderer because you had a vision. You think he paints pictures of dead women and has a book with a dagger in it." Inspector Seps shook his head. "None of this will stand up in court."

Well, if he was going to put it that way, then he was right about how crazy all of this sounded.

"If you can get to that room and see if Shona's picture is there and her ring, then you'll have proof. I saw a bracelet with the name Melanie in my vision. Do you know the name of the girl who was killed yet?"

"There have been a few names mentioned of missing persons. As yet we haven't made a definite identification. The name you mentioned piques my interest, but you're not giving me much to go on."

"But, you came anyway," Cara said, slightly irritated.

He nodded, unsmiling. "I'll give you an hour. After that, I'm headed back to the station. I'm not involving anyone else. Your proof is a bit strange to say the least. If we find anything, I'll call for back-up."

When they arrived, Cara rang the doorbell. Vincent answered. His smile disappeared when he saw she was not alone.

"Cara, I wasn't expecting you to bring someone with you."

"This is Inspector Seps. I asked him to come. He's been looking into my cousin's murder. Boscombe, the man she worked for, mentioned your name. I told Inspector Seps I knew you. I was sure you wouldn't mind him asking some questions."

"Of course not, do come in. I'll be happy to help."

As Cara expected, no one else was there, not even Stephan. Vincent led them through to his office.

"Please. Take a seat, Inspector. I'm ready to answer anything."

"Ms. O'Donovan wasn't quite accurate in what she said.

In fact, she made some statements to me today that could indicate you had some involvement in the murder of Shona Williams."

Vincent glared at Cara for a moment before he regained his composure. She shivered. She was the lamb, he was the lion, and she was in his den. *Stay calm*, she told herself. She was safe. She had a policeman with her. Vincent was too clever to risk anything.

"There must be some mistake. I don't believe I ever met her. Cara did mention she had a cousin who worked in Bath, but I never pursued it any further."

Vincent's eyes narrowed as he turned towards her. "Cara, I thought we had a professional relationship. Personally, I can't understand how you could have any grounds to think I could be involved in any way with your cousin's death."

"What about the room with paintings of the women you've killed?" Cara blurted. She had intended to keep quiet and let the Inspector do the talking, but she had a sinking feeling in the pit of her stomach that Vincent would worm his way out of everything. She couldn't let that happen. He might come after her. Well, Seth had better be a good protector.

"Inspector, I like to paint," Vincent said. "I can assure you that I don't paint dead women. This is all very melodramatic, but I'll be happy to show you my studio."

Cara followed them upstairs. The room was the same as before with paintings around the walls. One painting was on an easel. It was covered up. Before Vincent could protest, Cara ran over and pulled off the sheet. It wasn't Shona. In fact it was just a rough sketch and the face was not clearly defined.

Her heart sank. She couldn't be wrong. She couldn't.

Too much depended on this. Inspector Seps came and stood next to her. Vincent covered up the sketch.

"I think I've been very understanding so far. You've come into my house. You accused me of being involved in a murder. Now, you touch my private possessions. Inspector, unless you would like to obtain a search warrant, I believe it would be appropriate if you leave. Have no doubt. I will be talking to my lawyer about this visit."

"I'm sorry we troubled you. Ms. O'Donovan has been under a lot of strain recently. We've had no success in this investigation. We won't bother you again." Inspector Seps mobile rang. He walked away from them, past the easel and towards the window. "Excuse me one moment."

Sensing Vincent staring at her, made the hair rise on the back of Cara's neck. She kept her gaze on the Inspector. Her hands were clammy and the bravado of earlier had completely disappeared.

"And that's a definite identification. I'll be there soon." Inspector Seps turned back. "I need to return to the station. Please excuse us, Mr. Blatchford."

Cara wanted to scream, but it wouldn't do any good. She had played her hand and needed something else.

As Inspector Seps walked around the easel, he stopped and peered down.

Cara moved next to him and saw a paint brush on the small shelf at the bottom of the picture. Next to it was a blood splattered bracelet with the name Melanie engraved on it. Being frozen to the spot and having a lump in your throat wasn't the best option right now, but it was all Cara had.

"May I ask you where you came by this bracelet?" The Inspector looked up at Vincent who had approached and stood beside him.

Vincent didn't answer. Instead, he swung the large glass jar that he'd held behind his back. The inspector fell to the floor. Blood from a gash across his forehead spread on the cream carpet. Vincent smiled down at the body on the floor.

Cara reached into her bag for the dagger. It might be her only chance.

"You're wasting your time. It won't work on me. You have to be immortal and I'm the only one left. I'll prove it to you." He lunged forward, causing the blade to be pushed into his chest.

She let go of the dagger. She spun. She ran for the door. He was on her before she reached it. He knocked her down. His hands closed on her throat. She kicked and thumped as hard as she could. No effect. For once she wished her mother was outside and could hear her screams. As he squeezed tighter, the image of his grinning face disappeared.

---

CARA FELT something hard beneath her back. Where was she? Vincent leaned over her. She opened her eyes but struggled to focus. He was saying something, but she couldn't concentrate. She drifted out of consciousness again.

Next time he appeared there was a stinging sensation in her arm. She tried to move. She couldn't. Staring at the wooden beams of the cellar roof, she forced herself to concentrate. Her arms were bent back at the elbow and there were cords around her wrists.

Vincent stood beside her. There was an intravenous needle in her arm. She tried to move her feet. Cords cut into her ankles. Tears welled in her eyes and ran down the sides of her face. Before, when she had been sick, she imagined dying. The scenario had her mother and father sitting in the corner looking appropriately sad.

Daniel and Jeff, and more recently Matcher and Seth would tell her not to give up. She intended to keep Seth from dying, but now she would be the next victim. She shivered.

"Are you cold? I would do something. There hardly seems any point." Vincent moved away and sat next to a small table set up with wine and glasses. He picked up the glass and smelled the aroma. A smile of contentment came to his face as he sipped. "You know my recent kills haven't been as rewarding as they used to be."

"You're insane," Cara whispered.

"It's most frustrating," Vincent ignored her. "I like killing. I think it was something I inherited from my father. My mother was often sick when I was young. Father had needs and gratified them with the servants. There was one who used to be nice to me. Her name was Harriet. She made the mistake of saying no to my father."

Vincent sipped his wine. "I was ten years old when I hid and watched him beat Harriet to death with his belt. I shed a tear, but only one. The excitement I experienced observing her death took over. My heart was beating so fast I thought my father would hear it. It made me hard. The thought of your impending death is doing the same. I started with animals and birds, and then eventually progressed to humans. I had friends once who were equally willing to partake in the killing, but alas, they're no longer here." Vincent stood up and made his way towards her.

"You won't get away with this." She spat at him. The spittle landed on his arm. "Someone will stop you."

"I don't think so, Cara. Not now, I have you. You look

like Rosie from long ago. I searched for her sister the next day. She was gone. I wanted to kill her as well as an insurance policy in case the immortality started to fade. Someone said they saw her board the coach for Bristol. I wandered the streets there, looking for a sign of her, but to no avail."

"She was smarter than you thought," Cara hissed.

"A ship left for Cork the day after I killed Rosie. As time went by I assumed her sister was on board. Needless to say I didn't find her, though I spent many months trying. Then all these years later, one of her descendants is here to give me the gift I've been waiting for." Vincent finished his wine.

"I'm not giving you anything."

"I couldn't believe my luck when I saw you at Kathleen's book launch. I wouldn't have to share the power this time and I'd be able to live for another 500 years. Kathleen was most annoying. She died before I could kill her. If I didn't know better I'd have said she did it on purpose."

"She won. She defeated you. So will I." Cara wouldn't give him the satisfaction of seeing how afraid she was. "Why have you waited so long?"

"I like to plan things, and there were a few problems. You were right by the way. I had painted her."

Vincent went over to the far side of the cellar and came back with a painting. It was Shona and tied to the frame was her butterfly ring. "She was one of the problems. She damaged my dagger. It's my own fault. I wanted to play with you by killing someone close to you. By the way, I hope you appreciated my work."

He leered at her and smirked. "I hear you had to identify her body. She didn't have your beautiful and unusual eye coloring. I knew she would only give me temporary respite. I needed you, dearest Cara. The party was an excuse to get to know you. Of course you've brought everything forward."

Vincent sneered as he walked across and placed his hand around her neck and into her hair. "It was very rude of you to get the police involved, but I'll think of something. He is out cold. I don't think he'll come to the rescue any time soon."

"I know that someone will stop you, some day." She turned her head. She tried to bite his hand.

He laughed as he slapped her face and jerked away. "I intend to travel again. It's been a long time since I was in South America. No one notices another dead body amongst the drug dealers over there. I'll be able to kill as many people as I want."

He walked over and inserted the syringe into the intravenous access in her arm. He withdrew blood and squirted it into a small dish. Pulling the sheet covering her body back, he stared at her. His face showed no emotion as if he was empty of feelings. It filled her with fear as she tried to control her breathing.

"Your skin is so pale, but we can always add a bit of color." He ran a finger across her scar. "I see I'm not the first to cleave your skin apart. Don't worry. I can assure you I'll be the last."

She tried to move. It caused the ropes to dig deeper. Vincent dipped his finger in the blood and started to draw on her. She guessed that he would be tracing the lines he intended for his incisions. He picked up the dagger from the table beside her, the dagger she knew too well. She didn't want to die like this.

She wanted to grow old with Seth. She wanted to see Daniel and Jeff marry. She even wanted to reconcile with her family.

"It was so kind of you to bring the dagger. Seth was to bring it to me." Vincent placed his hand on her breast and squeezed hard.

She winced, but refused to show any other reaction. She wouldn't let him win any more than he already had.

"You've become intimate with him, haven't you? I watched the way you two looked at each other during my party. How fitting that he repaired the dagger that performed the deed. I wonder if there's a way to draw him here. I could render him unconscious. Then, I'd call the police and say he had come here as a jealous lover and murdered you while you waited in naked my bed for my return. They would have caught the slasher-killer and would be happy. That plan will still work. I could find you all here when I returned and I restrained him. I could say he told me he killed your cop friend because he caught him in the act."

It took every ounce of strength she had, but she had to let him know he would not succeed. "You won't get away with this."

"Oh, but I will. I've started over many times as a new person. This was the first time in many years that I actually used my real first name. Anyway, it's exciting to recreate yourself."

Pain seared through her as he cut across her forehead. She tried to wrench away. He held her face firmly with one hand. He cut again and again. The blood flowed into her hair and eyes. It blurred her vision.

She saw him climb onto the table. He straddled her body. Was he going to rape her? No, it was worse. She struggled not to scream when the blade bit into her chest. Then he dragged the tip of the dagger toward her breast. She couldn't hold back. Agony speared through her. She screamed.

She thrust her hips up to try and dislodge him in a last ditch effort. It only excited him more. He laughed. Another slice. The world darkened. She felt the knife enter her chest. She couldn't scream anymore. She couldn't fight anymore. At last it was all over.

# TWENTY-FIVE

Matcher had watched Cara drive off and then put his arms around Rachel. "Whatever it is, trust me we can deal with it." He noticed a black garbage bag at her feet. Rachel bent down to pick it up as he opened the door to the house. "What's in it?"

"My clothes and stuff. I'm sorry, I didn't know where else to go. I'll find somewhere else as soon as I can."

Matcher took the bag and went upstairs. Thankfully at this time of the day the guys wouldn't be in. He dumped her stuff in his room. She sat on the edge of his bed with a box of tissues beside her while he went and made coffee. Her aura was full of swirling colors showing emotional turmoil and fear.

"It's about last night, isn't it?"

"Yes, but not really." Rachel blew her nose loudly.

"You know I don't know anyone who can blow their nose as loud as you. It's a somewhat odd, but funny trait."

She smiled and her aura relaxed a little. "I think last night was one of the strangest nights of my life. That was some of the weirdest stuff I've ever seen. If I hadn't been there I'd say your friends were crazy, or I was on a movie set with special effects."

"Was it us? Look, I didn't know it was a first time for you. I wouldn't have pushed it, you know."

"I'm not upset about that Matcher. I should have told you that I wanted to since we met."

"You're kidding me. You've stayed at friends' all night before, haven't you?"

"Yes, but my step-dad didn't believe I was just staying at Cara's. He came there this morning and saw me leaving with you. When I walked in at home, Mum wasn't there and neither were my stepbrothers. My step-dad walked in. His knuckles were red. That meant he'd given mum a belting last night. I should have been there. He tended to lay off her if I was around." Rachel sipped her coffee.

"Go on," Matcher encouraged.

"I went to my room but he burst in. He called me a whore and said horrible things about Mum. That he had only stayed because he thought he would lay something a bit younger, but didn't want spoiled goods. He said the kids were probably not his anyway. From the look of you, I probably had AIDS. I'm sorry."

"Rachel, that's just him. I've had so much sickness in my life, I'm not going to take any risks. As far as I know I'm clean. If I had thought there was any chance I wouldn't have."

"I know."

"He said I was to get out. When I tried to pack my suitcase, he grabbed it from me and emptied it all over the floor. He said I could take my stuff in a garbage bag. I just wanted to be out of there. I think Mum and the boys must be at

Aunty Meredith's, but I don't know. I'm sorry, Matcher. You have all this other crazy stuff. You don't need me like this now."

Matcher went and got the phone. He gave it to her and left Rachel to talk to her mum. Why is it when you think your life is insane and can't get worse it does? He wasn't sad she was here. He had loved every minute last night. The guys were right. She did have a good rack. Shit, he was an asshole thinking that right now. Everything was crazy. Cara trying to get Vincent locked up. Seth getting Daniel to stab him, and surviving.

Rachel had hung the phone back up and came back to Matcher's room. She lay next to him on his small bed. They just cuddled for a while saying nothing. He knew she would talk some more when she was ready. Her aura was glowing so much more since she had talked to her Mum. He didn't want to jeopardize that.

"Mum said she was sorry. She said she has let me down. She let us all down. She said she never believed she deserved my dad and then Pat was the only one interested. She always thought it had been a fluke. When things went wrong, she felt that was the way it should probably have been in the first place. I told her I'm staying with friends for a few days and then I'll sort something out. I think she guessed it was you, but said nothing," Rachel went quiet. "Can I stay?"

"Yeh, the guys won't mind. We could try and get a place together, or you move back with your Mum. Whatever's okay with you." Matcher hoped she would stay.

'I know it's daft, but I liked being at Cara's with her crazy immortal man, and you seeing stuff around people. Your place and Cara's are the two places that feel good to me right now. Thanks for everything Matcher." Rachel reached up and placed her hand on his cheek.

It felt nice, and he knew where it would lead. His mouth came down and touched hers. Her lips parted and he wanted more. He knew he should be thinking of Cara now, but he needed this and so did Rachel.

Matcher yawned and stretched. His arm had gone dead. He was spooning Rachel. His little bed wasn't so little after all. It was dark even though the curtains were open.

It was the TV on in the other room that had made him wake up. Looking at his clock beside the bed, he could see it was eight. Hell, he had meant to phone Cara. He was worried she would have gone back to Vincent's on her own.

Easing himself out of bed, he found his mobile and called her number. No one answered. He had to go and check. If she wasn't there, then he would go to Vincent's. He started to dress.

Rachel turned over and yawned. "Are you going to Cara's?"

"Yes and don't ask, because you're not coming. You have had enough crap today. I'll sort this out. I'll tell the guys on the way out your staying for a few days."

Seth's bike was out in front of Cara's apartment. The lights were not on in her flat. Maybe they were in bed, but Matcher didn't think so, not on a day like this. He should have been there for her. He just hoped she had not done anything foolish as he pressed the buzzer.

No answer. He pressed it again. He wouldn't take his finger off until someone answered or the neighbors called the police.

SETH'S HEAD thumped with the buzzing. Why the hell wouldn't the noise stop? Opening his eyes felt impossible. Had someone weighted his eyelids with coins? He was at Cara's, but when he finally opened his eyes, he couldn't see her anywhere. Why didn't she answer the door? He tried to stand. His knees gave way. He fell forward onto the floor. The room spun. The buzzer droned on incessantly.

He finally managed to stand, stagger to the door and answer the intercom. "What?"

"Seth." Matcher's voice echoed through the intercom. "Let me up."

Seth pushed the security button, opened the apartment door and stumbled back to the couch. When Matcher entered, he turned on the lights. Then, he checked all the rooms.

"You look like shit. I can guess what she gave you. My cupboard used to have the same concoction of sedatives and pain-killers when I was sick."

"Where's Cara?" Seth asked shaking his head in a bid to clear it of double vision.

"My guess would be she's gone back to Vincent's. What time did you get here?"

"I don't know." He wanted to throw up.

"Think, damn it, Seth." Matcher grabbed his shoulders and shook them.

Seth's head started to clear. It was the anger building inside. People didn't touch him unless he said so. His hands went into fists. What was going on here? Matcher looked scared.

"Come on, Seth. What time was it?"

"Five, I got here at five."

"It's nearly nine. Come on, you need to splash that face of yours and wake up. I'll drive you. You're in no fit state to ride that great monstrosity of a bike at the moment. I'll tell you what happened this morning on the way."

Matcher helped him up from the seat and dragged him to the bathroom. With his head over the bath and cold water running into his hair, Seth started to recall what happened. Why had she drugged him?

When he returned to the living room, he found Matcher with a pile of paper in his hand. "Cara didn't tell you everything," the younger man said.

"I figured that much out for myself. We need to go."

"Not yet." Matcher met his gaze. "The other night she told us about a book she'd stolen from Vincent's. This is a copy of the pages. She put the book back on the night of the party. She believed Vincent was the killer. She didn't want you to know. The book says if you try to kill him, you'll die yourself."

"That wouldn't be such a bad thing."

"To you maybe. When we went to Vincent's this morning, she thought she saw some evidence that would link him to the most recent murder. Other people have lost loved ones too."

"Then why are we standing here wasting time?" Seth snatched the papers from Matcher's hands.

Matcher paused in the kitchen to grab a torch. "I know where the spare set of keys is kept and I saw the van down front. You can read on the way."

Seth sat in the van and started to read. All the years had led to this. He thought he would be angry. Instead, he was scared, not of Vincent, but at the thought of losing Cara. If Vincent hurt her, dying would be the easy solution to this situation. Matcher didn't interrupt him as he read. They pulled in around the corner from Vincent's house.

"I just thought of something. If she left the van behind, how did she get here?" Matcher asked.

"There's your answer. That's the police inspector's car. I've seen it outside of Cara's flat before. I'd like to think it's a reassuring sign. If Vincent's been alive as long as I have and can't be killed, he won't give up easily.

# TWENTY-SIX

Pain, the agony she was in meant she was still alive. Her heart beat wildly. Her breathing was too rapid. She wanted oblivion back. A voice cut through the agony. It was Matcher.

"Cara."

He leaned over her. He tugged at the rope tethering one of her wrists. As she gazed up, she saw him disappear from view. There was a dull thud. Had someone hurt him? Thrown him into a wall? She tried to raise her head but her body would not respond.

Anger welled inside her. It wasn't like anything she'd felt before. Not the anger at the injustice of losing her baby, or her parents indifference, or people hurting her friends. It was sheer violent rage at something being taken.

Then it was gone again. Warmth flowed through her. The discomfort eased. She must be dying and soon the hurt would be gone. The ache finally eased. She was leaving this world for good. The realm between life and death were close. Welcoming darkness beckoned. Someone called her back. A face appeared in the black surrounding her, but this time it wasn't Matcher.

It was Rosie. She didn't want someone in her head who had loved Seth as much as she did. It was an unworthy thought. Still, it was true. Death was near. He would live on to love someone else. She didn't want to live forever. She had just wanted to love him now. Why couldn't they leave her alone? The voice in her head was insistent.

*Cara, come back. Seth needs you. He'll die without you.*

It was the only thing anyone would say that made a difference. Matcher, where was Matcher? In some part of her brain, she remembered seeing him.

*Seth is here, Cara. I wanted my killer to pay. I made Seth stay because I was angry, angry at him, angry at life. Anger's a powerful emotion and I thought it was right. He's learned to love again with you. Let me heal you. I know Seth.*

*If you're gone, he'll want to die. His rage will turn him into something dark. I never understood the depth of his feel-ings. He was so scared to open up to anyone, but he opened to you. Each time you've been together, he's given you a part of himself. We haven't much time.*

Cara found herself floating near the ceiling. Her body below her was a mass of skin and blood. The blade was still partially embedded in her chest. Seth bent over her.

"I love you, Cara. I'm so sorry. I let you down." He pulled out the dagger and turned away.

The muscles in her chest clenched in spasms. Her real body arched off the table. She was healing. It was a slow process as if someone was using a red hot iron to seal her skin. The slashed edges joined together as if by some invis-ible surgeon. She watched as her real body's jaw tightened as she clenched her teeth against the onslaught.

*You must return now.*

Cara glanced to her side and saw Rosie.

*Save him for both of us. If Vincent dies I'll be free. I'm sorry, Cara.*

What was she not telling her? Why was she sorry? It wasn't her fault. *Will Seth live?* Cara sent out the thought.

*He can live but he may not remember. He may return in his mind to the night I gave him the power. You will have to make him remember your love.*

Now, there was noise, suffering, and the smell of spilt wine and blood. She couldn't ask any more before she was thrown back into her real form. Cara tensed every muscle in her body. The torment rippled through her again. Her body strained. She gasped for air in her lungs as if she had never breathed before or would again.

Her head rolled to the other side. She saw Seth's back. She tried to call out. No words came. He raised a hand in the air, his fist coming down. She heard a thump and a groan. He turned to pick something up from the floor. It was the dagger in his hand.

When he lifted his head, Cara saw bruises on his face, a swollen right eye and blood dripped down his chin. If only he would look at her, she could stop this madness. He moved and she saw Vincent, stripped to the waist and tied to the chair. His face didn't look much better than Seth's.

"Is this bringing back a memory for you, Vincent? I'd forgotten how bad this could feel."

"Who are you?" Vincent asked between groans of pain.

"Me." Seth laughed. "I'm just another long-lived man like you. Did you think you were the only one? It's ironic. I've wanted to die for so long. Something you did to Rosie stopped that. Now I wanted life again. You've taken away Cara. She was the only one who could have kept me from killing you."

"Rosie," Vincent said. Then, he chuckled, blood dribbling from his lip as he did so. "That whore. What were you? Her pimp?"

"I failed her. Now, I've failed Cara."

"Were you the blacksmith who repaired the dagger back then? Twice, you've fixed the blade to kill the women you love. Rather careless, don't you think?"

"You're right. I should've done better by both of them. So, there's only one thing left to do now."

Cara watched as Seth took the dagger and cut into Vincent, slicing him from neck to navel. He gritted his teeth but didn't cry out.

"Look at yourself. You can't do this." Vincent caught his breath for a moment.

Cara saw Seth glance down at his own chest. A line of dark red soaked into the gray t-shirt. Seth laughed, a crazed sound that saddened Cara. He cut again across Vincent's chest, the same way Vincent had marked his victims over the years.

With each cut, Seth's own t-shirt became soaked with blood. Tears coursed down her cheeks. She struggled to yell but, nothing happened. Seth kept laughing through the pain as Vincent screamed with each new cut.

Lifting Vincent's hair, Seth sliced into his forehead three times. Blood ran down over Vincent's face like a curtain of red.

"You'll die too. Don't you understand? I can give you anything. I'm rich. Don't throw away living forever. We can share her power. Just help me finish the ritual. Say the words with me."

No tears were left to fall down her cheeks. Seth placed the point of the blade on Vincent's chest above his heart.

With all her strength, Cara tried to call out. Only a whisper escaped her lips.

"No." The word came in a gasp. The blade was plunged in and blood bubbled from Vincent's lips. His eyes rolled back and he was finally gone.

Seth pulled out the blade. He let it drop to the floor. His knees buckled beneath him. He looked at her. For one moment, their gazes connected. He smiled and collapsed to the floor.

This wasn't fair. Rosie had said she could save him.

"Matcher." She screamed his name over and over and finally it seemed to bring him back to consciousness. Now her voice came back when it was too late.

Matcher stood beside her. He was so pale. He looked as if he would faint. She needed him to be strong. He started to undo the ties on her hands and legs.

"What the hell's happened?" He was shaking.

"Help me over to Seth."

"You don't want to see him." Matcher placed the sheet around her shoulders.

"It's not too late. She said I could save him." Her legs touched the floor and gave out. Matcher supported her. She felt so weak. When she looked down, she still saw blood on her body. Her wounds had healed but she was still giddy from the effects of the blood loss.

Seth lay by Vincent's feet. His face smeared with blood from the cuts on his forehead as his blank eyes looked up. His tanned skin looked ashen. She felt for a pulse at his throat. It was still there, but thready.

Rosie had said she could save him, but how? The dagger lay on the floor. The blade glowed with the power it had consumed. She had an idea. Whether it would work was another thing. Her hands shook. She picked up the blade and sliced into the palm of her hand.

"Shit, Cara. What are you doing? You've lost enough blood already."

Matcher tried to drag her away from Seth, but she stayed firm.

She ripped open the front of Seth's T-shirt with the dagger. She placed her bleeding hand on the wound on his chest. Nothing happened. She wasn't going to lose him, not now, not after everything they had been through. If she couldn't have Seth, then why the hell did Rosie save her?

Cupping her hand she let the blood pool in her palm. She dipped her finger in the sticky red liquid. She painted over the wounds on Seth's body. He shuddered, but nothing more. His blue lips parted as he tried to pull in air. He was still alive, that was enough.

Cara leaned over his bloodstained face and breathed into his slightly parted lips. The reaction was immediate. He inhaled, making a gurgling noise in his throat.

"What the fuck," Matcher yelled, as he moved away.

"I'll second that statement."

Cara turned to see Inspector Seps standing on the bottom step of the stairs. There was awe, not fear in both his and Matcher's faces. When she looked back at Seth he was glowing. The same luminescence was on her skin.

As each wound healed, Seth arched his back. His fists clenched, but no screams came forth. When the skin edges of the final wound joined together, he relaxed. It was only when Matcher hugged her that she realized the glowing had stopped.

Seth didn't move, his eyes remained closed. His chest raised and lowered with each intake of breath. That was all she needed for now.

"One day, I'll tell you what I saw in your auras, but not now," Matcher said, "Hell, Cara. I thought I was fucked up till I met you."

Seth's eyes opened as he struggled to speak. His voice sounded as though he had chewed on gravel. "Cara."

It was the most beautiful sound she had ever heard. He remembered her. That was all she needed to hear. The hand that grasped hers held more strength than she would have thought possible of a man so near death.

"I'm here, Seth. I won't leave you." She smothered his bloodstained face with kisses.

"Look this is all romantic, if somewhat gory at the same time. I mean you brought him back from the almost dead and all. We still need to get out of here. You two may have forgotten that we have a dead body two feet away from us. Plus a Police Inspector watching." Matcher said.

Cara knew she shouldn't, but she found Seth's smile contagious as he looked at Vincent's dead form. She would be happy to watch worms weave their way through Vincent's skin. The dagger lay beside Seth. She felt an almost irresistible urge to hack away at Vincent until all that remained were shreds of what had once been a human being.

Cara looked towards Inspector Seps. "What are you going to tell people?"

"I need to call this in. This goes against all my years of work but no one will believe it anyway. I say we move the body upstairs to his studio. Clean up down here as best you can. Grab that painting of Shona too. I'll then give you ten minutes to get out of here." Inspector Seps rubbed his forehead. "I should have retired last year when I had the chance."

Cara dressed as Matcher grabbed tablecloths from a pile

nearby and started to clean up. He shoved the cloths in a garbage bag as Seth helped the inspector with Vincent's body.

"I'll say it was an anonymous tip off. When I got here he knocked me out. When I woke up he was dead. One of you should write a note left by someone saying he was killing him for revenge for murdering his wife in the past. With the pictures upstairs plus Shona's and the keepsakes, no one will shed a tear that someone played out the same scenario on him."

"Our blood's everywhere." Cara said. "What about our fingerprints, hair, DNA?"

"We will clean up so that nothing is obvious. If they do come down here they will just find multiple blood types, including Shona and Melanie. The others I will suggest were probably just other victims. I must be mad. I have forty years on the force and I've never seen anything like this. I don't want to again either. Do I make myself clear?"

## TWENTY-SEVEN

Seth lay in the back of the van as they drove away. His body ached as if it would never be whole or free from pain again. Looking up, he saw Cara glance back over the seat at him. The rage he felt when he entered the cellar and found Vincent had been overpowering. Matcher had run to Cara, but Vincent threw the boy across the room like a rag doll.

The urge to rip Vincent limb from limb was strong, but it wasn't enough. Hurling Vincent into a wine rack and seeing him collapse to the floor, wasn't enough either. When he turned to Cara, Seth accepted he was too late. She was bloody and lifeless, a knife impaled in her heart.

As he pulled the dagger free, he knew what had to be done. Vincent would die and so would he. It would all come to an end. It had been foolish to ever expect more. Overpowering Vincent was easy, too easy.

As he plunged the dagger into the other man's chest, the darkness of death drew Seth too. A voice he hadn't heard in so long called to him. It was Rosie's telling him to return to Cara. He remembered floating above his dead body with Rosie's ghost next to him. He'd watched Cara cut herself and paint his wounds with her blood. What had he done to deserve such love? This wonderful woman made his heart soar with affection for her

*She loves you so much, Seth. Don't leave her like this.*
*I'm sorry I couldn't save you, Rosie.*
*You have. He's gone and I'm free.*

Cara had breathed life into him. He watched as a beam of light shone from her and attached itself to his floating form. She was drawing him back. He could sense in her mind how much she loved him. His lungs felt as if they would explode as he was drawn back into his body with a jolt. His body arched off of the floor in pain. It meant he was alive.

---

SETH'S HEAD ached as things came into focus. He must have passed out. He was in some kind of moving contraption that made a strange burring noise.

"We're almost home," A woman said. She reached down and grasped his hand. Did he know her? It was dark in the vehicle and he couldn't make her face out.

Home, a picture of a cottage with a forge came to mind. The vehicle stopped and they made their way inside a large building and upstairs. He had expected home to be the cottage. The woman helped him to the bedroom and sat next to him on the bed.

He couldn't keep his eyes open any longer. "I need to go home. Take me home."

"Later. First you need to shower and then rest. It will be all right, Seth. We'll go home tomorrow."

She knew his name. She had eyes like Rosie. One blue, one green but she wasn't Rosie. He had a feeling something bad had happened but the thoughts were just out of his reach as he blacked out again. He stood in the cubicle as the water sprayed him. Everything was strange. The way the water flowed, the lights. His mind struggled through a haze to make sense of it. Peering in the mirror he saw fresh cuts on his body. They were the same cuts he had seen on Rosie. What was happening here? He made his way to the bedroom and hoped sleep would bring some answers.

CARA SLEPT for a few hours after her shower washed away the blood from her body and hair. What she needed now was food. Seth didn't stir as she got up and left the room. Rachel was in the living room and Cara wasn't surprised. If she were Matcher, she would have wanted some closeness and normality around her. When he saw her, Matcher said Daniel was on the way over with Jeff and wanted to know what happened.

When the other men arrived, Cara told them everything and was amazed they actually believed it. It was official. Her friends were now as crazy as she was. The phone rang. Cara picked up the receiver and listened, then agreed. After she hung up, she said, "That was Inspector Seps. Says he needs to talk to me down at the station. This is going to be interesting."

SETH FELT as if he'd been pulled backwards from a dream to wakefulness. A woman perched beside him on a bed. She smiled at him. He didn't know her, but she had a beautiful smile and reminded him of Rosie. If he hadn't been a married man, he could have been tempted by a smile like that. Then, it all came back to him. His wife was dead and Rosie was missing.

Where was he? He should get himself home, sober up and find Rosie before something happened to her. He would never forgive himself if it did.

A light shone above him. It was like nothing he had seen before. A white globe glowed with no evidence of a flame. What was this place? Who was this woman?

"Where am I?" He saw the look of concern pass over the woman's face. She had expected him to know her.

"What do you mean, Seth? You're at my flat." She reached out and touched his arm.

He pulled away. How did she know his name?

"Who are you?" He watched tears form in the woman's eyes.

"What do you mean? I'm Cara."

The name triggered pain. Agony coursed through him. He curled up in a ball, hoping the sensation wouldn't tear him apart. Flashes of memories came to him, disconnected pictures. One thing he remembered was his home, his cottage. He remembered Rosie coming to him in a vision. She was dead. He turned to Cara.

"Can you take me home?"

Through silent tears, she nodded.

---

CARA WAS glad Jeff agreed to ride Seth's bike back to the cottage. Seeing it out in front of the block of flats for the past month had been like having Vincent twist the knife he stabbed into her all over again. Jeff looked well now. It was fun to see Daniel find out something new about his partner. She could see them both out riding some big bike now.

Daniel had driven the van out to the cottage. Janet showed them where to park the bike around the side. She had been polite. She offered them tea and her famous cookies, but Seth stayed in the forge.

"He rarely comes out. Then again, he never did much before. He said he remembers me. At first. I didn't think it was true but now it's different. Maybe my cooking has brought back some memories." Janet shrugged her shoulders.

Cara thought being at the cottage would help the anguish, but it made it worse. How could he not remember what they had together? She wished this was a dream, but she never seemed to wake up. Janet kept talking to Jeff and Daniel. Cara couldn't focus on what they were saying. Maybe, if she ran out there and threw herself into his arms he would recall something. A hand touched hers. It was Janet.

"I was just saying. I don't know how you managed to get him home that day. I struggle to get him in the car. He used to love that bike. Don't know if he'll ever ride it again now. He acts like he's never seen a car or bike before."

Cara heard a door slam outside. Her heart beat wildly even if her brain told her differently. There was no point in getting her hopes up.

"He knows you're here. He won't come in. He goes to ride Dart about this time every afternoon. Then, he goes back to the forge. I've told him he's a fool. He was lucky to find someone like you, but he doesn't understand. If I was him, I'd be locked up by now I'm sure. A person isn't meant to live as long as him."

Cara needed to go, but had one more thing to do. She reached inside her handbag and pulled out an envelope.

"Can you give him this? I've written down everything. Maybe, it will trigger something. If it doesn't, then at least I tried." Cara didn't bother to keep back the tears.

Janet walked around the table and hugged her. "I don't think I should be half as calm as you, my dear. I'd have grabbed a rolling pin and smashed some sense into that stupid head of his."

"I would if I thought it would work."

As they walked over to the van, Cara couldn't ignore the sound of a horse galloping nearby. She remembered the first day they had been together. They had watched his beautiful warm blood running around the field. It seemed like another lifetime. She was a fool but couldn't draw her gaze away from the field near the cottage. He pulled the horse to a halt at the gate.

Their gazes met for a moment. Cara wanted to fool herself, but she couldn't. There was no look of recognition there. If anything there was anger.

Sitting in the van, she fumbled with her seatbelt. Why did it choose now not to work? She turned to Jeff and Daniel. "For God's sake. Get me away from here."

# TWENTY-EIGHT

The world was at her feet. Well, hers and Daniel's feet to be more precise. The business had been all that kept her going this last six months. She had accepted that she would never have another man in her life except Merlin. She would become a crazy old cat lady. Her silly old cat had lived through all her traumas blissfully unaware. She would do spells and watch Seth in her mirror. After a while she stopped. She realized she was doing herself more harm than good and had to move on.

She'd spent long hours organizing menus, cooking, and arranging staff and equipment for their functions. They routinely did large gatherings now. In a strange way, all the new business had been a blessing.

Everyone mothered her for a while, until she screamed and told them to back off. She had survived losing a baby, almost dying, and an incredibly old serial killer trying to murder her. She would survive living without Seth. At least she'd keep telling herself that. Perhaps one day she might actually believe it.

Inspector Seps had come around to see how she was

getting on. He said they accepted Vincent had been the killer. No one was sad that someone had knocked him off. The investigation into who had killed him wasn't getting much attention. There was always some new job on the horizon. He was definitely looking at retiring and had bought a little cottage in the South of France. The experience had made him realize life was too short and he needed to enjoy it.

Jeff had invested in the company. They didn't have to prepare food in their apartments anymore. They had a base now, a small failed restaurant. They were purchasing equipment that in the long run would save them on hire fees.

Daniel was still trying to convince her to go into the wedding business. So far she had managed to fend him off. The thought of seeing happy couples tie the knot wasn't something she could cope with right now, unless it was Jeff and Daniel of course.

Matcher took their bookings. He was becoming invaluable at organizing things. It meant paying him more, but he was worth it. Cara still tried to do as much preparation as possible especially for the small meals. Their prices had gone up with their increase in bookings, but none of the clients complained.

She and Daniel sat at her breakfast bar. They were discussing options for a meal for her mother and father. She had managed to put them off for months. The idea of driving past Vincent's house was almost as bad as going to Seth's cottage again.

Why did her stomach still turn over at the thought of Seth? At heart, she knew she was a hopeless romantic. She had foolishly believed life would turn out well.

The phone rang. She jumped. It was stupid. It wouldn't be him. It never was. This time it was perfect Peter Connor from *The Evening Post.* What on earth did he want? Even while he attempted to listen in, Daniel continued to pretend to check on menus.

"That was Connor," Cara said when she hung up. "He wants us to do lunch for him at *The Post* on Thursday. He has a TV executive coming that's doing a series on local chefs and their businesses. He wants to include us."

Daniel was reaching for his mobile phone as she spoke. He would be texting Jeff no doubt. "That's brilliant, Cara."

"I'm not so sure. He mentioned that it tickled the fancy of the TV executive that we cooked a murderer his last meal. I'm sure he only suggested us because he thinks there's a story in this. I want to leave that behind, Daniel."

"This is too good a deal to pass up. Vincent's old news now."

Cara stiffened at the mention of his name. Daniel was right though. This was what they had been striving for. She just didn't have the heart to tell him she didn't care anymore. Then again, if she didn't keep busy with work, she might give up altogether.

"Okay. I didn't say I wouldn't do it, did I?" Cara answered.

<hr>

ANOTHER THREE MONTHS and still no phone call. *Stop waiting, you fool.*

The TV program had been filmed. Jeff, Daniel, Matcher and Rachel were coming around to watch the show with her.

Cara had two bottles of bubbly in the fridge. She thought they would be used for drowning sorrows rather than celebrating. She knew she had come over badly.

Daniel shone as usual. She had to swallow her words. They all came over well, even when she had been asked about her most famous meal for the notorious slasher-killer.

Daniel came in with a funny line. "You could say our meals are to die for."

The presenter laughed and replied, "Well, if this was my last meal, I'd be going as a happy man. Who knew turkey and pheasant pie could taste so good. That Dingle Delight is a winner too."

After the show, the first bottle of champagne went down easily. The second was following quickly on its tail.

"Before we all get too merry, I want to say something." Daniel stood up.

"Yeah, we know you're the best chef in the world," Matcher called out.

"That's true. It isn't what I wanted to say. Surprise, surprise. Two years ago we started this business and it's gone beyond what we imagined. I know the sky's the limit. I also know we'll all pull each other down, if we get too big for our boots."

"Get on with it." Cara teased sticking out her tongue at Daniel who did the same in return. "So mature."

"It's just that we achieved this while losing someone close to us. We've been through more than people deserve to go through. Anyway I'll stop rambling. I know Cara will agree with me. I wanted to raise a toast to Shona."

They all raised their glasses but Cara could only sip as they cheered. He knew how to make her smile and hugged her.

"Also to all of us, and the fact that we're still sane, well sort of, I think," Daniel said.

"Are you sure you are?" Rachel giggled.

"And another toast to you, Cara. I don't know where you get your strength from, but we could all do with some."

Cara smiled. She didn't feel any strength at all, just a numbing loss she covered with work.

"I think that's enough from you for one night." Jeff grabbed Daniel's arm and pulled him back down beside him. "Now, there's something I'd like to say."

Daniel looked confused which made Cara smile. Jeff took Daniel's hand in his.

"Daniel, I want to ask you something that's been on my mind for a while. I wanted to do it with our friends around. I'm hoping I'll get the right response." Jeff got down on one knee. "Daniel Peter Kenner, will you marry me?"

Daniel's mouth hung open. It was the first time Cara had seen him speechless. It was wonderful. Rachel looked like she was going to cry and Cara would join her.

Daniel still hadn't said anything. Jeff raised an eyebrow in a questioning look.

"Yes. Oh my God, Yes." Daniel hugged and kissed Jeff.

More champagne was opened. For the first time in a long time, Cara thought she had something to look forward to.

"Can I be a bridesmaid?" Rachel asked, causing Matcher to shake his head.

"Only if Tecquin will be an usher?" Daniel said, grinning at Matcher.

"Is that your first name? It's lovely. Why don't you use it?" Rachel asked.

"Got whacked too many times at school. It didn't exactly fit my image. Yes, I'll be an usher, but you'll pay for that, Daniel."

"I'm really happy for you both," Cara said. "That doesn't mean I want to do the catering. I expect to be guest of honor though." She hugged them so tight. It was good to have nice things happening. It called for more bubbly. To hell with the hangover champagne always gave her.

The phone rang and she jumped as always. She would have to stop this. It was silly to keep thinking it would be him. Tonight showed life was changing. That was the way it would go.

"Hello." Someone was talking. Cara couldn't hear who it was over the noise of everyone celebrating

"Janet, is that you? Just one minute." She didn't need to say anything. The room went silent.

"I'm sorry I didn't mean to interrupt you, Cara. You sound like you're having a party. I just wondered if you could pop over and see me."

"See you?" Cara felt dumb repeating the words.

"I'm off to Paris soon to stay with Henri. I wanted you to see something before I go."

"Will Seth be there?" It hurt to say his name out loud.

"His buyer is coming from London the day after tomorrow. He'll be out all day."

"It's just…"

"I know dear, it's hard. I don't know how you've coped."

"I'll see you then." Cara had to stop the conversation before the tears came.

---

CARA PICKED up her keys and put them back down again. Why had she agreed to go today? No good would come of it. She would just rub salt in an old wound, which was a silly thing for a chef to do. She would phone and tell Janet she wasn't coming. It was the past, better left there.

As she picked up the phone, the intercom went. It was

Matcher. She let him in the apartment, made him coffee and they sat down.

"Cara, I need to talk to you about the night you saved Seth before you go there today. I would have said something the other night, but I think we were all a bit too pissed to say the least."

"Go on."

"I saw your auras combine and it was about the only good thing I observed that night. Seth had always looked grey before. When you breathed into him, it was as if the air you put in was coming out of his mouth as a glowing mist. I mean you were shining like a bloody beacon. It was good for you. Because when I walked into the cellar, you had no color in your aura at all. Whatever happened to you while I was out cold worked wonders?"

She had never told anyone about Rosie. She wasn't sure why.

"The lines on his body you touched glowed like sunlight. Both of you were shining. Light shone out of you and pulled his spirit back. Your bodies were so white, it hurt my eyes. I saw your physical bodies. Above them were, well it was the two of you and you were entwined. You were like beautiful white ghosts I could see through. It was hard to see where one of you started and the other finished. Even Inspector Seps saw it. I don't think he would have gone along with all the crazy shit otherwise."

"That's wonderful, Matcher. It doesn't change things. He still can't remember."

"All I'm saying is, don't give up. If there's such a thing as a person having a soul mate, he's yours. I saw it that night."

She wanted to believe what Matcher said but it would mean a few hours of hoping and then nothing. A person could only cope with so much nothing.

"Okay. I'll go, but don't expect miracles."

---

CARA COULDN'T STOP SHAKING. Parking outside of his cottage made it all so fresh again. It brought back memories of the first day when she'd seen him here and they admired the roses. How could they have gone through so much and yet he couldn't remember anything? Rosie had warned her this could happen. She had told her to try and make him remember. She had with the letter but it hadn't worked. What was she supposed to do? Beg someone who thought she was a stranger.

Looking at the bush surrounding the gate she thought about Rosie. She said they would have time together, but couldn't say how long. In truth, Cara thought, she had nothing. She had a memory, but he didn't even have that.

What was the point in beating the bad guy and going through everything if she didn't win something, anything? She was supposed to get the guy. That's what happened in stories, only this was real life.

That was it, she decided. She couldn't face this. She didn't want to be around anything that would remind her of Seth. She turned back to the van. Whatever Janet had wanted to show her, it didn't matter.

"Cara," Janet called out, as she beamed at her from the front door of the cottage. "I'm glad you're here. Come inside."

Cara slowly smiled back. Did it matter if the owner of the cottage thought she was some stranger who rambled on about insane things? Things like great sex? Someone who had actually said he loved her and for the first time in a long time, she had believed it. He had even made her start believing that she loved herself.

The kitchen was as always a comfortable place to be. Janet put the teapot down and opened the tin containing her cookies. Every step hurt, seeing this place and not holding Seth, or kissing him. He had made her smolder. She wanted those emotions back, but that wasn't possible.

"I saw you on the television the other night. You're a natural in front of the camera, you know. I think some of those chefs put on an act, but not you." Janet poured the tea.

*"Everybody was probably yawning away. Did Seth see it?" Stupid woman, why are you asking? If he had, he obviously didn't pine for you and rush to the phone.*

"I told him when the show came on. Like most evenings he spent the night out there. After what happened, he may have changed in some ways. As to being a sullen, grumpy loner, that hasn't changed. Before I take you out there, I need to talk to you."

Janet glowed. She might be sixty, but she was animated. At twenty-nine, Cara felt tired and jaded. She had been wrong to come here. "Listen, Janet. I'm sure that you're well-meaning, but..."

"Don't 'but' me anything. Honestly, I think you are as stubborn as he is sometimes," Janet scolded.

"Okay, I'll listen." Cara stared into her mug.

"I knew about Seth. I accepted what he told me years ago. Most people would have said I was mad. That didn't matter. He was long-lived, but he was dead in a way. Nothing touched him. He was like a dog that's lost its owner and had been left to pine. Then you came along and stirred things up." Janet smiled.

"That was never my intention. I was only just holding it together myself back then."

"Seth told me about you losing the baby. Lost one myself once. It's hard." Janet reached a hand across and touched Cara's.

Biting her bottom lip, Cara tried hold back the tears. "What do you want, Janet? Otherwise I'm going home. As lonely as that place might be without him, it hurts being here."

"Cara, he doesn't know you're here. He's like most men, no matter how long they live. They can't see what's right in front of them. He loved you."

"Please don't say that." Cara's tears fell.

"I read your letter." Janet reached across and lifted Cara's fringe. "Until the last few weeks I would have said he still couldn't remember. Now I think there may be a chance for both of you again. I brought you here to see something. When you've seen it, then make your decision on whether you give up on him."

"What decision? I've never given up on him but he doesn't want me." Cara followed Janet outside, wanting to get this over and done with as soon as possible. "The statues? They're gone."

The garden looked just like any cottage garden without them. It was winter and most of the flowers were gone but everything was green and lush from the rain.

"He sold them," Janet said. "He made a pretty penny too. That's one of the things his manager is talking to him about today. People are placing orders. Seth never did two the same. He insists he meets with prospective buyers. He said he doesn't feel that keen on sculpting so it will cost them an exorbitant price. His statues were always different. They called to you and made you feel things."

Cara was genuinely glad he was being successful. What they had lost in love they were both receiving in wealth and fame. She had worried initially how he would cope with today's world? He had survived well even though he had no memory of all those years that had passed. Another kick in the teeth, another area he didn't need her.

Walking towards the forge, Cara remembered the last time she was there. Seth had kissed her and taken her back to the cottage. They had talked about Vincent and the dagger, but she had kept secrets to protect Seth.

It hadn't helped her in the long run. She had lost him. A deep ache caused her to catch her breath when she remembered the passion of their lovemaking. She had never been able to get enough of him, but he remembered nothing. At least with their lovemaking, she had taken enough of his power to save him.

"He's started to ride the bike again. Went out there one morning two weeks ago and started it up. Five a.m. it was. If he has to get his memory back about things, couldn't he do it at a reasonable hour? Gave him hell I did when he got back from his little joy ride."

Tears stung Cara's eyes again. If he could remember the bike, why couldn't he remember her?

## TWENTY-NINE

Entering the workshop, the familiar smell of the forge hit her. Smoke, the coals, and that tang of metal she almost tasted on her tongue. His tools all hung neatly on their hooks on the wall. A few blades were on the worktable. It was as if she trespassed on his private space.

"Well, don't stand at the door, Cara. It's over by the far window. He keeps it covered with this tarpaulin, so I'm not meant to see it. I'm going to Paris for a month. I wanted to know what it was before I left. He knows I'm nosy, so I don't know why he bothered." Janet walked over to the large gray lump.

Cara longed to run. She was nothing to him now. She should give him privacy. Walking away, she heard the swish and rumble of the cover being removed behind her. She stopped. She clenched her hands and closed her eyes. *I can't do this. It's not fair to him.*

"Seth." Janet's voice echoed through the forge.

Cara instantly opened her eyes. There he was, but he wasn't looking at her. He stared at the place where Janet stood. Cara knew he didn't love her anymore, but she didn't want him to think badly of her. When he glanced at her, she struggled to read his face, but his eyes showed nothing. Cara opened her mouth. She couldn't speak. To see him and not be with him was making her heart feel like it was physically breaking in two.

Janet walked past her and stood in front of Seth with her arms folded. Cara knew she shouldn't have come. Whatever chance she had with him, was now gone.

Janet unfolded her arms and wagged her finger. "I'm not going to apologize. Don't bother asking. I'm going to go and pack. If you haven't sorted yourself out when I return from Paris, you can live on your own. I ordered a taxi for the morning to take me to the airport. Don't worry about driving me." Janet slammed the door as she left.

Cara gazed at Seth, willing him to look at her. He just stared at the floor. Her heart beat faster. If she let go of the bench she grasped, her legs would give out. Nothing had changed for her. She wanted him as much now as the first night they made love.

The van was out front. What caused her to be fixed to the spot like superglue? Him. She wanted to be near him for a little while longer, even if he ignored her. This was pointless. I won't cry she thought as she bit her bottom lip.

"I'm sorry. I didn't mean to intrude." Cara forced her body to step sideways. She just had to get past him, get out of here and get on with her life. Seth grabbed her forearm as she slipped by him. She winced as his fingers dug in.

"Wait," Seth said, his voice so low it was almost a growl. He released her arm.

Cara hesitated, pulling her arms across her chest. The sensible side of her brain said, keep moving. Her legs didn't feel like they were going to obey her brain right now so she stood still. There was silence. She couldn't gaze at the floor any longer. She looked straight at him.

He didn't see her. He was looking past her at whatever Janet had uncovered. Eventually, he glanced her way with what she thought was uncertainty in his eyes. If he didn't remember her, she wanted out of here. She took another step to leave.

"Please." His hand came to her arm, only gently this time.

"Please what, Seth?" Saying his name, she trembled and hoped he couldn't feel it. He looked so sad. It would be easier to cope with his anger or indifference than his vulnerability.

"Please forgive me for hurting you. I didn't understand. As things became clearer, I thought it was too late."

What the hell did that mean?

"Too late for what?"

"For us."

"For us? The last time we spoke, you didn't know who I was." Was he playing with her after all the pain?

"I thought the statue would have shown you."

"I haven't seen it. I was leaving before Janet could show me." Now, she was too scared to turn around. "I felt as if I was intruding. I couldn't do that to you. You may not remember me, but I like to think I honored what we had." She took a deep breath.

"Do you trust me, Cara?" Seth said as he held a hand to her cheek.

Nine months. Never so much as a phone call. She had convinced herself she meant nothing to him, that she had never existed as far as he was concerned. It was better than dealing with rejection. No one said her name the way he did. His voice so low and powerful it made her heat up to her very core with need. And now he was asking this.

She couldn't cope with being hurt again. Everyone said she was strong, but she didn't want to be anymore. "I trust you more than anyone else I've ever known."

He smiled at her words and her heart began to hope against hope once more.

"Close your eyes." Seth moved behind her and placed his hands over her eyes.

All these months of saying she was coping without him were gone in an instant. His skin touched hers. It was like electricity, little shocks running over her. He turned her around and gently coaxed her to move forward.

She shivered as his body pressed against her back. She had spent so much time just dreaming about him holding her, caressing her. Then, she would wake up angry with herself for letting those feelings consume her. His breath warmed the back of her neck. She wanted to lean back and let his lips slide over her skin.

"I want you to see what I remembered and why I'll never let you go again."

Cara held her breath. It was what she wanted to hear, but for one moment she was afraid. Seth removed his hands and stepped back.

She gasped. It was them. They were making love. He'd captured the moment in pure white marble. They sat naked, entwined with each other. His arms were around her waist while he kissed her throat. Her hands rested on his shoulders. Her head arched back. She knew that expression. He had caused it on her face on more than one occasion.

She moved away from him. She had to, so she could think. She walked around viewing the statue from all angles. It was sensual, erotic and beautiful. Seth's memory had come back, all the way back, to their first time together.

She wanted to touch the statue, but more so she wanted to touch Seth. Standing on the far side of the sculpture, he leaned against his work bench. His hands gripped the edge so hard his knuckles were white. He kept his eyes on the statue.

He was so big and strong. Sometimes, he appeared like a little lost boy. Walking over, she stood in front of him so he had to look at her. She hoped she wouldn't regret what she was about to say. Then again, she was lucky to be alive. She was a survivor.

"I love you, Seth. I never stopped loving you." She leaned forward. She brushed his lips with hers. She hadn't realized the floodgate of emotion that action would release. Pulling back, she looked into his eyes. The depth of passion she saw was so intense it almost scared her.

"I thought you were a dream for so long," he said. "I wouldn't listen to Janet. I just knew that I had been thrust into this world I didn't want to be in. I wanted Rosie and I felt the guilt of losing Annie. You weren't real."

Cara felt the pain of that day when he had stared blankly into her eyes. Seth took her hand in his.

"It was as if they had just died. It was fresh, as if I had never grieved. Then there was you. I didn't understand where you fitted in. I was angry that a stranger intruded on my grief. I should've been dead. Rosie, Annie and other memories were the past. I couldn't get back to them."

"I never wanted to cause you any pain."

"No one ever did, Cara. Don't you see I was the lucky one?" Seth laughed as he gazed at her. "I just left agony in my wake, including you."

Silence descended again. He was right. He had caused

her pain. All those months of sadness after Vincent's death were there. Could she just let it go?

"You read my letter?"

He nodded. "It meant nothing at first, and then a few weeks ago memories started to return. Come with me." He took her hand.

They walked back to the cottage in silence. The kitchen was empty and they headed upstairs. Cara heard a chuckle come from the room at the end of the corridor as she entered Seth's bedroom. Janet must be chatting with Henri. If they had lasted this long, Janet might be moving to France permanently.

Cara thought about her life two years ago, post Tony. If anyone had told her about the future with Seth then, she would have said they were insane, especially if they had mentioned his past. He still held her hand as they sat down on the edge of his bed. She never wanted him to let it go.

The night they had first made love, she had been content if it had been just great sex. Now, she didn't know how she could cope if this all fell apart again.

Seth went over to his dressing table. He removed something from one of the drawers. "These are my past."

He placed two pictures in brass oval frames in her hands. One photograph was Rosie. The other was a young dark-haired woman. Cara held the photos wondering what was expected of her. These were women he loved, and they had loved him.

Seth had made her care after a long time of not feeling anything. She had fought Vincent and won. Then, she had lived the last nine months as if that hadn't happened. Now, Seth showed her these women. She was confused.

"I remember everything, Cara, everything about them

and you." Seth took the pictures and placed them face down on his bedside table.

"You didn't call or come see me."

He pulled a chair across and sat in front of her. Taking her hands in his, his eyes locked with hers. "Up until two weeks ago I couldn't remember you. The night it came back I was going to go to you. I got on the bike and drove to your apartment. I couldn't go in. I had hurt you and you had a new life. I thought the right thing was to let you go. I have worked on the statue day and night since then. You have to believe me when I say I was going to ask you to take me back."

"All I've wanted was for you to remember me." She was trembling again.

"I no longer have the luxury of trying again in the future to get things right." Seth's hand came up and cupped her face. "You wrote that Rosie didn't know how long we would have together. I'm afraid I'll fail again."

Cara remembered the rough texture of his hands mixed with the gentle touch of a man who worked metal. He leaned forward towards her, his lips slightly parted.

She wanted those lips. When they touched hers, it was like a shock rang through her body. She wanted more. Thrusting her tongue into his mouth she matched his passion. He picked up on her need and pulled her to her feet.

As they kissed, their hands gently roamed over each other's bodies, remembering the feel of each curve. She relished the hardness of his arousal pressing against her. When they broke apart, she found she was breathing hard. She wanted him so much. That hot aching sensation was building in her. He smiled down at her as he scooped her up and laid her on the bed.

Nine months of pent up passion was released as he lay beside her and started to remove her clothes. Her hands fought with his. She needed him naked. She wanted him in her. To be joined with him again, to know that their love had survived everything.

With their clothes gone he stopped for a moment as he lay beside her and stared at her new scars with sadness as his eyes watered. His hand traced her wounds as she touched his. So much had been shared but now they could be together.

She reached up and brought his head down to her so their lips touched. She wanted more as her tongue entered his mouth to get closer. He lay on her and the feel of his body naked against hers made her want to cry with joy. As their kisses became more passionate he entered her and caused her to gasp. She had never thought she would feel this again. The feeling as he moved in her was intoxicating as their bodies joined. She thought the sensations could not get any stronger but they kept building more and more. Her whole body tingled with the power running through them both. Then they both screamed out in release.

As they lay there in each other's arms their bodies still connected she heard him chuckle.

"What is it?" she asked.

Seth raised himself up onto his elbows and smiled down at her. "I was wondering if what I remembered when I was sculpting was in fact true. Now I realize it wasn't. This is more, Cara, so much more. I never want to lose you again. I want you to be my wife."

"I have no intention of ever leaving and I most definitely accept your offer." She slipped her arms around his neck, smiling up at him. At last they were together and they would be for the rest of their lives.

# ABOUT THE AUTHOR

Australian author **Maggie Mundy** lives in Australia with her husband. She has always loved reading fantasy, paranormal, and contemporary romance books and decided the stories in her head needed to be written—it was either that or start on medication.

She writes hot, sexy men and women who have troubled pasts and are looking for their soulmate. She may make them suffer along the way, but you always get a happy ending.

Maggie believes romance can be fun to read and write, but it's exciting to spice it up with the uncertainty that comes with suspense where the rules can be broken.

# ACKNOWLEDGMENT

I would like to take this opportunity to say thank you to all the people who have made this book possible with their help, support, and encouragement.

Extra thanks go to my husband, Alan, and daughters, Jenny and Rachel. They never doubted I could do this even when I did.

Thanks also to my critique partner, Delwyn Jenkins, who has been one of my greatest supporters, and has always been generous in sharing her time and knowledge. To my friend Leesa Bow who is always there to listen to my doubts and keeps encouraging me.

www.ingramcontent.com/pod-product-compliance
Lightning Source LLC
Chambersburg PA
CBHW060945120726
47910CB00002B/500